Murder, Fantasy, and Weird Tales

Eighteen Short Stories

by Rosemary and Larry

Mild

Coauthors of the Dan and Rivka Sherman Mysteries
- *Death Goes Postal*
- *Death Takes A Mistress*

Coauthors of the Paco and Molly Mysteries
- *Locks and Cream Cheese*
- *Hot Grudge Sunday*
- *Boston Scream Pie*

Coauthors of the Adventure/Thriller *Cry Ohana*

Magic Island Literary Works • Honolulu, Hawaii • 2015

i

Interior book design by **Larry Mild.**
Cover design by **Marilyn Drea,** Mac-In-Town, Annapolis, MD.
Original cover painting by **M. Santini** (Circa 1950)
Photos by Rosemary Mild

"**The Perfect Poison**" first appeared in *Mysterical-E*, on-line magazine (2014).
"**Assault and Battery**" was awarded 1st prize, short fiction, MD Writers'
    Association.
"**Seeing Red**" first appeared in *Chesapeake Crimes: Homicidal Holidays,*
    Wildside Press (2014).
"**The *Joss* at Table Twelve**" and "**Adrift on Kaneohe Bay**" first appeared in
    Mystery in Paradise, 13 Tales of Suspense by 13 Masters of the Genre
    (CreateSpace, 2013).
"**Dream Channels**" first appeared in *Scribble*, MD Writers' Association
    literary magazine (Vol. I, Issue 1).
"**Picture Imperfect**" and "**Just a Little Bite**" first appeared in *Corner Club*
    Press, on-line magazine (Vol. I, Issue 3, July 2011).
"**The Telltale Art**" first appeared in *Crime and Suspense*, on-line magazine
    under the title "**Art by the Numbers**" (July 2007).

Library of Congress Cataloging-in-Publication Data
Mild, Rosemary P. ; Mild, Larry M.
Murder, Fantasy, and Weird Tales, A Collection of 18 Short
    Stories
Mild, Rosemary P. ; Mild, Larry M.
ISBN 978-0-9838597-6-5
First Edition 2015

10 9 8 7 6 5 4 3 2 1

Dedication

For our beloved grandchildren—
Alena, Craig, Ben, Leah, and Emily

For our wonderful children—
Jackie and Myrna

For our marriage—soul mates, partners, lovers

Acknowledgments

We could fill an entire volume with the names of loyal fans of our books. You are all precious to us and give us the ultimate push to continue our writing. We owe special thanks to the following for their expert editorial input:

Ron Darby and **Al Izen**—for their valued advice.

Joe DeMarco—Editor of *Mysterical-E*.

Donna Andrews, Barb Goffman, and **Marcia Talley**—Editors of *Chesapeake Crimes: Homicidal Holidays*.

Sherry Audette Morrow—Editor of *Scribble*.

Lourdes Venard, Laurie Hanan, and **Gail Baugniet**—Editors *of Mystery in Paradise, 13 Tales of Suspense*.

Tony Burton—Editor of *Crime and Suspense*.

Disclaimer

Murder, Fantasy, and Weird Tales and the short stories herein are entirely works of fiction. The entities, plots, and events depicted are of the authors' imagination and invention. All characters are fictitious and any resemblance to living persons or persons having lived in this century or the past few centuries is purely coincidental.

Murder, Fantasy, and Weird Tales
Table of Contents

Murder, Fantasy, and Weird Tales
Table of Contents (Continued)

*Author's Note: "The Lost Art of Lake Como" contains true details of how the original (front cover) oil painting was actually acquired by Larry and his late wife, Hannah, in 1951. The story goes on to reveal their apartment and living arrangements for a seven-month stay in Naples. Rosemary and I cherish this 46"x 21" painting, which hangs prominently in our living room today.

——*Larry*

Compulsion!

These short stories of **_Murder, Fantasy, and Weird Tales_** explore the strange obsessions and compulsions gnawing within most of us. Whether to commit murder, dream wildly, or just wander out of the box, we're all tempted, but who acts on these urges and why? Meet the **Novice Killers**, the **Hits and Misses**, the **Fantasizers and Dreamers**, and the **Art Lovers.** Join them as they venture into these realms.

Novice Killers

Meet those finding revenge sweet and sour. What turns these perfectly amiable citizens away from their peaceful existence and makes one-time murderers of them? Is it a need to pay back for a miserable relationship? Is it a desire to possess greater riches in life? Or is it an overwhelming whim to steal a special prize? And what else does greed, envy, and spite spawn?

The Perfect Poison
Assault and Battery
Seeing Red
Adrift on Kaneohe Bay
The Busybody

The Perfect Poison

Kalliss Industries was a small, privately owned pharmaceutical firm, whose successful financial base included four well-accepted pain medications. This profit center paid for the research facilities in the red brick building on Division Street and, after expenses, left enough for a tidy semiannual dividend. The firm's current effort was directed toward Lukertuchus, a muscle relaxant, whose main ingredient was extracted from a rare poisonous plant root grown in southern China. It was a complicated process, depending on serial catalysts and structural modifications accomplished at the molecular level. Of course, the toxic byproducts had to be managed safely during its manufacture.

Dotty Frettersome, research assistant to Dr. Fritz Bendz, was conveying Geraldine, a white lab rat with pink eyes and whiskered nose, back to its cage. En route, her cell phone erupted with an irritating ring tone. Dotty had her master's degree and was only months away from her Ph.D. But Dr. Bendz still treated her like a glorified gofer, assigning her to transport lab animals and dispose of the unwanted byproducts. Occasionally, he allowed her to perform a rodent autopsy, which he found too distasteful for his lofty status as vice president of research and development. Early on in her employment, he scolded her for naming the rats. "Don't get personal with the study subjects," he said. "You'll lose your objectivity and skew the results."

Despite his abuse, he relied on her meticulous research and incorporated it into his professional articles.

The ring tone blasted a second time. Dotty shifted Geraldine to her left hand and then into the pocket of her lab coat. With her right hand, she fetched the cell phone from the opposite pocket and flipped it open. Caller ID told her it was her sister, Hermiony.

She pushed the talk button. "Hey Hermy, what's going on?" Thus began a long, comfortable chat. The lanky lab assistant with boyish face, but surprisingly large breasts, leaned up against the counter, crowding Geraldine just enough to make the little one seek new space. The counter proved to be an easy hop—so easy that Dotty didn't notice the animal's desertion. Minutes later, she stuck her hand in her lab coat pocket to check on Geraldine and discovered the escape. "Gotta go now, Hermy. Pressing business."

She scanned the room. At the other end of the countertop, she found the escapee just about to stick its nose into an open Petrie dish, half-filled with a clear liquid. Dotty dropped the cell phone into her pocket and raced to the other end. Too late! Geraldine had already tasted the potion. Dotty picked up the little fuzz ball, wiped its tiny nose with a Q-tip, and gave it the once-over to check out its well-being. The rat seemed okay, so Dotty returned it to its cage.

Geraldine looked back at her through the bars, then tilted its head as though it were experiencing an internal change. Suddenly, the furry thing keeled over and died on the spot with its little feet straight up in the air. No wriggling, no gasping, no squeaking. Just dead.

Dotty opened the cage, removed Geraldine, and tested for its vital signs. She found none. The only apparent anomaly was that the wee body had experienced a sudden, phenomenal temperature loss. Dotty spent the rest of the day identifying the clear liquid and performing an autopsy on the departed rodent. Within ten minutes of death, the corpse had almost reached ambient temperature—the temperature of the environment—for a *live* lab rat. There were no signs of the errant liquid anywhere in the blood or body parts. All the organs were of expected size, shape, and consistency. So how had Geraldine died?

Dotty was baffled. Had she—and the hapless Geraldine—stumbled upon the perfect poison? She slid her hand under the elastic net covering her tucked-in braids and pulled on her right ear lobe as she pondered what to do next.

Dotty knew she had to report the disaster to Dr Bendz, but feared his reaction. With good reason.

Staring at her with the humorless black eyes of a crow, he said, "You let the animal get loose? This is not responsible conduct in my laboratory. But since the damage is done, you'd better perform a second and third experiment to confirm your findings." Before turning to leave, he threw fat on the fire. "Don't let it happen again. Escaped animals don't exactly enhance this laboratory's reputation. Or yours either."

Dotty stood frozen to the spot, unable to come up with a credible response. After all, she'd been on a personal phone call. She wasn't anxious to sacrifice more lab rats, but an order from the boss was non-negotiable. She stored most of the mystery solution in a glass bottle with a cork stopper and left a portion in the Petrie dish to examine potency over several days and weeks. She selected Alex as her next subject because it had bitten her the week before and Calvin after that because of its defiant attitude, even after getting fed.

Dotty's findings were identical. She kept exacting logs of all her work, including photographs of the unfortunate corpses. When she was done two weeks later, she filed the results and stored the original sealed bottle in a refrigerated glass cabinet.

Time passed under more pressing work and study. The dilemma of a perfect poison soon passed from her conscious memory—because personal love life intervened. Sister Hermy wanted to fix her up with a bowling friend of her husband's, one Brian Manik. Dotty's reflexive reaction was "No, no, no!" She'd never had a successful blind date, and the very idea made her stomach churn. She always seemed to scare men away. When they found out she'd graduated from high school at fifteen and college at nineteen, majoring in organic chemistry, they fled—with an "I'll call you" that never came. But when Hermy showed her a photo of her husband and Brian holding up a bowling trophy, Dotty caved. Brian Manik looked like an agreeable hunk in his league T-shirt, with defined pecs and biceps and a wide, freckled smile. She had a sudden moment of panic. What would this cute hunk want with a lab-denizen, a Plain Jane like her?

Not to worry. On their first date Brian found the combination he was looking for in a woman: breasts and brains. By the fifth date they had become quite close, intimate even, and several dates later they moved in together at her apartment.

Their cozy conversations turned passionate, but not in a sensual way. "I hate my boss" became a mantra that appeared to bind them together. Dotty had just earned her Ph.D. and was now Dr. Frettersome, but her milestone degree didn't improve her status in the lab. "I still get all the dirty work," she complained, "and Dr. Bendz gets all the glory."

Brian sympathized, but he really wanted to talk about his own job at Quality Antiques on Poplar Street. His boss was a rigid, unreasonable man, a tyrant by the alliterative name of E. Elders Everthane. No one, not even Brian, knew what the initial E stood for.

Brian Manik, his second in command, had bought a thirty-percent piece of the business when old Everthane had a cash-flow problem. The boss was now eighty-six years old, came to work every day, and still bullied all his employees, even Brian. But Brian had bought in and stayed this long for a good reason. He and Mr. Everthane had an written agreement that the lucrative business would become Brian's when the old man died.

To Dotty, that contract meant her boyfriend had a promising financial future. Calling on her objectivity as a scientist, she assessed his potential as a husband and decided he was a "Go." He was more of a jock than a brain, but his sincerity and cuteness made a good impression in the antiques business. His carrot-red, neatly cut hair, sport coats, and earnest demeanor gave customers confidence. Nothing sly or oily about him; no image of hands rubbing together at the prospect of an authentic Chippendale chair sale.

But at home in their living room his tone changed. "I'd like to shoot the old bastard," Brian said, as he formed a gun with his hand and pulled the imaginary trigger. "Like this. Pow!"

"Wouldn't poison be simpler?" Dotty asked, having no idea where those words came from. She had always considered herself a churchgoing, moral person.

"Sure," he replied. "But what I say to you here stays here. I'm just venting, babe. No matter what the method, murder is murder. I don't want to go to prison for life for something that will be mine a short while later anyway."

"What if you could get away with it? That is, with no chance of being caught?" Dotty's voice dripped with saccharine. "I'm being hypothetical, of course."

"Sounds like pure fantasy to me," Brian said, "and pretty grisly at that."

"Not really, dear," Dotty murmured. She looked glamorous, lounging on the sofa in a velvet pants outfit. Her light brown hair, unbraided for her lover, fell softly around her shoulders. "I happen to know of a perfect poison that leaves no trace."

Brian jerked his head up. "What?"

It was now a matter of pride, so Dotty revealed the details of the mysterious potion: how it cryogenically swept through the victim's system just long enough to inhibit the flow of oxygen to the body's essentials and left no internal clues as to the primary cause of death. She also described her three autopsies.

"Wow!" Brian was flabbergasted. "You're only kidding, aren't you? Surely, you'd never do anything that evil. Would you?"

"Of course not, silly," Dotty chuckled. "I wasn't suggesting that you actually commit murder."

The subject changed after that, and the relationship bloomed for more than a year, during which time the sweethearts married.

In the lab at Kalliss Industries, things weren't so lovey-dovey. Dr. Bendz went out of his way to throw Dotty for a loop and keep her guessing. On Valentine's Day he brought her a two-pound box of Godiva chocolates. On her birthday he gave her a bouquet of roses. But when his newest journal article came out, she saw that he had deleted her name—even though she had done ninety percent of the research. *The Lord giveth and the Lord taketh away,* she thought with bitterness. How should she handle a two-faced boss? She had no clue.

A few days after the Maniks' first wedding anniversary, Dr. Bendz, out of the blue, turned on his researcher. "Your work has gotten sloppy!" he charged.

"Excuse me?" she said. "When? Show me! My logs are precise and accurate."

The hawk-nosed Dr. Bendz glared at her, a predator nailing its prey. "Nothing specific. Just careless."

Dotty stifled her natural reaction of "That's a lie!" It would have buried her career for good. Instead, she spun about and fled the scene, swallowing tears of helplessness and winding up in the room housing the cold-storage cabinets. Palms pressed against one of the doors, she rested her forehead on the frosty glass while she sobbed in frustration. Slowly, anger replaced tears, and her vision cleared. *What's he trying to do? Get me fired,* she decided, *because I'm a threat now that I have my doctorate. I'm accomplishing most of the research.*

So what should she do about it? What *could* she do? A list of revenges flashed through her head. Sabotage his next research paper by stuffing it with false data? That could take a year or longer. Puncture the tires on his Jaguar? That would be childish; besides, she'd probably get caught. Suddenly, the cold air brought her to her senses. Why was she thinking so far afield when the answer might be right in front of her?

Her glinting blue eyes focused on the bottle of poison she had placed in storage eighteen months earlier.

A palpable aura surrounded this bottle of evil. She felt it physically. It seemed to beckon her, speak to her. *"Dotty, Dotty, you can get even. You can get rid of him. Just a drop of me in his iced tea and then you can be in charge of this whole lab."*

She opened the glass door, reached in, and retrieved the bottle. Placing it on the counter, Dotty then shifted her attention to another glass cabinet, the one closest to the lab door. A black and red thermos bottle sat on the top shelf, tempting her to proceed. She brought the thermos to the counter, set it beside the poison bottle, and unscrewed both the outer cover and the inner cap.

At this point Dotty unsealed the poisonous contents, squeezed a rubber bulb of an eyedropper ever so lightly, and stuck it into the clear liquid. A minuscule amount trickled into the snout. *More than enough!* She shifted the dropper to the top of the thermos and gently pressed the bulb once more. A single drop elongated, then disgorged itself and fell to its malevolent purpose. A second drop joined the first for good measure. Dotty wore a crooked smile as she recapped the thermos and returned it to its original spot in the end cabinet. She did not feel evil, as she had expected. Instead, she rode a spectacular high. It felt good to lose all her angelic inhibitions. Then, without conscious reason, Dotty did a strange thing. Using a hypodermic needle, she filled two small glass ampoules with the poison. She placed the two deadly ampoules in a blue pillbox. Next, she rinsed the dropper and needle in the sink and disposed of them in the toxic-waste bin.

Dotty was about to return the re-corked poison bottle to its proper shelf, when she thought, *No one knows of my secret research into the poison. The only records of its existence are my own laboratory log books.* She took the lone bottle to the sink. Turning on the hot water, she poured the contents down the drain, rinsed the glass bottle thoroughly, and sent it through two cycles of the sterilizer. When the cycles were done, she placed it on the shelf with the line-up of brand-new bottles. Dotty stuffed the incriminating log book into her briefcase for later incineration, took a fresh serialized log book from the bottom file drawer, and marked it with the same serial number as its predecessor.

Dotty darted out the back door of the cold-storage room and entered the area housing the rat cages. She spent the next half-hour feeding the little ones and caressing their soft white fur as she worked. Walking back through the cold-storage room to get to the main lab, she picked up her briefcase and made a shocking discovery. The red and black thermos had been removed from the cabinet. Dr. Bendz must have returned from his senior staff meeting. Casually striding past his open door, she saw him seated at his desk. He had the half-filled thermos cup in one hand and several pages of a typewritten report in the other.

Dr. Bendz lifted the cup to his lips and took a sip. Resuming his reading for an instant, a look of surprise reshaped his face and literally froze. His head dropped rigidly against the back of his leather chair. His crow eyes locked in a vacant stare. The papers slid to the desk; the fingers retained their clutched posture.

Dotty strode into his office as if she'd been summoned there. Slowly shutting the door, she inched around to his chair, reached out, and felt his brow: icy, blood-chilling cold. A shudder spasmed through her own body. She couldn't call for help yet, not with *the* major symptom still prevalent. At last, Dr. Bendz's hand relaxed and dropped to the desk.

She gasped for breath. Her lungs felt short of air. Her heart seemed to be punching against her chest wall. Did she have time to complete her mission? What if someone knocked on the door? Ten minutes later, she felt his forehead once more. It was still cold, but she detected a slight warming. She repeated the procedure at two more ten-minute intervals. In between, she moved to the alcove housing Dr. Benz's own lab equipment. She ran a spectral analysis of the coffee remaining in the thermos cup to ensure that no trace remained in the coffee. Thirty minutes later Dotty was perspiring.

It was nothing short of a miracle that no phone calls had

come and no colleagues had knocked on the door. She tried her boss's forehead once more: almost normal, and the entire human corpse had relaxed. She had to act quickly now, before rigor mortis and lividity set in.

Dotty slipped out of his office to her own desk and set her briefcase down. Then she hurried into the hall and screamed. Her voice came out so loud and shrill and true that she inwardly congratulated herself. Doors flew open and employees flooded the hall. Dr. Harold Winslow arrived first and Dotty fell into his arms, shaking and sobbing.

"What's wrong, Dr. Frettersome?"

No response—calculated so.

"What's wrong?" he repeated. "Dotty!" He put his hands on her shoulders and shook for a response. "Dotty!"

"He—I think he's dead," she slobbered, backing out of his grip.

"Who's dead?" Dr. Winslow asked.

"Dr. Bendz," she gasped. "At his desk."

"What's going on here?" a new voice demanded. It was Dr. Armond Kalliss, the founder and CEO of Kalliss Industries, arriving from his plush corner office.

"It's Fritz," Dr. Winslow said. "Something's happened to him."

Kalliss's secretary, Gaileen Plumber, was right behind him and immediately took charge of the sobbing Dr. Frettersome, while the two men hurried to check on Dr. Bendz. Thus began the long procession of curious employees, medical technicians, police, crime scene investigators, and the coroner's cronies. The general consensus was that poor old Fritz's heart gave out. The coroner would sort out the specifics during autopsy. The second consensus was that the old bastard was really a great guy—"A true professional, loved by many," Dr. Kalliss said. "He'll be missed by all who knew him." The second consensus, was, of course, a corollary of the maxim "Remember the dead with saintliness and respect, even if there was none while they lived."

Gaileen insisted on driving the distraught Dotty home. Before leaving the office, Dotty grabbed her briefcase and clutched it on her lap as if it were a lifeline. Gaileen guided her into the living room, and settled her on the couch before leaving. As soon as Gaileen had departed, shutting the front door behind her, Dotty ran to the window to make sure the secretary's car had pulled away from the curb.

Now Dotty turned her attention to the incriminating log book she had brought home in her briefcase. First, she piled two pressed-wood logs into the fireplace. Next she balled-up pages of yesterday's newspaper and tucked them around the logs. With two wooden matches, she started a fire that soon burned hot and high. She pulled out her secret research documents. The notebook pages came apart easily, and she fed them one by one into the fire, where the flames licked them into oblivion. Afterward, taking no chances, she raked through the ashes with a fireplace poker to verify that no remnants remained.

Alone in the apartment, she could hardly wait for Brian to come home. She had to tell someone what she had done or burst. Brian was the only one she could trust. He'd understand. And when her husband came through the front door, she leaped into his arms and kissed him on the lips with great passion.

"To what do I owe this sudden affection?" he asked. But without waiting for an answer, he cocked his head and sniffed. "Dotty, I smell smoke."

"Yes, sweetheart, but not to worry. It's been a busy day. I have so much to tell you."

Brian stepped into the living room and walked straight to the fireplace. "Why do we need a fire? It's June, for God's sake, and it's hot as hell in here." He pulled off his jacket and threw it over the arm of a wing chair.

"I know, I know," Dotty said, her voice soothing. "I had a few documents to get rid of." She took his hand and pulled him toward her. "Come sit down. I have really big news." She plopped herself on the couch and tried to pull him down next to her.

He remained standing, his muscular body rigid.

"I did it," she said. "I went ahead and did it. I finally got up the courage to do it."

"Do what?" Brian demanded. A frown creased his forehead as his patience grew thin.

"I killed the bastard. Poisoned him from head to toe."

"Who? What? Where would you get poison?" Brian's voice squeaked.

"Remember months ago I told you about the toxic substance I discovered in the lab? How it instantly killed one of my white rats? I joked about it and said it was the perfect poison." Dotty's face flushed from chin to forehead; her blue eyes glittered.

"Well, I put two drops of it in Dr. Bendz's iced tea. Darling, the lab will soon be mine, all mine."

Brian sat down hard. "You're kidding me!"

"No, I'm not." Dotty then related the details: blow-by-blow, or rather, drop-by-drop, reveling in the re-telling of each moment; enjoying how she had committed the deed.

He listened, shaking his head in disbelief. By the time she finished, panic had set into Brian's brain. "Dotty, are you out of your mind? You could get caught. You could go to jail for this. For life!"

Dotty had thoroughly prepared herself for her husband's reaction. "Sure I could, but I *won't* get caught, because the poison doesn't exist an hour later. It leaves no trace—there's not a mark on his body. Everyone thinks he died of a heart attack. I was the one who discovered the body and reported the death. Why on earth would they suspect me?"

"Dear wife, how can you be so cocksure of yourself? Almost anything can go wrong. It's Murphy's Law."

"Okay, Brian. Let's wait three months and we'll see what happens. If all goes well, we can have a go at Mr. E. Elders Everthane." On the coffee table sat a small blue box. She flipped the lid open and showed him the two tiny ampoules nestled inside.

"Nothing to it. See?"

"Nothing to it? You want *me* to knock off *my* boss?"

"Why not? You told me you wanted to shoot the man. This way is a lot neater all around. No gun to buy and get registered. No noisy gunshot. No blood."

Brian's breathing came fast now. He sprang to his feet. "What's for dinner?"

* * * *

In two weeks, the police concluded their investigation, determining that Dr. Fritz Bendz died of sudden heart failure. Dotty received the appointment she craved: as Acting Director of both the laboratory and the Lukertuchus project. But her exhilaration faded when she discovered that the appointment was temporary. It would only last until Dr. Kalliss found a celebrity researcher to replace Dr. Bendz. In the interim, she decided that she needed to enhance her reputation and prove Dr. Kalliss wrong; she deserved the permanent position. Dotty accomplished several technical breakthroughs and made a successful presentation to the corporation's board of directors. Her work soon put her on a first-name basis with Armond Kalliss. He dropped the word "Acting" from her title. All her chips had fallen in place.

At home, she let months pass without further mention of doing away with Mr. Everthane. During her own calculated silence, a turmoil brewed at Quality Antiques on Poplar Street.

Brian arrived for work one Monday morning to discover carpenters swarming around his office, which was situated next to Everthane's. On a closer, more horrifying look, Brian saw that the wall between their two offices was being torn down. Everthane himself materialized at his left shoulder, startling him.

"Good morning, Brian," Everthane began. "I'm making a few changes around here. I need a larger office, so if you don't mind, I've expanded into yours. I've relocated yours elsewhere."

A cold sweat began under Brian's armpits. Their offices were behind the retail floor, which occupied 1,500 square feet. Where could he possibly go?

"I've established a great corner for you in the storeroom.

Very cozy and private. You'll like it." An unmistakable hint of irony lay behind the announcement.

The storeroom? Below street level! That S.O.B.! Brian descended the staircase to his new quarters. He hadn't realized it before, but the only light filtered through the narrow windows just below the ceiling. His mahogany desk, swivel chair, and tall file cabinet filled one dim corner. To get there, he had to weave his way around the shop's huge inventory: a 19th century English sideboard; a Louis XVI-style tub chair; a 1940s lacquered highboy; a Chinese 18th century painted cabinet; a set of gilt rope-and-tassel nesting tables. And much more.

Brian thumped down into his chair and breathed deeply to collect his composure. Forcing him into the storeroom was humiliating—definitely a demotion. For the first time since Dotty's shocking news in their living room, he began to stew and brood over the potential benefits of the perfect poison. By nature he was an amiable, low-key kind of guy. He'd needed an impetus to commit an act of murder. Now he had one. The old man had no idea that he had broken the last straw on Brian's back.

The next morning, Brian—supposedly still second-in-command at Quality Antiques—left the house with the small blue box in a pocket of his sport coat.

He had spent hours the night before hashing over a viable plan. His boss drank neither coffee nor tea nor soda. Occasionally, he did sip directly from the spout at the water fountain. This presented a problem until Brian remembered the bottle of Cutty Sark in the bottom drawer of Everthane's desk. He'd seen it surface, with a Waterford crystal highball glass, whenever the old man made a major sale. That morning Everthane left the shop at 11:30 for a business lunch. Brian stole into his lavish new office. Removing the liquor bottle, he unscrewed the cap, and broke one of the two ampoules from the blue box over the bottle mouth. He recapped the bottle, shook it, and returned it to the bottom drawer of the desk. He slipped the pillbox back into his pocket.

Business was slow for the next two days: a few odd-lot gilded Dresden plates; a signed Czech figurine; and a period French end table. But on the third morning, the old man sold a 17th century Italian armoire in only fair condition for $46,000—of which 34% percent was profit. Brian was certain the excellent sale would trigger a drink from the Cutty Sark stash, but Everthane seemed content to go without it.

The suspense was driving Brian crazy. He went to lunch and returned. Still the old man was puttering around the shop in a good humor, greeting patrons with enthusiasm. At six o'clock, Everthane told him, "You can go on home. I'll close up for the evening."

This is not normal, Brian thought. *I'm always the one to turn off the lights, lock up, and set the alarm.* With his nerves on edge, he entered the Manik apartment, headed straight for the bedroom, and slapped the pillbox—with only one ampoule left—down on the dresser top.

"Hey, grumpy!" Dotty said. "What's with the sour puss?"

"I laced the old goat's Cutty Sark three days ago like you told me to, but he hasn't touched it yet."

"Easy, Brian. I suppose he's just waiting for something to celebrate. Didn't you say he likes to take a nip after a big sale?"

"That's just it. He had a humdinger of a sale this morning, but didn't touch the bottle afterward. And he was exceptionally cheerful the rest of the day. It's like he knows what I'm up to—and that's freaking me out, Dotty. I can't take another day of this."

"Calm down, darling," she said. "We have to be patient. Mr. Everthane isn't going to neglect his bottle for long. Let's have dinner. We're having T-bone steak, and we'll watch a few hours of television. You'll forget the whole nasty business."

"Yeah, sure I will," Brian said with a scowl. "What'll we watch? *Criminal Minds? Law and Order: Criminal Intent?*" His fears followed him to bed. Bad dreams wove through brief snatches of sleep.

A weary Brian skipped breakfast. He was too tense to eat, so he returned to the shop an hour earlier than usual. He was surprised to find the front door still locked. Everthane always got to work first. *Strange*, Brian thought. *The old goat has never ever missed a day of work.* Brian fumbled through his pocket for a key that he hadn't used but twice in the last fifteen years. He unlocked the door and punched in the code to disarm the burglar alarm. Striding a few yards into the shop, he realized that Everthane's door was also shut tight. He rapped lightly. No response. Knocking harder yielded nothing, so he turned the knob and moved slowly into the office.

Brian stopped in his tracks. He found Everthane seated at his desk, facing the other way. Apparently, he was perusing the accounts ledger laid out on the credenza behind the desk.

"Good morning, sir. Sorry about barging in like this, but I had to open up this morning. Your—"

Everthane didn't respond, didn't turn around, didn't even twitch a muscle. For a split second Brian wondered whether he was hallucinating from lack of sleep. Stepping to the side of the desk, he stared at his boss's face. It had taken on a gray pallor unlikely even in a man of long years. The bottle of Cutty Sark stood opposite the ledger, its level considerably lower than when Brian had tampered with the contents. His boss appeared to be dead, but Brian felt no relief, even though he had waited four days for this very result.

He slowly backed out of Everthane's office and trudged downstairs to his own desk in the storeroom, where he called 911. The Emergency Medical Technicians arrived and made it official. Because they could find no apparent cause of death, they brought in the police and crime scene team. Brian's anxiety settled like painful gallstones into his gut.

Over the next two weeks, the investigators found nothing toxic in the open scotch bottle and even less on or in the autopsied body. So taking Everthane's eighty-six years into account, they pronounced him dead of natural causes.

Both Brian and Dotty were thrilled with the outcome. That is, until an audit revealed that Quality Antiques was deeply in debt. Everthane had been tapping into the business equity for some time to feed his obsession with high living, including a recent purchase of a villa in France. Months later, when the accounts were settled and creditors paid off, the debt had consumed all of the recent sales. The business bank account contained a mere $1,300. Brian felt sick. Even the best pieces in their inventory would have to be heavily discounted. There wasn't much left of Quality Antiques on Poplar Street.

And all these years he'd thought he would be inheriting a flourishing business.

Things were not going much better at Kalliss Industries. The Food and Drug Administration had repudiated one of Dotty's banner breakthroughs. Though her employment wasn't in jeopardy, Armond turned personally cold. "Dr. Kalliss to you, Miss Frettersome." She soon learned he was searching for someone new to head up her lab.

The once-solid Manik marriage soon turned south, with husband and wife in constant agitation over what they had done. Worse still, their evil deeds had reaped meager rewards. Each blamed the other for their ongoing regret. A wedge of mistrust and hate insinuated its way into their daily routines. Separately, secretly, Dotty and Brian began checking the contents of the little blue pillbox—sometimes as often as twice a day. Then one day, instead of one remaining ampoule, the box was empty.

A crisis they couldn't possibly predict had occurred one Thursday, when both the Maniks were at work. It was the day their weekly cleaning service came to their home. Maizy Dubrowe, from Immaculate World, was vigorously vacuuming the bedroom floor. Her elbow accidentally bumped the blue box off the dresser onto the floor. Curious, Maizy knelt down, opened the box. and fingered the strange-looking ampoule. It was so small and slippery that she dropped it on the thick-piled carpet, where it rolled near a bed caster. After a futile search on her knees, Maizy merely shrugged. *How important could a tiny thing like that be?* She returned the empty pillbox to the dresser top. As she continued to vacuum, the roar of the machine masked a slight clicking sound—as the wayward ampoule got sucked up into the vacuum's entrails.

Maizy did not report the incident to her employers. She reasoned that it might cost her her job.

Dotty discovered the missing ampoule the very next morning; Brian that same evening. Each suspected the other of nefarious intentions. At first, their mutual wrath drew boisterous accusations. As the burning ire stepped up, notch by notch, deafening silence and hurtful sneers became commonplace. Neither accepted food nor drink from the other, nor was the refrigerator a safe place to store food. They drank like animals: with their mouths gaping open at the kitchen faucet. They ate alone at fast-food joints on their way to and from work.

Two factors kept the Maniks from divorcing. One, financially they couldn't afford to live apart. And two, they needed to keep a suspicious eye on each other. One could say that the Maniks had created the perfect poison: a suitable life sentence for themselves, far worse than that imposed by any formal justice system.

§

Assault and Battery

The silence frightened her. "Ernest, is it running?"

"Is what running, dear?"

"The motor. I can't hear anything but a hum. Is something wrong?"

"Of course the motor's running, Vel. We're moving, aren't we?"

Oh, yeah, we're moving all right, but in the wrong direction, Velma thought. She had expected to be back home in Annapolis by now, not driving aimlessly through Maryland's desolate Eastern Shore farmland. Gazing out her passenger-side window, she watched the Silver Queen cornfields parade by, the towering stalks heavy with August ears marching toward them, menacing, walling them in on this snaking, narrow road. If she were to roll down the window and reach out, she could practically touch the coarse husks housing the fat ears, the brown silk. The very thought gave her the shivers.

"Let me explain, Vel."

Oh-oh! My know-it-all engineer husband is about to deliver another of his interminable discourses. I couldn't care less about all that useless detail.

"This is an EV, a totally electric vehicle, and the motor

hums. It's supposed to. You can't expect a car to know lyrics, so it has to hum." His fine-boned, angular face relaxed into a smile at his little joke. "Our EV is quiet, efficient, and nonpolluting. And we're the first couple on our block to own a totally advanced, state-of-the-art 2016 model."

"Is being first all that good, Ernest? Have they worked out the insects yet?"

"Insects?"

"You know, the bugs, whatever." She tossed it off lightly, making a concerted effort to breathe normally and crack through the tension.

"Very funny. Of course. Think of us as pioneers, Vel."

"The pioneers had to endure hardships, Ernest. After five years of marriage, you should know I'm not good at that. The only hardship I'm willing to endure is a too-firm mattress at the Hilton."

A frown drew his sand-colored eyebrows together. "Must you be so obstinate? Open that pinhead brain of yours. Conservation is more than a buzzword. We're doing our part to save the planet. Remember, we'll get a tax break for buying this little gem, too."

"Okay, okay, enough is enough. Now take me home."

"Hey, woman, you pestered me to take you antiquing. Like we really need more of that junk. I should send you to Knick-Knacks Anonymous."

"I bought three fine pieces of carnival glass at a good price. Is that a crime?"

"Yeah, in a way. But at least I did what *you* wanted. Now it's *my* turn. I want to test this baby out in the wide open spaces. It's our new car's maiden voyage." He repositioned his skinny frame in the driver's seat, and leaned forward, eagerly gripping the wheel.

For heaven's sake, Ernest, it's not a Formula One. She didn't voice her sour thought. He wouldn't have listened anyway. *What I wanted was so simple: just one stop over the Chesapeake Bay Bridge to visit the Old Schoolhouse Antiques Shoppe. How could I have made such a mistake? I should have known he'd turn a little shopping excursion into a Tour de Grand Prix far from home.*

Ernest, intent on maneuvering the tricky road, chose not to acknowledge the turmoil brewing anew inside his pretty wife. He took perverse pleasure in taunting this five-foot-ten woman with the coppery ponytail, athletic body, and generous breasts.

The far-away outdoors spooked Velma, threatened her, and filled her with anger and hostility. Lately, even breaching the bounds of their own cozy neighborhood of clapboard houses set her fear in motion. Her shrink had said these feelings probably stemmed from some agoraphobic root. She couldn't nail the exact date when this anxiety had burst like a noxious weed into the orderly garden of her brain. About a year ago, she guessed, impelling her to quit her sales job at Sports Authority. It had not only cost her a job, it had definitely put a crimp in their marriage.

Today, as the miles droned along, Velma's chest tightened. Shifting an inch or so in her seat, she felt the constriction of the seat belt and shoulder harness. Even with the windows up and the air conditioning on, she couldn't help but inhale the sickening scents of crops, fertilizer, and tractor dust. They mingled with the overbearing new-upholstery aroma—an aroma she felt sure came in bottles to be squirted into virgin cars by dealers just before a test drive.

This new car business was all Ernest's fault. Right after breakfast, he had hustled her to the Hontoya dealership, forcing her to miss her morning Bowflex workout. Now Velma's athletic body felt stiff and deprived. She loved her home gym with its power rods and resistance routines. It fit right into a corner of their bedroom, and after just a few months she felt herself already building new strength. The best part was she didn't have to leave the house to jog or join some health club and exercise with obnoxious, smelly strangers.

Velma missed their macho, roomy SUV, even if it did devour gas. Oh, the Hontoya Orange looked nice enough—even cute, like a sparkly metallic fruit. But it felt so puny, so cramped.

There wasn't room enough to stretch out her long, muscular legs, even with the seat pushed as far back as it could go.

She broke the silence. "Didn't the salesman say we could go seventy to ninety miles on a tank?"

"Charge. He said seventy to ninety miles on a battery charge."

"Charge then. Do we have enough whatever to get to the next gas station?"

"Of course. The charge duration is a big improvement over the 2015 models. Besides, we just left the Hontoya dealership a few hours ago. We're fine. Relax and enjoy."

"What happens if we can't make it home? Think about that." She tried to suppress the tremor building in her voice. "What if we get stuck out here in this godforsaken place?"

"It's not gonna happen, dummy. We just head for the first EVC. If you must know, that's the Electric Vehicle Charge facility at the nearest gas station."

"What if they haven't installed an EVC facility out here in the boonies? I mean, what if they haven't gotten around to this area yet? What then?"

"All the service stations are required to have them. It's a state law now that there are four million EV's running around— more coming, too."

She threw him a sly look. "Four million? There goes your pioneer fantasy."

"Okay, so we're not the first ones in the whole universe. Forty-three states have EVC laws now."

"Does Maryland?"

"I think so. Anyway, it won't be long before all the states are on board. At the EVC facility, they slip the tired old battery out of the car's quick contact case and slide a fresh zinger replacement in like a flashlight cell. Then they charge up the one you leave behind, test it, and resell it. Any clunkers they just junk. The system is efficient. No more than five minutes per stop with the new loader gurneys. It takes about the same amount of time as the old gas-ups."

Velma's hazel-yellow eyes widened, cat-like. "So it's really an ER for cars. What if they don't have any good batteries left?"

"They always have batteries, although you might have to wait two hours for a charge when a facility is overwhelmed."

"What if you get caught on the road with two bad ones?"

His slender fingers clenched the steering wheel. "Vel, the system is foolproof. You use a metered charge pump. Every third utility pole along the major highways, and other roads too, is supposed to have one. Of course, if you get careless, you can always call EVC road service."

Velma studied her husband's intent profile. When they had first met, she'd felt a magnetic attraction to this slight, sandy-haired man with the fair complexion and tortoise-shell glasses that enhanced his intellectual aura. She often teased him: "I ask you the time and you tell me how to make a watch." It was a second marriage for both of them, opposites attracting—she the more physical, he the more brainy. But lately, she realized this fascination was wearing thin. For months now, they'd been scraping each other's nerves like worn-down brake pads. How much longer could she tolerate this arrogant side of him: the lecturing engineer who documented and pounded home every statement, thereby winning every argument?

The lonely miles ran by. Velma stole a glance at the dashboard just as the gauge on Battery One crept out of the green into the amber warning zone. Her heart began to hammer. As if to suppress it into behaving, she hugged herself, large hands gripping upper arms until the flesh turned white. "It's time for a charge," she said. "Don't wait too long or we'll get stranded."

"Hey!" Ernest shouted. "Got it covered, Ms. Worrywart." A sudden gap in the oceans of corn revealed a small intersection with only one icon of civilization, but a welcoming one: an EVC charge facility.

The gray cinderblock building bore the usual splashy posters that adorned gas stops with lures of "Lotto & ATM! Jumbo

Hot Dogs! Cappuccino! Donuts!" A palpable relief shot through Velma. Ernest pulled up to the EVC trailer beside the building. A Flemish-looking, broad-chested man in T-shirt and bright green coveralls strolled to their car. Velma tried not to stare at this wannabe version of Jean-Claude Van Damme. His half-smile conveyed what? Insolence? Indifference? She couldn't tell, but something about him transfixed her gaze. Her hands flew to the back of her head and unclipped the barrette imprisoning her ponytail. With practiced fingers, she released the thick sheaf of auburn hair and let it fall loosely around her face and shoulders.

"Hi!" Ernest sang out. "Fill 'er up!" Then he grinned sheepishly when he realized his *faux pas*.

"Premium, Deluxe, or Regular?"

"Uh . . . what's that all about?"

"Premium, Deluxe, or Regular?" repeated the attendant.

"I'm, uh, not sure," Ernest stammered. "We just bought the car this morning. The Battery One warning light came on." The blue veins in his wiry neck tensed as he realized he didn't have the answer to the question.

The attendant jumped to his customer's rescue. "I'll have a look-see to check it out."

Ernest threw an anxious glance at his wife, expecting it to be met with an accusing I-told-you-so. Instead, he noticed her hair, now fluffed out and feminine, and her cheeks tinged with a rosy glow.

Reaching under the dashboard, the attendant pulled two levers. In the panels normally occupied by rear doors, four hatches—two on each side—sprang open, exposing the two batteries lying laterally in their cavities. Labeled One and Two in large gold letters, the batteries were cylindrical—each one about four feet long and two feet in diameter.

The attendant bent his tall, twenty-ish frame almost in half and squinted as he read the identification plates. "You're driving with two Original Issue Deluxes right now," he said, backing away. "Do you want another Deluxe grade, Number One?"

"Sure, the Deluxe will be fine," said Ernest.

His wife almost shrieked. "Shouldn't we get the Premium? We wouldn't want to get stuck in the middle of nowhere, would we?"

"Can it, Vel. Deluxe will be fine."

"Age? . . . New, One, Two, or Three?" the young man asked.

Ernest's narrow shoulders hunched. "This is our first EVC battery swap. What do you recommend?"

"Older is cheaper, but I recommend you stick with the first year and call it an even-age swap. That way you get the best for your money."

"Do it," said Ernest.

Sunglasses perched on her head, Velma's dark, feathery lashes flickered as she cast the hunk in green coveralls a coquettish smile. He responded with a wink before rolling an empty gurney flush up to the open hatch on the passenger side. From the driver's side, his biceps swelling, and leaning hard into it, he pushed Battery One out of its compartment onto the locked-wheeled gurney on the opposite side, then sauntered back to the passenger side and pulled the gurney a foot or two out of the way. Wheeling about, he disappeared inside the building's shadowy bay and returned moments later, slowly pushing another battery-laden gurney, which he positioned next to the first one. Cleaning the battery terminals and contacts with a large brush, he locked his sharp blue eyes on the sexy lady.

She unsnapped her seat belt so she could turn to observe the proceedings and gawked in fascination at the torpedo shapes as they lay side by side on their gurneys.

"Wow!" she gushed. "They sure are humongous."

Ernest scowled. "I assume you're referring to the Jolly Green Giant's muscles."

She grinned. "Of course not, hon, the batteries."

"They weigh about a hundred-fifty pounds each, but so what?" asked Ernest, watching the young man complete the swap and slam the four hatches shut.

"They take up an awful lot of room. We could use more space back there."

"There's just the two of us. Whoa! Is there something you're not telling me?"

"Don't be ridiculous, I'm not pregnant," she snapped. "But it would be nice to have room for groceries, at least. That trunk is a joke. I could hardly fit the antiques bag in. What's the guy doing now?"

"Laser-scanning the labels on both batteries."

The attendant loomed over the driver's side. "That'll be $48.50, including road and sales tax."

Velma squealed. "You're kidding! That's just as much as an SUV fill-up. Ernest, I thought you told me we'd save money."

Her husband threw her a vicious look, then turned back and signed the charge slip.

"It sounds more expensive than it is, ma'am," the young man interjected. "It's true that you would save more on the slow charges you do overnight at home—about three dollars per. But this way's more convenient." He flashed her an impish grin. "Have an electrifying day." Behind Ernest's back, he blew Velma a kiss.

Ernest hummed the car onto the two-lane road and opened the speed to the maximum recommended—fifty miles per hour.

"Which is it, Ernest?"

"Which is what?"

"What we're going to get on this charge. Seventy or ninety miles?"

"Oh. It depends on whether we're going uphill or down, how fast we're traveling, and how much weight we're carrying."

"How do we know if we're going up hill or down?"

"For pity's sake, Vel, what kind of idiotic question is that?"

"Ernest, don't be so insulting. I mean on a really gentle grade. Shouldn't there be an indicator on the dash or something?"

"We don't need all that data. All I have to do is keep my

eye on these two battery gauges, and that'll keep us out of trouble. Why don't you take a nap? I can take her home from here," he said. "Eighty miles and we're in our own driveway."

"Best idea you've had all day." She tilted her seat back, drew up her knees, and positioned her sneakers on the dash as a footrest. Her husband flinched at such disrespect for their pristine new vehicle. He was about to scold her when a succession of light snores told him she was asleep.

The miles clicked away, and the Battery Two gauge declined accordingly. Twelve miles later, the gauge pointer dropped into the warning amber region. Ernest threw the switch back to Battery One, the unit the attendant had just installed. Immediately the EV slowed down. The Battery One gauge dropped into the red zone. Ernest felt a stab of alarm, but maintained his cool long enough to switch back to Battery Two. The car picked up speed again as he scanned the horizon for the next EVC station. Five more miles, still no station. In spite of his increased pressure on the accelerator, the EV decelerated. Ah, the utility poles! He remembered them just in time and rolled to a stop in front of one of them.

Velma continued to sleep. Her husband climbed out of the car and read his new vehicle manual on the subject of utility pole charge pumps. Following the step-by-step instructions, he located the retractable orange charge cord, coiled just under the Battery One compartment. Unrolling the vinyl covered cord, he clamped it to the charge pump. Next he read: "Insert one quarter (25 cents) for each fifteen minutes of charge time." Ernest reached into his pocket for coins. He spread them out in his palm: one dime, two nickels, and three pennies. He tried these coins, but to no avail. Apparently, it had to be a quarter. He flung open the passenger door. "Honey, wake up. Please wake up." He shook Velma's hefty shoulder.

A rush of thick heat blanketed her. She blinked. "Are we home?"

"Does it look like we're home?" he shot back. "We have a problem. The swapped battery doesn't work, and the other one is out of juice."

She sprang upright. "How could that happen, Ernest? You said the system was foolproof."

He jammed his hands into the deep pockets of his shorts, curling his fingers into fists so tight his nails cut into his palms. "I think that hunky EVC attendant you made the googly eyes at got distracted and put the old battery back in again."

"Now look, even if he did screw up, don't go blaming all this on me."

"I'm not the flirt in the family, *deeeear*. I'm not the one seducing strangers with the Lauren Bacall look, or is it Veronica Lake? So how about some help?"

For several moments she sat rock-still, staring straight ahead out the windshield. Resentment crawled and nibbled like a tapeworm inside her flat belly. When she finally spoke, her words sounded distant, disembodied. "You used to love it when I flirted, even with other guys. You said it turned you on."

"You're bringing that up *now?* Great timing, Vel. That was when we first met. But . . ." He sensed he was treading on dangerous ground, yet couldn't stop. "When a woman reaches her forties, that sort of thing gets . . . old. So now let's just drop it. I need some help here."

At first he thought she hadn't heard him. She continued to stare out the windshield. He was about to repeat his demand, when her body rotated slowly toward him. He cringed at an expression he'd never seen before, a dark cloud like a swarm of wasps ambushing out of nowhere. Her brows merged into a dangerous furrow that divided her forehead in half. Her full lips flattened into a red, scar-like line. Her eyes radiated a poisonous glow.

Then just as suddenly, the look passed, a switch flicked off. Standing before the open passenger door in the blistering sun, he wondered whether he'd hallucinated.

Sliding her sunglasses from the top of her head down over her eyes, she swung her agile body out of the car. She was only two inches taller than Ernest, but outweighed him by thirty pounds.

Breathing hard, determined to ignore the bleak expanse surrounding them, she stood with feet spread apart and hands on hips. "You're already hooked up to a pump. Why don't you put some more juice in? Isn't that why they call it the Hontoya Orange? Because it has to be juiced?"

Ernest scowled, in no mood for her lame jokes. "Who cares why? I need quarters to make this pump work. Do you have any in your purse?"

Velma searched her wallet, but found only a few dimes and pennies. She spilled the purse's entire contents out onto the passenger seat, shook her head, and stuffed everything back in. Looking up at the wires between poles, she said, "All that juice up there and not a drop to drink. Have you tried your credit cards yet?"

"Good thinking, dear. You have the semblance of a brain after all." He extricated his MasterCard from his wallet and approached the meter. But chewing gum blocked the scanner slot. Picking and probing proved useless.

"Now what?" he complained.

"Next meter, smarty-pants."

Ernest retracted the cord and returned to the EV. Turning the key, he heard the hum once more. In DRIVE, the EV inched ahead slowly, the strained hum sounding more bass-pitched as the vehicle crept on. Just past the second utility pole, the motor emitted its last grunt. Leaping out of the car, he stretched the cord to full length, but it fell yards short of the nearest meter.

"Any more great ideas, Vel? This is all your fault. If you hadn't been trying to seduce the Jolly Green Giant, maybe he would have kept his mind on what he was doing."

"My fault? I'm not Mr. Obsessive-Compulsive Conservationist." In a sing-song voice, she parroted his pitch to her at the Hontoya showroom: 'Think what we're doing for the world, honey. We're helping to reverse global warming, honey.' Riiiiight. Why couldn't we have bought a hybrid like every other couple we know? The Baxters drove all the way to Boston and back to Annapolis on eight gallons of gas. Five hundred miles on eight gallons, Ernest.

And they didn't have to stop even once at one of your wonderful EVCs, because hybrids use some gasoline and charge themselves up."

"That's all well and good, but it's yesterday's technology. We're on the cutting edge here."

As she drew a deep swig from her water bottle, a light bulb ignited in her gray matter. She plied open the glove compartment and whipped out a cell phone. "Hey, guy, we're in luck. We can call the EV station. They'll send their mobile charge truck to rescue us."

"Good! Here's the 800 number from the manual," he said. "They'll connect us to the nearest one." He hated it when she was right, but realized he hadn't seen another car on the road for more than an hour.

Velma punched the keypad, listened, and scowled. She punched again, harder. Nothing. She handed him the phone. "You try."

Ernest's index finger jabbed at the keypad, but the screen came up black. "The blasted battery's dead! Why do you think I told you to keep the cell phone in the house? To recharge it, that's why! Has it been recharged—ever?" He whirled away and, head down, paced back and forth in jerky steps, then stopped short. "Hey, here's another idea. If we jettison the dud battery, the car will be lighter and we can push it closer . . ."

". . . and charge up the good battery!" she chimed in. "Excellent! We should be able to handle that."

He reached under the dashboard and pulled a lever. Thunk! The hatches sprang open, exposing Battery One.

Working from opposite sides, she pulled and he pushed. The dud battery slid most of the way out of its compartment. He came around to her side, and together they hefted it out of the car toward the roadside drainage ditch. But after only a few feet, his back spasmed and his arms trembled under the weight, while she energetically carried her share.

"Hey, Gargantua, slow down!"

"I can't," she cried. "Whatever you do, don't drop it."

Ernest sucked in his narrow chest and lurched forward toward the ditch. Somehow, they made it, letting the battery drop with a thud.

"Vel," he panted, "it's illegal to discard old batteries this way. They contain toxic chemicals that leach into the groundwater."

"So we're littering once in our lives," she retorted. "So what?"

"It's irresponsible."

"We'll be civic-minded tomorrow and make a donation to the Chesapeake Bay Foundation. Today we have to push the car closer to the pole."

"Yeah," he said without conviction. He pressed a hand to his scalp. "I'm getting scorched. I left my prescription sunglasses and hat at home."

"So start pushing!"

"A lot you care if I get sunburned," he whined. "I'm a prime candidate for skin cancer and cataracts."

Velma wasn't listening. Waves of panic were sweeping over her. Icy globules of sweat oozed from under her arms down her sides, gluing her blouse to her clammy skin. The stiff denim of her jeans imprisoned her legs like lead casts. Her grating voice erupted. "We can't stay here forever. Do you think I like being stuck out in this wretched place? It gives me the creeps."

"It's just good old Maryland Eastern Shore farmland. Pretty nice, if you ask me. Somebody'll be along soon to give us a lift. Vel, you've got to get over this crazy fear of yours. You know what I think? You'd be a lot better off if you hadn't quit your job. At least it kept you busy. What the devil do you do in the house all day, anyway?"

"Shut up!" she screamed. "Just shut up!"

"Okay, okay!" He reached into the car, shifted into neutral, and released the brake. Then, with one hand on the wheel and the door open, he placed his shoulder on the door frame to push. From behind the car, she leaned forward with all her strength.

They pushed for ten minutes, but neither one voiced the glaring reality: they were on a slight but obvious uphill incline. The 2,000-pound car only inched forward.

"I've had it!" Ernest shouted. He flung himself down into the driver's seat.

Behind her dark glasses, his wife squinted into the blazing sun as a pair of huge crows settled on a telephone wire overhead. *Caaaawwww, caaaawwww.*

"Ernest? Are those vultures up there?"

"Don't be so stupid. We're not in the desert."

* * * *

Two days later, back home in Annapolis, Velma answered an insistent doorbell. Alarmed, she saw a policeman standing on the porch. He introduced himself as Officer Larkin and asked for Ernest.

"Oh, dear, I'm afraid he's away on a business trip," Velma purred, shifting on one hip to accentuate her low-slung jeans and clingy shirt. "I'm his wife. Anything I can do for you?" she asked, scrutinizing his powerful bulldog physique.

"Maybe, ma'am. That your Hontoya Orange sitting in the driveway?"

She swallowed hard. "Yes, Officer, it is."

"Your registration, please."

He followed her to the car and waited while she fished the white card out of the glove compartment.

Officer Larkin studied the registration, then compared it to a document on his clipboard. "I see it's registered to your husband. I'm afraid we have a summons for him. Local kids on bicycles found his abandoned EV battery in an off-road drainage ditch on the Eastern Shore and called the sheriff's office."

"But how could you have known it was ours?" she asked.

"The Department of Motor Vehicles keeps track of serial numbers on batteries. We traced the serial numbers back to this vehicle. Ma'am? It's illegal to dump a battery anywhere except at a hazardous waste facility. Any idea why your husband neglected to comply with the law? And by the way, EV batteries are usually too heavy to handle alone. Did you help him?"

Velma's feline eyes narrowed. "Won't you come inside for a cup of coffee, Officer? We can talk more comfortably there."

"Nice of you, ma'am, but no thanks. Please explain why the discard wasn't in the vehicle. There's room for two."

Velma batted her eyelashes and gave him a contrite look. "We were in a dreadful jam, Officer. The attendant at the EV station sold us a dud. We were stuck out in the boonies without any quarters for the charge meters on the poles. Our credit card wouldn't work. The doggoned slot was jammed with chewing gum. So we tried to push the car to the next pole. We junked the dud to lighten the car. But it was uphill. We couldn't push it far enough. Our cell phone battery was dead, so we couldn't call the mobile charge truck. I know it was terribly irresponsible of us to leave the battery, but we were desperate."

Officer Larkin suppressed a smile, but couldn't resist: "Quite a comedy of errors."

"Yes, but not funny at the time. Would you believe a mobile charge truck came along anyway, on a routine call for someone else? We flagged him down and had him charge up Battery Two, so we were able to get home. He never noticed Battery One in the ditch."

"Why didn't you just have him retrieve it for you?"

"We were so flustered and exhausted by then that we didn't think to ask him."

Officer Larkin noted that Velma hadn't shut the passenger door all the way. "Mind if I take a look?" he asked.

A lightning chill shot through her and her muscular body stiffened visibly, a reflex not lost on the policeman. "Of course not," she mumbled.

He flung the door wide and flipped the passenger side lever under the dash. The hatch to Battery Two sprang open. Satisfied, he closed it. He was about to accept the lady's offer of a cup of coffee when suddenly, a muffled, metallic thumping reached his ears, and he strained to locate its source. He leaned over the passenger seat, placed his hand under the dash on the driver's side, and pulled the lever. The Battery One hatch sprang open.

Officer Larkin stared. Neatly tucked into the compartment reserved for Battery One lay a man, wedged in as if the space had been specially designed just for his slender frame. Ugly purple blotches colored his bony face as he gasped for air. An orange jumper cable encircled his red-streaked neck.

Scowling, Velma understood the situation immediately. Her haste in stuffing her husband into the compartment must have loosened the garrote. She hadn't persisted with it long enough to finish the job.

As Officer Larkin freed Ernest from his intended coffin, Velma stood watching, detached and disgusted. *Ernest, you son-of-a-gun,* she thought. *Such a perfectionist, such a purist. Always lecturing and correcting me. Couldn't you have been gracious enough to let me do this one thing?*

In a choked, labored voice, her husband managed the last word. "Couldn't even get this right, could you, Vel?"

Officer Larkin drew Velma's hands together behind her back. As he cuffed her wrists, her fingers curled like claws, her eyes smoldered, and her brain boiled as it charged up with fresh tactics.

I'll get the best lawyer. I'll make bail. If Ernest thinks he's through with me, he's mighty mistaken. Hey, sweetheart, I'm just revving up.

§

Seeing Red

The doorbell rang. Elise Harrenton saved the accounting spreadsheet on her iMac and trotted to the front hall. A Fed Ex guy stood on the porch. She opened the door and signed for a nine-by-twelve tan bubble bag addressed to Mr. Charles Harrenton. Return address: Cartier Fifth Avenue.

Elise's heart quickened. Charles didn't often buy her presents, but the package was from Cartier. It had to be for her. She carried the package into the dining room, sat down in one of the upholstered chairs, and pulled the tab. Inside sat a long blue velvet box. Under it peeked out an elegant silver envelope. Her fingers tingled as she removed the velvet box. Setting it on the table, she sprang the catch.

Couched in white satin lay a pendant: a white-gold chain and an exquisite square-cut sapphire surrounded by diamonds. In the noonday sunlight, the gems winked at her with self-satisfied knowledge of their brilliance. Elise flipped her shoulder-length chestnut hair behind her right ear, a habit when she anticipated something special about to happen.

Reaching into the bubble bag for the silver envelope, she pulled it out, opened it, and read: "My darling Melanie. Thank you for the blissful Bermuda weekend. Your devoted Charles."

Elise's lean body grew rigid. She felt a burning in her belly, heartburn in her chest, her neck and face on fire.

She and Charles had never taken a trip to Bermuda! They'd barely traveled anywhere the past few years. He traveled all the time, working eighty-hour weeks running his Fortune-500 company. She'd put up with his insane schedule because she loved him. Only to find out that he loved someone else?

What had gone wrong? Didn't they have a secure marriage, with trust and all the rest, and even good sex? Every negative detail suddenly loomed as the villain. Was she spending too much time at the gym, carving her former plump self into a gaunt, athletic machine? Was it the faint varicose veins threading her thighs? Her smallish breasts? The fact that she'd miscarried twice and hadn't been able to conceive again? Whatever *it* was, she hadn't seen it coming. And there was no use denying that Charles was still a stunning man at forty: six-two, with dark hair and confident green eyes.

Elise stayed rooted to the chair for a long time, replaying in her mind the joke Charles had made of her life. What should she do? Confront him when he walked through the door tonight? Rant and rave? Throw things? Threaten divorce? It all sounded so clichéd. She deserved better.

At that moment she stopped brooding. Her breath quickened, and a seed began to germinate within the farthest reaches of her mind. Charles would be leaving soon for another month-long business trip, due to return home on Valentine's Day. She would have her gift ready for him when he returned. A gleeful smile crossed her face. Yes, it was time to redecorate.

But first she had an urgent task. She took the silver card down the hall to her office, photocopied it, and printed it out in color. For evidence. Whipping out her digital camera, she took two photos of the velvet box: the first one closed; the second one with the glorious pendant lying in the open box. She checked the two images, pleased that she had remembered to turn off the flash, enhancing the natural lighting and showing off the jewels to their best advantage.

Next, she jumped into her Porsche, zipped over to Office Depot, and bought a nine-by-twelve tan bubble bag, exactly like the one that had been delivered. Back home in the kitchen, she boiled water, and as the steam chugged out of the teakettle spout, she held the bubble bag from Cartier above the scalding puffs and steamed off the "From" and "To" labels. After allowing them to dry, she used thin coats of Elmer's Glue to affix them to the envelope she'd just purchased. Saying goodbye to the sapphire and diamonds, she snapped the box shut and tucked it inside the bag, along with the card. Sealing the bag with great care, she placed it on Charles's desk, under the pile of other mail that had arrived that day. Charles would probably kick himself when he realized he'd had the package sent home instead of to his mistress, but he'd also think Elise was too wrapped up in her accounting work to figure out what he'd been up to.

All the better for her plan.

But her strategy needed backbone. She just couldn't remember all the irritants that bugged her husband most. Maybe the Internet could help. Typing madly, she Googled "Phobias" and discovered a plethora of links, from simple definitions to studies in psychiatric and psychological journals. Scanning the websites, she singled several out. *Ereuthophobia. Ornithophobia. Pteridophobia.* Those three would needle him the most.

* * * *

February 14th dawned cold but with brilliant sun. Charles returned late in the afternoon, catching a cab at the train station, looking forward to a relaxed evening with his single-malt scotch and the NBA on TV. But when the cab pulled up to 1577 Larkspurr Lane, he wondered whether he'd given the driver the wrong address. Their conservative black front door was now a screaming enamel red—like a hooker's nail polish. The door swung open before he had a chance to use his key. Elise greeted him with a mock pinup-girl pose, in a filmy red teddy. As he stepped into the foyer, setting down his briefcase and luggage, she threw her arms around his neck. "So glad you're finally home, darling. Happy Valentine's Day!"

He tried an appropriate response, but it just wouldn't come. "Elise. The front door. It's so . . . garish!"

"Darling, welcome to our new décor." She helped him off with his cashmere overcoat and hung it in the closet. "How was your flight, sweetheart? You look beat."

"Snow in New York. Delayed takeoff. Nasty turbulence. In other words, not so great. But seriously, what's with the door business?"

Elise nuzzled a kiss on his neck. "It's *feng shui*, darling. The Chinese spiritual forces of wind and water. A red door symbolizes welcome—harmony with the universe."

"*Feng* hooey is more like it." Charles shook his head, spotting the new floor: a dizzying array of red and orange irregular shapes. "Jeez, Elise, isn't this kind of busy for a front hall?"

"Not really. Mosaics are the 'in' thing now. They call this pattern Sunset Blitz." She led him into the living room. "Let me give you the tour, dear. Ta da! Our new contemporary home. Quite electrifying and exquisite, I think."

Charles's jaw dropped. He couldn't speak. His eyes ached from what he saw. A tomato-red leather sofa, flanked by matching bucket chairs. On a glass coffee table, a tall vase filled with long-stemmed red and salmon rosebuds. An area rug edged in a broad border of Chinese red. He gritted his teeth at the sight of the freshly painted walls: wide vertical stripes of ruby red and maroon. The motif continued down the hall to the kitchen. "I guess I can get used to this stuff, if I have to," he mumbled.

His agreeable mood lasted about five seconds, until he noticed the hanging pots of greenery in each corner of the living room: voluptuous ferns overflowing with coiled tendrils. An involuntary shudder shook his body. "What the hell, Elise. Those damned things look downright snaky!"

It was then that he heard a squawking commotion in the kitchen. He turned pale. "Birds? In this house?" He raced toward the kitchen and lurched to a stop in the doorway. A tall cage stood beside the breakfast table. Two large parrots swayed from side to side on their roosts. Their beady eyes stared at him.

Charles broke into an icy sweat. "Elise, have you turned totally dense?"

"Sorry, dear," she murmured. "I thought they'd lend a little amusement to our marriage. We can teach them to talk, you know, all sorts of cute things. They're very smart."

"Get those friggin' beasts out of here! I'm going to change," he said, pressing his lips together to prevent escape of his ugliest thought. *If she's messed with our room, I'll strangle her.*

Charles entered the master bedroom, flicked on the light, and nearly fainted. He wished he were back on the road. The recessed lighting cast a sinister glow on the king-size bed. The headboard was covered in red and purple paisley; the comforter, shams, and sheets were scarlet, trimmed in purple. Vermillion curtains cascaded from ceiling to floor. And on the far wall, Elise had hung a large framed photo of parakeets.

Shivering, he tore off his business clothes and pulled on his favorite gray sweats. Would he at least be able to pee in peace? Opening the door to the master bath, he sighed with relief to discover the pristine white granite vanity top—until he saw that the shower walls were retiled in a throbbing red brick, and a potted fern sat perched on the toilet tank, its leaves curling—practically crawling—over the sides.

Dinner did nothing to soothe his anxiety. Crowded together on his Wedgwood plate were rare roast beef, a salad of grated red cabbage, and baby beets. Their juice stained the mashed potatoes nestled against them. Famished as he was, Charles pushed the plate away. It wasn't just the nearly all-red meal. He couldn't tolerate individual foods touching each other. He desperately needed a glass of wine, but not this one: burgundy, in a gleaming blood-red goblet. Then Elise handed him a long, slender box. *What can it be but a tie? How original is that?* And that's what it was. Tiny white polka dots on crimson silk.

"Elise, what the devil is this?" Charles pounded the fuchsia tablecloth with his fist. "Have you ever seen me in a red tie? Well, have you?" His face contorted and his cheeks flushed.

A twinge of genuine sympathy clouded her face. "No, darling, but I thought it would be a refreshing change. The stock market's been so bad, and the business news has been so gloomy. I thought this bright tie would cheer you up. It's an Armani, a special limited-edition. I'm sorry."

"Have you ever seen me in any suit or jacket that's not black, gray, navy, or brown?" He didn't wait for an answer. "Because I hate red! Don't tell me you didn't know that. And what's with the ferns and the birds and this revolting dinner? Are you trying to drive me crazy?"

Charles suddenly bent over, clutching his stomach. "I don't feel so well. Something's wrong." He bolted from the table and staggered into the guest powder room. Falling to his knees, he flipped up the toilet seat and vomited. His guts heaved and retched until, finally, his belly quieted down. He flushed and pushed down the toilet-seat lid. Then his head began aching as he took in the lid's new cloth cover: red and yellow stripes. Pulling himself weakly upright to the vanity sink, he turned on the faucet to wash his hands and face. That's when he spotted the cerise hand towels and—in a crystal bowl—cherry-red, heart-shaped soaps. Charles broke into a spasm of chills. He reached for his usual bottle of Listerine mouthwash, the citrus-flavored orange one. But what his eyes met with absolute horror was a bottle of Lavoris, in fire-engine red. Charles gasped and clutched his chest.

* * * *

Elise remained seated at the table, sipping her wine, smiling widely as she gazed at all the new touches in their house. *You deserve it, you louse, for cheating on me. And once your anxiety attack is over, I'll hand you the divorce papers—with a photo of that diamond-and-sapphire pendant attached. It should be enough to get me everything. Happy Valentine's Day.*

She strode to the powder room. The door was open. She

arrived just as Charles swayed forward, backward, forward—and crumpled to the floor. His large frame filled the tiny room.

She knelt beside him. "Oh, my God! Wake up, dear. Please wake up. Are you all right?" But she knew he wasn't. His face had taken on a ghostly pallor. His eyes had rolled up into his head.

Elise felt a stab of remorse. Yes, she had orchestrated her scheme to feed on his phobias. Yes, she had intended to make him suffer an anxiety attack before serving him with divorce papers. But a heart attack? And one severe enough to kill her strong, handsome, ruddy husband? She hadn't intended to take her revenge so far.

Then she remembered the stunning pendant he'd bought for someone else, and her guilt evaporated as quickly as it had come. Everything was working out—amazingly well, actually. Charles's death was quite a bonus. A fortuitous accident! His generous life insurance policy would set her up in comfort. Okay, so he hadn't bought the diamond-and-sapphire pendant for her. But so what? Now she could go out and buy herself one. Only bigger. *Happy Valentine's Day to me.*

Jolted out of her reverie, she scanned the rooms she'd transformed, and a fresh thought hit her. Now she could get rid of the gauche décor, those violent, head-splitting reds. And the ferns. And those annoying parrots. Win. Win. Win.

Elise sprang up, loped to the kitchen, and called 911. While she waited for the ambulance, she poured herself a large glass of white wine.

§

Adrift on Kaneohe Bay

Captain Rick Garvey stepped into the dinghy tied to the dock behind his Kaneohe Bay home. The title of captain was honorary, but Rick had earned it decades ago at the local yacht club, a well-respected marina on the windward side of Oahu.

The weather promised a relaxed day cruise: a robust but steady trade wind from the east-northeast, and a Delft-blue sky full of warm sun, punctuated with a few cottony puffs. Rick untied the tender line and rowed past the ancient Hawaiian fishponds out into the bay. His destination: the Cal 20 moored to a buoy some hundred-fifty yards offshore.

He secured the dinghy to the buoy and boarded the twenty-foot sailing craft he had dubbed *Downsized* after selling his larger Cal 30. He chuckled at a bit of irony here. The name "*Downsized*" barely fit on the Cal 20's transom. He should have chosen a smaller name.

Leaning over the rails, the perpetually tanned, balding senior moved the cooler, loaded with a couple of beers and a few bottles of water, to the larger boat. Despite his age, he lifted it with ease. His sinewy body was still muscled from decades of what he modestly called "fussing around" docks and boats. This was his relaxation: man against the sea for the next four or five hours. He would return by sundown, at the very latest. At least that's what he'd promised Peggy, his wife of fifty years. Oh, yes, Rick had also promised Peggy not to leave the bay because he was sailing alone. His children had grown up and acquired other interests, leaving him to sail solo much of the time. Peggy had plenty to worry about. She knew her husband still yearned to replay the earlier years of their marriage, when they cruised through choppy ocean waters to Molokai, Maui, and other outer Hawaiian islands. Kaneohe Bay was plenty big enough for sailing these days, Peggy argued. It stretched all the way from Mokapu Peninsula, the U.S. Marine Corps base, to the tiny conical island known as Chinaman's Hat eight miles away.   Today was of particular importance. It was Rick's seventieth birthday. Peggy had wanted to take him out to dinner or do something else special to celebrate, but he chose this glorious day for a sail as his birthday gift to himself.

An hour later, Rick was in his element. With both jib and mainsail full on his third westerly tack, he intentionally leaned to port and headed out the Sampan Channel. The boat ran fast with this high tide, and he sought to take advantage of it for as long as the depth-under-keel would permit. As he began to lay off the wind for an alternate tack, he noticed a dark shape on the horizon just beyond where the bay spreads out into the Pacific.

The shape grew larger and more defined as Rick continued to close the distance. Soon the strange object took the shape of another sailboat. But as *Downsized* approached, he felt a curious sensation and tightened his grip on the tiller. As the hull plowed through the churning waves, he did a double-take. What he saw was a nearly bare mast, with a few shredded rags where the sails ought to have been. Closing in on the craft, he noticed the mast bent at least fifteen degrees about halfway up. Two of the shrouds flopped freely as the surf rolled. The sailboat was about thirty feet long and seemed to be adrift, working its luckless way through a gap in the barrier reef between the bay and the ocean. It tossed and turned about and revealed its stern, with *Naut-a-Clue* emblazoned across it. Rick lowered his mainsail and edged in on momentum. There didn't seem to be anybody on board, but as the final distance narrowed, he noticed what appeared to be a thin fishing line trailing from a port-side cleat.

Fighting bobbing waves, Rick moved quickly as he lashed the two craft together, clamping a fender between the two boats with line fore and aft at the cleats. Trying to ignore his creaking joints, he struggled to maintain his balance as he climbed over the port gunwale. If Peggy had been with him, she would have begged him not to get involved, meaning not to get them into trouble, but to stay aboard their Cal 20 and call the situation in to the Coast Guard when they returned home. But Rick's heart was beating like *taiko* drums against his chest wall, and inside his head, curiosity urged him on—the same curiosity that had propelled his successful engineering career. He was a problem solver. Besides, he had stupidly forgotten his cell phone and had no other means of communication on *Downsized.*

He found his footing and succeeded in climbing aboard the renegade boat. As he straightened up, he jerked to a stop. A man lay facedown in the cockpit in several inches of water. He appeared to be *haole*, middle-aged, with graying red hair, arms limp at his sides, hands blue, and the prominent veins even bluer. He was barefoot and shirtless, wearing only once-white shorts. A white peaked cap lay upside down a few feet away. The body looked rather slender, unmuscled, with narrow shoulders. *Not a veteran sailor*, Rick decided. The legs splayed out. Noting the sun-scorched flesh on the man's back, calves, and arms, Rick speculated he must have been dead a few days. A fat wallet protruded from a rear pocket.

Rick pondered for only a split-second before pulling it out. A driver's license identified the man as Merwin MacAlbee, five-foot-eight inches, 180 pounds. Rick whistled. The centerfold of the wallet held $1,592. A business card revealed that Mr. MacAlbee was a partner in a Honolulu seafood restaurant called MacAlbee and Harada.

He braced himself in the sloshing water caused by the

boat's uncontrolled rocking, then gently rolled the victim over on his back and confirmed the man's face against the driver's license photo. The bare-chested body gave no indication of the cause of death—not a mark on him. *Perhaps a heart attack*, Rick thought.

While searching the small cabin, he checked out the galley: only about a day's worth of canned food and a can opener. Tucked into a slot above a fold-out writing ledge, he found the equivalent of a ship's log. He took the notebook out on deck, where the light was much better and sat down on a vinyl cushion to study it. The first entry was eleven days earlier, made as the victim set out from leeward Oahu. But the log revealed much more than the basic itinerary, weather, and directional settings. It also served as a diary. Mr. MacAlbee had planned a two-week solo journey at sea with no particular destination. But reading on, Rick discovered that the purpose of the sailor's cruise was to clear his head. Merwin MacAlbee had confronted his partner with charges of embezzlement and had given Len Harada fourteen days to return the money to their corporate account. The tone of the diary reflected a bitter anger over his partner's betrayal and a disgust with himself for not recognizing the signs—the drop in cash flow—a lot sooner.

Rick's pulse quickened. He felt as if he had walked, unwelcome, into a stranger's life. His eyebrows came together in a deep frown as he pondered the boat's unusual name. Did *Naut-a-Clue* have a specific meaning? Had MacAlbee named it immediately after he found out that his partner had skimmed off thousands of dollars from the restaurant? Or was it just a clever, whimsical pun he had given the boat years before, a wry comment on his own personal lack of sailing expertise?

For the most part, the entries described Mr. MacAlbee sailing in a great circle around Oahu, at least fifteen miles offshore. His last entry was three days ago. That entry contained no hint of anything wrong. The damage to the sails must have occurred after his death, during the big storm the day before yesterday. Rick surmised that the sails were probably old—but also weakened from the sun's ultraviolet rays and shredded while luffing wildly during the storm.

Now shadows fell as the sun began to set over the Ko'olau mountain range, so he rigged a stern line from his Cal 20 to the orphaned boat's bow cleat. He set sail—wing and wing to run with the wind at least partway to the Kaneohe Yacht Club. As a member, he knew which piers were for visiting boats. Once there, another club member helped him secure *Naut-a-Clue*.

Rick called the police and left to moor his own boat at his usual buoy and row his dinghy back to the family dock. He accomplished this in roughly forty-five minutes, plus a hasty briefing to his wife. A five-minute car ride brought him back to the club dock, arriving there just in time to greet the police.

Detective Frank Akiona headed the group. Rick immediately recognized the tall, burly cop with inky-black hair and keen dark eyes. He and Frank had taken the same marine biology course at the University of Hawaii a few years ago.

A three-man crime scene team pored over the boat and found nothing more than Rick had described. Camera flashes exploded right and left, and all the fittings were examined for prints. The body was carted off to the morgue, and the boat was declared a no-man's-land with yellow police tape. The crime team left for the night, leaving a uniform to guard the premises. Rick drove home to Peggy.

Over a cold supper Rick told her his story in detail. She rolled her eyes, but suppressed the urge to say "I told you so." But she was definitely ticked off. Three years before, he had complained of chest pains. An ambulance had rushed him to the Emergency Room and, after a few tests, the cardiologist had asked him: "When did you have your heart attack?"

An annoyed Rick said, "I've never had a heart attack."

"Oh, yes you have," the doctor said. Peggy would never forget that ugly scene. A stent was inserted to open up the blockage in the offending artery. Little did she know, her husband would think of that fragment of metal mesh as a green light to go about his sailing adventures, even if they no longer included ocean cruising.

They finished supper, and an exhausted Rick went right to bed. But he spent an uneasy night knowing there was something he'd seen and not mentioned to the police, but for the life of him he couldn't remember what. It haunted him like something he'd misplaced.

Just after eleven the following morning, Detective Akiona called, asking Rick to come on down to the station to sign a formal statement.

"Sure, Frank. By the way, how did MacAlbee die?"

"A preliminary toxicology screen says it was a quick-acting poison. A more extensive screen will be needed to identify the exact poison and its source. It's definitely a homicide. We studied the log and diary entries, and we've got the partner in for questioning now. So far he looks good for it, but the evidence is still circumstantial. We can't figure out how he managed it. We've got motive and means, but no poison was found aboard the boat. The unopened cans of food and drinking water were clean. I'm afraid we haven't been able to establish opportunity."

Rick cut in. "Mind if I throw in a comment?"

"Be my guest."

"I'm just speculating," Rick said. "I didn't know Mr. Mac-Albee, of course, but I read his log pretty carefully. I didn't get any idea that he was despondent or suicidal—more angry, I'd say. Was anything of value missing from the boat?"

"We have no way of telling," the detective said. "As you discovered, $1,592 was in his wallet—in large bills. That rules out robbery. Did you notice any signs of a third party on board?"

"No, no one," Rick answered. "It was weird. And sheer luck to encounter a sailboat in open seas, with no apparent sailing plan. But—" A thought flashed across Rick's mind, then slipped away. "Frank, before I come down to make a statement, would you allow me to have another look at the boat? Something's eating away at me. Maybe another look will trigger it."

The detective was quick to respond. "Of course. I hate that

dead-end feeling, if you'll excuse the expression. You can go over to the yacht club this afternoon, about two."

But Frank hadn't relayed permission to the officer guarding the boat. The guard used his cell phone to check back with the lieutenant before allowing Rick aboard. Even then, the officer was hardly cooperative. They finally compromised. Rick borrowed a pencil from him and used it to pull up the hardly noticeable fishing line tied to the port-side cleat. The skimpy remains of a dead *papio* dangled from the end of it. Rick examined it for a few minutes, then dropped the color-drained fish and line in the water once more, leaving the line tied to the cleat. Rick's blue eyes lit up behind his sunglasses. His heartbeat quickened, this time with fresh knowledge. He now knew how the victim was murdered. Not only that, Rick alone had the "opportunity" aspect of the crime all figured out. He returned to the clubhouse and called Frank from a pay phone. Detective Akiona decided to come and look for himself.

An hour later, Rick and Frank were on their way to the police station with the dead fish and nylon line in an evidence bag. MacAlbee's tackle box was in the police cruiser's trunk. Hook, line, fish, and box went to the crime lab immediately. Rick dictated his statement to a stenographer and waited around for it to be typed before signing the statement. Then he returned home.

The Garvey phone rang at three-thirty the next afternoon. It was Frank Akiona. "Rick, I owe you one. The lab did a second tox screen. The poison was tetrodotoxin, from a blowfish. Symptoms can occur as early as twenty minutes after ingestion: nausea, dizziness, numbing of the tongue, shortness of breath, even paralysis. If symptoms are untreated, death occurs in four to six hours. We're fairly certain the killer was the vic's business partner, Leonard Harada."

Blowfish, also known as pufferfish or balloonfish. Yes! Rick could barely conceal his feeling of triumph.

Frank explained how he believed Harada had administered the poison: via the fish hook. "When our lab people discovered that the fish had died from the very same poison, they examined the other hooks in MacAlbee's tackle box. They found traces of the poison there as well and became extremely suspicious."

"Wait a minute, Frank," Rick blurted out. "Wouldn't any poison on the hook be washed off, or at the very least, be so diluted in all that water, especially salt water, that it would be ineffective?"

"Ordinarily, yes," Frank said. "But Harada was quite clever in that respect. He coated the hook with multiple layers of poison, allowing them to dry in between. Then he sealed the poison in with an outer coating of clear fingernail polish. The fish teeth gnawed away the protective coating, exposing it to the deadly potion. Apparently, MacAlbee filleted the fish and discarded the remains overboard before preparing the meal and consuming it."

"If he got sick so quickly," Rick said, "wouldn't some of the fish have been left on a plate?"

"Well, friend, I can only guess. *Papio* is a small type of *ulua*, another food fish. Either he finished it all, or he deep-six-ed the remainder because it didn't taste good."

"Harada probably figured on MacAlbee eating the fresh food stores first," Rick said. "It would be a number of days out to sea before the man started to live off the ocean. A pretty good alibi, wouldn't you say? That would be a problem for you."

"Of course," Frank said. "That's what stumped me."

"Are you saying you don't have enough to make a case against the business partner?"

"No, I'm not saying that," Frank countered. "Thanks to you, my friend, we have now established opportunity for him to commit the crime. In a search of the Harada home this morning, the team couldn't find any trace of the poison. He probably took extraordinary care to get rid of it. But a half-bottle of clear nail polish turned up in his outside trash—same brand, same formula. The man lives alone. No potential female users. Oh, one more thing. A *skosh* bit of poison appeared on the brush applicator. Besides that, leaving his fingerprints on the bottle ties him directly to the hooks and the murder. That about wraps it up."

"Crazy, isn't it?" Rick said. "Blowfish properly prepared in a restaurant is considered a delicacy."

"Yeah," Frank said. "But only by diners who like living on the edge. The toxicologist told me that in restaurants where it's served, Japanese chefs are specially trained and licensed to prepare it. Believe it or not, some of the toxin is deliberately left in because it gives the diner a kind of euphoria, which is the whole point of ordering it."

Rick remained silent for a moment, taking in all this sinister detail, when Frank spoke again, this time in a much lighter tone.

"Hey, Rick! How about a beer one night next week? Or even better, a seafood dinner? It'll be on me—a thank-you for your help. And by the way, wasn't it your birthday this week? We'll make it a belated celebration. I know a great place in Waikiki. They serve excellent fresh fish."

Rick Garvey's weathered face suddenly turned seaweed green. "Maybe next year, pal."

§

The Busybody

Oh, nuts!" cried the freckle-faced teen as he failed to make yet another catch. The scuffed-up football had sailed clean over his extended hands and landed in the middle of Mrs. Sullivan's prized azalea bush, sending salmon petals flying. It settled there like a bird in a nest. The boy pursued it, but slowed to a cautious tiptoe across the perfect lawn, lest the old lady catch him in her yard. As soon as he plucked the pigskin from its nest, he saw the front room curtains flutter.

"Hey, guys, old lady Sullivan's seen us and she's gonna call the cops on us again for playin' in the street. We'd better take off or I'm gonna lose my ball—maybe for good this time."

"Cool it, man, we can get a few more plays in," called a teammate from the street.

Five minutes later, a police black and white turned the corner into the first block of Iris Lane. Eleven teenagers scattered and scrambled over neighborhood fences out of view. The cruiser drove slowly by the Sullivan house, made a U-turn at the end of the street, and continued on its way without a stop. It was their third response this week.

For as long as anyone could remember, Addie Sullivan had been the self-appointed neighborhood busybody. She had survived two horrific marriages: the first, a year of subservience to a tyrant who took offense when she punched back. And the second, caregiving to an ungrateful invalid. No more weddings for her, thank you. The griefless widow of sixty-eight thrived on vigorous housework, baking, gardening—and her all-time favorite hobby: armchair vigilantism. These activities rewarded her with a pretty fair share of muscles and entertainment.

Addie had been firmly ensconced in the brown-shuttered, yellow clapboard house at 825 Iris Lane when everyone else moved in. The lane actually dead-ended in 800's, so naturally, the neighborhood kids chose this block for stickball, touch football, and kickball. Addie delighted in calling the cops if they disturbed even one blade of her beloved grass. Her ski-jump nose automatically bent out of shape for the slightest hint of any community misstep, prompting her to notify city councilmen, the community improvement association, and the fire and police departments. Woe be unto a neighbor who left his empty garbage can out on the curb for a whole day after collection.

Addie's preoccupation seemed quite at odds with her looks, which newcomers expected—from her reputation—to be gaunt and severe. Far from it. With a head of wild yellow curls, Addie fancied makeup, even during her chores. She wore enough blush to rival Raggedy Ann; enough mascara, eye shadow, and frosted lipstick to compete with the Bratz girls.

And she certainly didn't think of herself as mean-spirited. Community-spirited would be more to her liking. During the daylight hours, her accusing eyes kept watch from the front porch rocker. After sundown she continued her vigil from an overstuffed recliner strategically positioned in the middle of the parlor's bay window. Some neighbors claimed she even used binoculars.

So it wasn't much of a surprise when Addie engaged Fred Tremaine in a confrontation. Fred had the nerve to park his autoparts business van in front of his house directly across from the Sullivan residence. Addie stomped into the street swinging her bamboo cane. She didn't need the cane; it had belonged to her second husband. But it made a nice psychological weapon, and she'd watched enough swashbuckling movies to brandish it with authority.

"You spiteful hooligan!" she shouted. "You know very well the Community Covenants and Restrictions don't permit the parking of commercial vehicles on the street overnight."

"Ish my truck and my house. Shcrew you, Missus Sullivan."

"Oh, so you're drunk again, are you, you miserable sot?"

"Ish none o' your meddlin' business, woman." He drew a step closer.

"It is when your wife cries from the terrible beatings you give her. I can hear the poor woman clear across the lane. Her crying keeps me up all night, you nasty bully of a wife-beater."

"So close your damn windowsh, you dumb witch."

Addie watched Tremaine's blood-red eyes stretch wide into a fearsome look. His puffy ochre face distorted, and he seemed to loom larger than his actual five-foot-eleven, so she did an about face and retreated into the safety of her house.

Fred remained in the middle of the street for a few minutes, but all he saw was two flashing eyes staring back at him from the moonlit bay window. A self-proclaimed winner, he smiled, turned and walked into his house. He apparently spared his wife that night, but Barbara Tremaine could be heard crying several nights afterward. Addie often reported the domestic disturbance to the police, but each time they showed up Barbara protested, "Oh, it was just a minor disagreement" and refused to press charges.

Fred continued to park the van out front. When Addie tried the police once more, they informed her that the so-called parking violation was a matter for their community association, as it was their covenant being contested. The fact that the association president had taken a month's vacation left her further frustrated. The police began to think of Addie as the boy who cried wolf. They responded to her calls, then placated her; now they ignored her.

But the van wasn't the only bone of contention between

these two neighbors. The Tremaines had two mean-looking Great Danes: Rocky and Hardplace. Fred went out of his way to walk the two huge canines on Addie's side of the street. He intentionally dallied in front of her immaculate emerald-green lawn for them to deposit their doggie do the size of soccer balls. She didn't dare go out to confront the man for fear of being attacked by those vicious beasts.

One pleasantly cool evening Addie had been dozing in the parlor recliner when something stirred her awake. Her watch revealed the late hour—twenty past midnight. She realized something strange was going on over at the Tremaines. The van? No. It had been parked across the street for a whole week now without having been moved. A second vehicle, a dark blue sedan, was parked at the curb as well. Addie noted that it wasn't there at 11:15 when she dozed off.

The front door of the house slammed shut. She strained to see through the darkness. Why hadn't they turned on their outside light? Then, as the shadows moved out into the moonlight, she saw two distinct figures: Barbara and another woman. *Most likely her mother, Grace,* Addie thought. *But what are they bumping down the steps? What is that huge bundle they're dragging up the walk?* Addie moved closer to the bay window, pressing her curious nose to the glass until, under the streetlight, she recognized two huge lawn-and-leaf bags duct-taped together with something unusually heavy inside—so heavy the two women had to stop every few feet to rest.

A thrill shot through Addie's spine. *There must be a body inside. Fred's body! The woman's gone and done it. The brute must have pushed her too far. And her mother's helping her get rid of the body. Bravo, Barbara!*

But wait! This was a crime! Addie drummed her polished nails on the telephone table, fighting the urge to pick up the receiver and notify the authorities. With a dramatic sigh, she allowed her righteous indignation to win out. *This was murder.* She had to call it in. *But will they get here in time?* she wondered. For a fleeting moment, she considered changing into her best pants suit to greet the police. After all, murder was a special occasion.

Addie returned to her watch post at the bay window and waited for the police. Barbara and Grace finished loading the body into the Chevy trunk. When they climbed into the car, she began to think they'd make a clean getaway. But then the driver's door opened again, and she saw Grace head back into the house. Addie saw her walk straight through the living room and bedroom without using lights, but then the bathroom light came on. Addie nervously squirmed about in her recliner until, finally, the bathroom light went out again, and Grace reappeared through the front door.

Grace got in and started the car, but before she could pull away from the curb, a black and white police cruiser nosed in, boxing the Chevy between itself and Fred's parked van. The Chevy wasn't going anywhere. Addie purposely moved to the porch so she wouldn't miss a thing—not one delicious word. She silently slid the rocker into the shadows and sat down.

One officer ordered Barbara and Grace to face the vehicle with their hands on the car roof, while the second officer took the keys from the ignition and searched the back seat. He found nothing. He proceeded to open the trunk and saw the two plastic bags. Slicing one open with a pen knife, he shouted, "Found something!" He'd discovered a dead body, but it wasn't Fred Tremaine's. The dead hulk belonged to Rocky, one of the aged Great Danes. The ladies were allowed to drop their hands. Neither officer could suppress a chuckle.

"Okay, ladies! What's this all about?"

Barbara Tremaine explained that Rocky had died two days earlier. She tried to wait for Fred to come home from a four-day auto-parts seminar in Detroit, but the corpse began to smell up the garage too much. She'd called the veterinarian, but he couldn't send anyone for the corpse until tomorrow afternoon when he had extra help. If she could manage to wrap poor Rocky in plastic and bring him in, the vet said, he would quickly dispose of ripe Rocky in the pet crematorium. Barbara sighed. "Rocky's ripeness simply couldn't wait until tomorrow afternoon, so I called Mom to help."

Addie overheard it all and felt a flash of embarrassment—an emotion almost foreign to her. She slunk back into the parlor unseen and went to bed without turning on a single light in the house.

At ten o'clock the following morning, Barbara appeared at the Sullivan front door, her round face flushed with fury. "How could you, Addie? Why did you call the police on me? Some neighbor you are."

Addie first apologized and then confessed what the scene appeared to be in her eyes. Suddenly, amid the tension, the two of them saw the humor of the situation and began to laugh. Addie invited Barbara in for tea and apple cake. That night became a turning point, a friendship, something rare for both women.

Over the next few weeks, they often shared tea and cake in Barbara's kitchen, although never when Fred was at home. Barbara soon began to talk openly about her marriage troubles. Fred had a girlfriend with whom he drank and gambled, and made no effort to hide this relationship. There weren't any auto-parts seminars in Detroit—only frequent pleasure junkets to Vegas and Atlantic City. The beatings came when he returned home broke, despondent, and stinking drunk.

"Why do you stay married to that bum?" asked Addie. "I'd have thrown the loser out years ago."

"It's his house, and I've got no place to go," Barbara replied. "We married before I finished high school. Addie, I don't even know how to go about finding a job, let alone being qualified for one. I've put on a little weight, and with money so scarce, I can't afford to replace any of my old clothes. I'm trapped."

"Why does *he* stay with *you* then?"

"His girlfriend won't have anything to do with him when he's broke, so he comes home to me. At least he has someone to cook and clean for him."

"And you're his favorite punching bag, too." Addie enjoyed

her mothering role, but deep inside felt exasperation. She'd rarely seen Barbara smile; life was passing her by. Underneath the misery, a rather pretty middle-aged women was hiding with fair skin and a plump but shapely body.

"He wasn't always this way," Barbara insisted. "He used to be sweet and gentle. I think he just feels trapped in his going-no-place job, so he takes it out on me."

And you let him, Addie thought. She gave a start when Hardplace hobbled into the kitchen. The once-proud coffee-colored dog could barely move across the floor. Hardplace laid his twelve-year-old grayed head on Barbara's lap, and she took his solemn face in two hands, looking lovingly down into two large sad eyes. She stroked his fur. Hardplace circled once and lay down at her feet.

"I thought the dogs were Fred's," said Addie.

"They are, but he's neglecting them...I mean him lately. Besides, I'm the one who feeds the poor guy."

"But aren't Great Danes ferocious?" Addie asked.

"Not at all," Barbara murmured. "They're sweet as pie."

Another embarrassment. Addie had feared them for years for no reason at all. She even forgave them for pooping on her grass; that was all Fred's fault.

The friendship ebbed whenever Fred decided to be in residence and flourished again while he chose to be on junket. Addie always knew when to call; the van would be parked out front during the daylight hours. Barbara actually seemed content with the current state of her marriage and studiously avoided talking about it. But she had no such qualms about her friend's private life. Slyly, she asked about Addie's second husband. "You nursed him for so long. Did he leave you anything in his will?"

"His *will?*" Addie snorted. "His *won't* was more like it. He was always saying, 'You won't get this, you won't get that 'cuz you're not a good wife.' Can you believe it? My dad, may he rest in peace, bought me this house."

One scorching summer night, Addie heard Barbara crying

through the open windows. Alarmed, she crossed the street, rang the Tremaine doorbell, and pounded until Barbara answered.

Amid red face and streaming tears, Barbara announced that Hardplace too had gone to the inevitable doggie heaven.

That wasn't all. "Oh, Addie," she wailed. "Fred was due home this morning, but he phoned instead to say he's leaving me for good. Told me I can have the house and everything in it."

Hmmm, Addie thought, *sounds like a pretty nice outcome to me.* She hugged her friend. "Where's Hardplace now?"

"He's out in the garage, all packaged up just like Rocky was. Here, I'll show you." Grabbing a handful of tissues, she turned tail and walked down the hall, through the kitchen, and out into the attached garage. Addie felt compelled to follow.

"When did it happen?" she asked.

"Yesterday morning. I found him sprawled at the foot of the stairs when I got up. I tried to clean him up. He made an absolute mess. I've already called the vet, but I have no way to get him there without some help."

"What about Grace? She helped you last time."

"Mom went to Miami Beach last Thursday with her mahjong group." Barbara wiped her reddened eyes and blew her nose.

"I'm not sure how much help I can be, Barbara. I'm not very strong."

"Baloney! I've seen you hauling bags of mulch and topsoil around. You're a lot stronger than I am. Please?"

Addie nodded helplessly. She actually worried more about getting dust and dirt on her rhinestoned jersey.

"Oh, thank you, you're such a dear. We'll take Fred's van. It'll be so much easier." Barbara yanked her garden cart free of its hose attachments and dragged it to the bundle, securely wrapped in two lawn-and-leaf bags. She then pushed a weighty cardboard box up to the two-wheeled cart for stability. The women positioned themselves at opposite ends and lifted. A push of the button sent the garage door into the overhead, allowing them to drag the loaded cart out under the overcast nighttime sky. Barbara unlocked the van's rear doors and swung them wide. Because of the cart's height, they only needed to lift the bundle about eighteen inches to slide it into the rear of the vehicle.

Addie wished her friend a hasty good luck and spun about to return home.

"You can't leave me now!" Barbara protested. "Not when I need you most—to come with me."

Addie couldn't stand the tears and reluctantly slid into the van's passenger seat, wishing she hadn't agreed so quickly. Neither woman spoke during the twenty-minute ride to the vet. Barbara backed up to the double doors at the rear of the facility, and they climbed out.

"Wait here, I'll go around front and get Doc Evans," Barbara said. "He'll give us a hand."

A few minutes later the double doors flew open, and Doc Evans pushed a gurney up to the rear of the van. He and Barbara hoisted the bulky bundle onto the gurney and rolled it back into the work area. A reluctant Addie followed, wishing she were back in her recliner with a tall gin and tonic. The vet and gurney came to a stop before a huge iron furnace. Its heavy access hatch lay open, ready to receive their bundle.

"Is it as bad as last time?" Doc asked.

"You can look if you want, Doc, but Hardplace has been lying around in our hot garage at least one more day than Rocky did," said Barbara. "I had trouble keeping my dinner down the whole time I wrapped him up."

"It won't be necessary. I'll take your word for it."

Doc pulled the drawer-like tray out of the furnace. He and Barbara rolled the package from the gurney on to it. Doc slid the drawer home and closed the hatch, sealing it with four lock-down levers. He spun a series of dials into the red areas and pushed the large green start button. They heard a series of loud snapping sounds as the huge high-temperature oven roared into action.

"That's it, ladies. The whole process takes about thirty minutes. You can wait around another hour for everything to cool down and then you can take Hardplace's ashes with you. I can sell you an urn, too. They range from fifteen to seventy dollars."

"That won't be necessary, Doctor," Barbara replied. "The dogs belonged to my husband, and he seems to have lost interest in them. But please send me the bill for this."

"I understand. Well, I'll just have to take care of things here, won't I?" he said with an expression of profound concern. "You have my sincere condolences. Good evening, ladies."

Half an hour later, the two women hugged on the street in front of the Tremaine house and Addie returned home. Almost dizzy from their ordeal, she sank into her recliner, feeling all the endorphins that go with having done a good deed. She awoke the following morning, startled to find herself still in it, feeling oddly refreshed and not at all sore from sitting up all night. Only one thought intruded. Bake! One of her chocolate *babkas*, a rich coffee cake, would cheer her friend up.

"Surprise!" Addie trilled on the front steps, waving the warm cake under Barbara's nose.

"Ooo! That smells yummy. I've got a fresh pot of coffee on." She led Addie into the kitchen. "That was a nice thing you did for me last night," Barbara began as she filled both cups and set the pot back on the burner.

"Glad to be of assistance, dear," Addie replied, then took up a discussion on how the Ruperts family left their garbage cans on the street the whole day. Of course, the Ruperts' sin led to the overt shame of Cassandra Peach, who paraded around the house in her altogether while she vacuumed—blinds pulled up and all.

The coffee klatch, richly laced with more neighborhood gossip, saw no signs of ending when a curious scratching noise rattled the basement door.

Addie gasped, "What's that?"

"Oh, that's Fred," Barbara murmured as she rose from her chair.

"Fred? You mean he returned home last night?"

"In a manner of speaking—yes." Barbara opened the basement door, allowing an elderly Great Dane to hobble, click, and scrape across the ceramic kitchen floor.

"Good grief! It's Hardplace!" Addie shuddered, not knowing whether the ghostly sight of the dog or the grating noise made by his nails on the tiles upset her more.

"Don't be silly," Barbara giggled. "We disposed of Hardplace last night. This must be Fred."

Some joke. Addie threw a frantic glance toward the back door. She should probably make a run for it, but couldn't bear the suspense. "*What*...I mean *who* was in the lawn-and-leaf bag, girl?"

Barbara didn't answer. She stroked the specter-like Great Dane and scratched him behind one pointed ear. His long floppy tongue slobbered a kiss on her bare knee.

"Dear Lord!" Addie shrieked. "You went and done the brute in? You murdered your own husband? How could you? You could've divorced him!"

"Oh, I didn't actually murder him. It was an accident. Fred had been drinking cheap wine all morning yesterday. You know, the sort that comes in a jug. At noon the louse chased me up the stairs with a belt in his hands, looking to wallop me with it. He swung several times on the way up, missing me each time except for once—here." She pulled up her ruffled sleeve and showed Addie an ugly red welt on her forearm.

"So what happened to Fred?"

"On the last step he lunged for me and lost his footing. Fell all sixteen steps and hit his head on the landing wall."

"Was he still alive?"

"I don't know. At that point I was too confused."

"Why didn't you call for help? The paramedics or the police or someone?"

"I don't know. Part of me wanted him dead—free of him for good. Part of me wanted him alive so he could take care of me and earn a living for me. There was *some* good in him and I could love that. So I just sat around all afternoon, staring at him staring back at me with empty eyes. By evening, I got worried that the police would think I had actually murdered him."

"You poor, poor dear," Addie responded automatically. But then she noted that her friend didn't look so pathetic or miserable. The hunched shoulders had evaporated. Barbara stood tall, almost transformed. No more severe ponytail; her thick brunette hair fell free around her face. Gone were the grubby sweat suits. She actually looked spritely in cutoff jeans and fire-engine-red T-shirt.

"I didn't want to go to jail," Barbara explained. "Then I remembered how Mom and I handled Rocky. So…" Her voice grew perky. "I strapped Fred's body over double with two of his favorite belts. Nothing but the best for Fred. Then I slipped a lawn-and-leaf bag over each end and sealed the two bags in the middle. In fact, I bagged and duct-taped him a second time to be sure and stop that awful odor. His loss of interest in eating—that's what drunks do— had brought his weight down to a point where I could actually handle his body…fold him in half so he'd appear more like one of the dogs. Very thoughtful of him."

"Did you have some sort of plan?" asked Addie.

"Not really. That is, not until you came calling."

"I don't understand."

"Without Mom, I had no way of getting our precious package to the vet and crematorium. When you showed up on my doorstep, it was like manna from heaven. You were such a doll to volunteer. I could never have done it without you."

Addie's palms went damp. Her heart accelerated like a Mixmaster on high. "If it was an accident like you said, you should have gone right to the police. I'll call 911 now."

"Are you crazy? I waited too long—too many hours. They'd never believe me. No, you will *not* call the police!"

"And why is that? Are you threatening me?" Addie shot out of her chair and stood with hands on her hips in defiance.

"Let's just say you're involved—personally. Like I said, I couldn't have done it without you. I believe it's called aiding and abetting or maybe accessory-after-the-fact. I'm not sure which, but you are definitely in this with me now. So, no, you won't be calling the police."

Addie's temper and gold hoop earrings flashed in the morning sunlight. "Some friend you are. I'm no such thing as accessorizing. I'm completely innocent. There's no way anyone would believe that I'm involved in such an ugly scheme."

Barbara's usually reddened eyes gleamed with mischief. "Doc Evans's testimony might prove to the contrary. He saw you as a working accomplice. Sorry, old girl, but you hafta know that I'm grateful."

All the steam suddenly vented from Addie's defiance. Her arms collapsed to her sides. She fell back into the kitchen chair and absently inhaled the coffee aroma. She suddenly thought, *No more kitchen chats, no more pleasant encounters in the street or at the market.* The very idea of spending the rest of her days alone in the porch rocker or the parlor recliner—with the binoculars her only companion—seemed ridiculous now. *If Barbara doesn't feel guilty, why should I?* Addie flipped two generous slabs of *babka* onto the dessert plates. A smile broke across her face. "I have to admit, it was quite a lot of fun helping you and all, and I did enjoy the excitement. You do think we'll get away with it, don't you?"

"Get away with what? I don't know what you're talking about," smirked Barbara. "More coffee?"

"Yes please." Addie's gaze fell on the arthritic dog sprawled out asleep next to Barbara's chair, its chest heaving laboriously. "What happens when poor Hardplace has to go to doggie heaven? Won't Doc Evans smell a rat?"

"There are more vets in town than just Doc Evans. It's not like you have to have a death certificate or anything. And you'll be there to help." Barbara rested her free hand on Addie's shoulder as she poured the coffee. "Won't you?"

With a forkful of cake poised halfway to her lips, Addie grinned. "Naturally! What are partners for?"

Hits and Misses

Meet the deadlier of the species, the female professional hit person: Dr. Robin Priestly, Psychiatrist, and Dr. Jennifer Anne Willmont, Dentist. Neither is mob-related. Don't let their professions mislead you. These two kill for reasons you'd never imagine.

Deadly Remedies
Standby

Deadly Remedies

Dr. Robin Priestly doled out gems of domestic advice as a popular call-in television personality—a psychiatrist dealing primarily with the battered. In her early forties, she kept her dark brown hair short and off the face to enhance her plain yet kindly features, the motherly look so conducive to communicating with a patient. Piano legs, glasses, and a thick waist supported that look. Her demeanor, coupled with strong vocal chords and an air of authority, gave comfort to her callers. Robin dressed the part, too: formal business suits, pastel blouses, and practical heels.

Surreptitiously, she accomplished another, much-needed service to the community: she did away with evil people who preyed on their spouses. Somehow, *hit person* seems a little harsh in describing this self-appointed guardian of the abused, but what else could you call her? Her TV show aired five times weekly for seven months of the year. By choice, her medical practice normally ran just under two dozen patients. Being single and otherwise disentangled, she enjoyed a great deal of free time for her extraordinary ministering.

Robin wouldn't just kill indiscriminately, and she never asked for payment. Her lucrative practice and broadcasts provided a more than satisfactory lifestyle. It wasn't the killing so much as righting a wrong that yielded sufficient reward in itself. Her Priestly justice had to include something symbolically appropriate. Robin liked to think of the snuffing out as a good deed: taking the lives of bullies in exchange for giving life back to the abused. Not exactly Robin Hood, but close.

The enterprising doctor had little trouble finding domestic disasters to champion. Robin's call-ins poured out their pitiful woes without hesitation, relying completely on assumed anonymity. However, Caller ID usually yielded the poor soul's telephone number, and hacking into the phone company's reverse directory uncovered their names and addresses—hardly identity theft, but again, close.

The problem became one of selection. Who was trapped in the most dire situation? Who did the good doctor believe she could help most? Robin took copious notes as she listened and spoke. Her broadcasted advice was sound and heartfelt. Often she urged these women to get a divorce, but they usually gave some rationalization for staying in the marriage. Whatever her advice, it generally went unheeded. The fear factor, lack of money, or just low self-esteem nearly always stood in the way. Was it any wonder then that she resorted to the more invasive technique? Even *this* wasn't always the ultimate answer. Many returned to identical relationships afterward. Hardly a sterling batting average, she admitted.

"Hello! Dr. Priestly here. How may I help you?" Carla, the third caller of the Thursday afternoon show, seemed to be particularly desperate. Her husband had broken her leg with a baseball bat because he didn't like the smelly codfish she'd prepared for his dinner. He'd reluctantly taken her to the emergency room, where they set her leg in a heavy cast and sent her home with crutches. Despite her serious injury, the husband expected his wife to continue cleaning, cooking, and attending to his sexual demands. As a precaution, he locked her crutches in the closet when he went off to work each morning, so she couldn't run away. If she complained, he rewarded her with a backhand across the face. The woman claimed she loved the man and didn't want to leave him. Her question: What could she do to please him so he'd stop beating her? Good grief! What misplaced love! There were a half-dozen more callers during the thirty-minute show, but none so terribly in need.

An hour after Dr. Priestly closed the mike and walked out of the studio, she had the name and address of this battered, befuddled wife. Robin spent much of the next three workdays observing, from a distance in a rental car, the daily routines of Arthur Bailey and his wife. Carla was easy—she never left the house. How could she?

At 6:30 each morning, Arthur left for his job at the United Cement Company. He drove a wet-cement mixing truck from the mix silos in the company's supply yard to various construction sites. Finishing his morning rounds at 11:15 a.m., he sat in the truck for an hour consuming a brown bag lunch. His afternoon deliveries ended at precisely 3:20 each day, when he peeled off his splattered coveralls and swapped his crusted Boondocker boots for a pair of clean loafers. His spanking new Dodge Ram pickup would arrive at Danny's Irish Pub over on Alder Street shortly after 4 p.m. He sat in the corner booth with three or four beer-drinking buddies for the next two hours until, one by one, they left for home, leaving him to drink alone. At this point, the sociable Arthur turned sullen, so his last drink comprised a double shot of whiskey in a hefty stein of draft beer.

How the brute succeeded in driving home without killing or maiming himself puzzled Dr. Priestly at first. Following him at a safe distance, she discovered that his route was on a mostly deserted country road.

No later than 6:45 he'd stagger up the front steps and slam the front door to the tiny gray Cape Cod house at 231 Beale Street. As dusk fell to darkness, Robin crept up to the house and hid behind a sprawling juniper bush. She heard raised voices, scuffles, slaps, and the crying that ensued.

Dr. Priestley's plan began to gel into a prescription for extinguishing Arthur Bailey. On Wednesday, soon after he had left for his first delivery, Robin confidently strode through the gate of the United Cement Company yard in coveralls, baseball cap with her hair tucked in, and heavy work gloves. She quickly located Arthur's prized pickup, parked well away from the silos and any human activity. He was protecting it, she reasoned, from the fine cement grit that could injure his precious red paint job.

The popular psychiatrist had skills unknown to her patients and radio audience: she'd learned auto mechanics from her older brother when she was in high school. Those skills were about to serve her well. First, she slid on her back under the truck. Next, using an ice pick, she punctured small holes in the two rear brake lines to trigger slow leaks—leaks that wouldn't increase until the brakes were pumped several times. As an afterthought, Robin also drained the steering box of a good deal of its fluid, knowing that manual manipulation was still possible, although significantly more difficult.

That night Robin followed the red pickup as Arthur left work. She observed him struggling with the steering wheel on the way to Danny's Irish Pub. But predictably, his caution gave way to a much-needed drink, and he stopped there anyway. Robin waited, and at 6:40 Arthur exited, wavered, and stumbled his way to the tampered truck. Squeezing in behind the wheel, he started the engine, apparently too blitzed to remember his difficulty steering on his way there. His route home was a straight shot down Alder Street, ending in a T at County Road 12. The Dodge Ram bucked and jerked as Arthur pumped the brakes and ultimately came to a halt at the stop sign.

Wrestling the wheel hard over, he drove left onto the county road and took advantage of the two-mile straightaway to accelerate to sixty miles per hour. In a flash at that speed, he reached the dangerous half-mile-long S curve that skirted Cattail Creek in one direction and Potts Quarry in the other. Too late, Arthur realized he had no braking power remaining. Eyes wide open with fresh fright, he put all his adrenalized strength into commanding the truck to the right of the creek. But when he tried to reverse the steering wheel and turn it to the left to avoid the quarry, alcohol delayed his reaction and fuzzed his reflexes. Arthur and his speeding vehicle sailed through the air into space, dropping seventy feet into the quarry pit. Standing water at the pit's bottom swallowed the truck, ensuring no possibility of Arthur's survival. Observing the result with satisfaction, Robin returned home riding on a high. She read the newspaper account on Thursday morning. "Robin the Just," as she referred to herself, indulged in a heartier than usual breakfast.

The following Friday, another call-in on her TV show met Robin's dire-need parameters.

Daphney Worchek had called in to say she enjoyed being a homemaker and she excelled at it. However, being a good wife came much harder. Life would be so good if she didn't have to deal with her discontented, abusive husband. Trips to the hospital emergency room for dislocated elbows, pulled muscles, and strained rotator cuffs happened too often. There didn't have to be a reason, but he'd soon invent one, so that *she* appeared to be the guilty one. Eleven months earlier he'd shoved her down the basement stairs, resulting in a serious back injury. The Worcheks had no spare cash for the much-needed physical therapy. Poor Daphney wasn't sure any love remained in their marriage at all. She had no special training or work skills beyond her comfortable domestic domain, so she couldn't really leave. How could she ever make it on her own?

Lech Worchek eked out a living in insurance sales for a supervisor who bullied and belittled him for his deficient production. His coworkers actually called him the "Slack Work Chek." Skinny and only five-foot-four, Lech possessed the little-man syndrome, often turning on his sales colleagues, trying unsuccessfully to bully them. Having nowhere else to take out his work frustrations, he turned on his petite and frail domestic partner, Daphney. Lame apologies afterward couldn't begin to compensate for the misery she endured.

Robin remained on-air to hear the frivolous complaints of a housewife calling in merely to get more personal attention. Out of the studio and back in her office, Robin went to work on Daphney's cause. The battered victim ventured out only to the supermarket, the cleaners, and for an occasional walk round the mall.

Most of Robin's surveillance activity focused on the husband. Lech Worchek spent much of his workdays making cold-calls to potential clients. Not possessing a car, he rode city transit to close the infrequent policy contract he'd stumble upon. Like a habitual gambler reluctant to leave the gaming tables, Lech extended his work hours, believing the next cold-call would produce the hot response.

Observing that he used the same public transit system to go to and from work each day, Robin found little opportunity in that routine; too many witnesses. She chose his office for the application of the Worchek remedy. He nearly always stayed at least an extra hour, to about 5:30 p.m.

By 4:55 p.m. on the following Wednesday, Robin had finished applying a thick coat of clear petroleum jelly across the top three of twenty-two uninterrupted steel steps that led to the first-floor concrete landing of the old insurance building. Removing the slimy garden gloves and depositing them in a clean baggy, she pocketed the bag and proceeded along the upper hallway to the elevator. She taped a yellow "Out of Order" barrier ribbon across the double doors, ducked under it to step inside, and touched the ground floor "G" button.

Robin chose a vantage spot on the opposite side of the street where she could observe the first-floor landing of the building she had just exited. A glass door and two glass side panels exposed the well-lit landing. At roughly 6:05, she saw Lech's head smash against one of the glass side panels. Considering the awkward position of his head, Robin had little doubt that his neck had been broken. She walked away pleased and elevated in spirit.

The newspaper account called the death an accident; *a hasty, wrong assumption,* Robin thought. The police certainly would have found the "Out of Order" ribbon and the petroleum jelly. As a precaution, she decided to lay low for a while. During the next six weeks, she continued to screen her call-ins, but took no action on the deserving few—five to be exact. One in particular, a Charlotte Remmie, appeared to stand out as most dire. Six weeks to the day, the enterprising doctor emerged from hibernation.

Charlotte Remmie described herself as an overweight but otherwise attractive mother of two, trapped in a twenty-year-old "nonmarriage." Her husband, Warren Remmie, was a good provider, but much of his disposable income just seemed to disappear. His money problems didn't bother her. She had inherited wealth, stashed away in hidden bank accounts where he couldn't get his irresponsible hands on it.

As her pounds mounted and months went by, Warren spent more and more time away from home. "On business trips," he always said, but he never explained what for or where. They seldom spoke and rarely touched each other, and that was fine with her, too.

Suddenly, a change came over him. Warren began spending more and more time at home, talking to her and touching, too. But not in a kindly way. He criticized almost everything she said or did. His behavior was so overt that a frightened Charlotte began to notice a sinister pattern and called in to Dr. Priestley's show with almost daily reports. Warren routinely played with the clocks so she'd miss numerous appointments. Her kitchen utensils, pots, and small appliances moved drastically from cabinet to counter or even the basement on a daily basis, as did the clothes in her dresser drawers. He usurped and modified her letters before posting them. He intercepted her phone calls with ridiculous reasons why she couldn't come to the phone. She soon figured out his goal: a campaign to prove her insane.

Oh, my, this is bad news, Robin thought. *He must have learned his techniques from Charles Boyer in the movie* Gaslight.

Charlotte also learned that her husband had dropped numerous hints among their family and friends, strongly suggesting that she belonged in a loony bin.

When Robin asked what motive Warren would have for launching such a devious campaign, Charlotte had a ready answer.

Her husband had somehow found out about her hidden bank accounts and intended to take control of them, via a power of attorney once he had her committed. She was sure another woman waited out there for him. He couldn't rightly kill her because all the money would wind up in their children's trust under a bank trustee. Charlotte didn't know how much more of his mental cruelty she could take and wanted to know what could she do to thwart his monstrous plot.

Dr. Priestly laid out some of the options available to Charlotte. Chiefly, take the kids and move from the house; hire a private investigator to gather evidence to support a divorce with cause; and contact the police for criminal action. Charlotte started to sob and one by one declined all of these sensible alternatives because of the disturbing effect it would have on the children. Her crying interfered with the conversation, so the troubled caller abruptly hung up.

Robin decided to tail Warren Remmie, and to her great surprise on the second night, he led her to Bebbete Evington, the other woman. Bebbete wore a wedding ring, so it followed that they would consummate their trysts at a nearby motel. As a literary agent, Warren traveled some, but spent the majority of his business hours on his cell phone, in no place in particular. Therefore, Robin concentrated her exploring at the Remmie household. Using powerful binoculars, she noted that he usually ended his day with an amaretto liqueur nightcap while standing in the dining room at the sliding glass doors. Facing the outside, he usually appeared to be deep in thought, looking at nothing in particular.

Even after several days on the task, Dr. Priestly still wasn't exactly sure what to prescribe for the cruel and wayward Warren. Finally, on Tuesday, she decided to focus on his nightcap as a first course of remedy.

On Wednesday morning, while Warren was at work, Robin met with poor Charlotte at the Remmie home, and the two of them laid out Robin's new plan. She gave Charlotte some chloral hydrate, a Mickey Finn in a paper packet to slip into the liqueur bottle that Warren chose for his nightly drink. After he passed out, they would remove his clothes, carry him to the car, and deposit him naked on the steps of the Springly Sanitarium over on Maple Way. They would ring the bell, then dash to the car and disappear. "Who would believe Warren after *that* went public?" asked Robin.

Charlotte was skeptical. She worried that Warren, a smooth talker, could eventually be released, return home, and accuse *her*. But Robin seemed so confident of the plan that the wife didn't voice her concern. The two women had a drink of the delicious amaretto liqueur to seal their pact. Then Robin reached for the bottle again, this time to remove her prints, but Charlotte had already picked it up and seemed to be wiping it clean.

Late Wednesday evening, Robin returned to the Remmie house and took up her watch under the oak tree, where she observed Warren consuming his nightcap. Minutes later, she saw him fall to the carpet. Quickly, she re-entered the Remmie home through the back door left open for her by Charlotte. Robin fully expected to find Warren collapsed on the floor in front of the sliding doors. He was there all right, but when she checked his pulse there wasn't one. Warren Remmie was dead. How could that be? All she had provided Charlotte was a packet of chloral hydrate, a Mickey Finn. As Robin turned to scan her surroundings, the dining room chandelier bloomed in her face, blinding her momentarily.

Charlotte stood before her and spoke first. "What's the matter? He's passed out, isn't he, just the way you planned?"

"No, he's not unconscious. Your husband is dead and I can't explain it."

Charlotte began to scream. "You killed him! You killed my husband!" Her screams pierced the night air. As lights came on throughout the neighborhood, she reached for the phone to dial 911.

A shocked Robin ran out the back door, jumped in her car, and sped home. What had gone wrong? She tried to conjure up an alibi, but nothing would come to her. Bursting into her house, terrified and confused, she saw only one answer for herself: she had to run. She took down an overnight bag and started throwing a few things in when she heard banging at the front door. She headed for the back door and threw it open only to find a woman standing there.

"I'm Sergeant Diane Freemount from Homicide."

Robin slammed the door in her face.

A male voice, from the kitchen, said, "That's no way to treat the good sergeant. She's quite a fan of yours, Dr. Robin Priestly. The sergeant watches your show all the time. She's the one who put two and two together."

"And who are you?" asked a stunned Robin, realizing she'd left the front door unlocked.

"Lieutenant Phillip Childs. Homicide," he said, pointing his Sig Sauer P226 weapon directly at her.

"Homicide?" Robin cried. "I didn't kill anybody."

"Mrs. Warren Remmie claims you put poison in her husband's nightly drink."

"How could she possibly think that?" Robin asked calmly. "How could you blame such a terrible thing on me?"

"She insists you tried to convince her to help you kill her husband the way you did all those other husbands."

"What other husbands?" asked Robin.

"The diligent sergeant can answer that one better than I can," replied Lt. Childs.

"To begin with," said the sergeant, who had slipped in the back door, "I was routinely assigned to interview the wives of nine suspicious murder victims over the last six months. Statistically, that's nearly three times the normal murder rate for Nickels County. More than half of these stories sounded so familiar that I went back to check if they were, in fact, your very own call-ins."

"But that's only circumstantial evidence," protested a smug Dr. Priestly.

"Then there are the phone records tying all nine of these directly to you—plus the studio's routine recordings of your show," explained the lieutenant.

"Still circumstantial!" Robin insisted, as the sergeant cuffed her.

"Hardly," returned the lieutenant. "According to the Assistant District Attorney, there's such an overwhelming amount of circumstantial evidence that no jury would fail to convict. It's so far beyond the realm of coincidence that there's no other explanation. You have the right to remain silent. Anything you say can and will be used against you . . ." He continued reading her her rights.

"I want a lawyer!" Robin demanded.

"It's first-degree murder," the lieutenant cautioned. "If you cooperate, we can recommend that the prosecutor take the death penalty off the table." He knew it was a lie; in their state the worst she could get from a circumstantial conviction was a life sentence.

"What would you like to know?" Robin asked cautiously.

"I'm curious," said the sergeant. "What did you give the husband?"

"I didn't give him anything. I gave Charlotte a small packet of chloral hydrate, along with a dose of hallucinogen to dump in his drink. The most you can charge me with is complicity."

"What was the hallucinogen for?"

Robin switched on her most professional demeanor. "I admit to nothing. But let's take a hypothetical case. Say a wife had a husband trying to, literally, drive her insane. What would be an appropriate way to get even with him? A lovely thought would be to deposit the unconscious brute on the doorstep of a sanitarium so that he'd awaken ranting and raving. He would surely be incarcerated, hopefully for life."

"You had all that in mind for this guy?" asked the sergeant.

"I'm not going to answer that," said Robin.

"You'll answer that," said the lieutenant, "and a whole lot more when the ADA sends you for a psychiatric evaluation. How's that for appropriate?"

"I want a lawyer!" she repeated demurely.

* * * *

Warren Remmie's body was hauled off to Forensics, where the medical examiner performed a preliminary tox screen. To Lt. Childs' surprise, no chloral hydrate or hallucinogen was found. What *was* found was a heavy dose of pesticide containing a cyanide derivative. Dr. Robin Priestley was convicted of murder. No circumstantial evidence there.

At the trial, Charlotte—in black with tear-stained cheeks—expertly played the role of grieving widow. Nobody would ever know what really happened that night. She had made a sham of wiping off Robin's prints on the bottle and then switched her own pesticide for the knockout potion Robin had given her.

Mrs. Remmie had endured all she could from Warren, but had no idea how to kill him without being blamed. When Robin offered to rescue her and laid out the plan, Charlotte knew *her* problem was solved. Double-cross the good doctor.

Standby

Jennifer Anne Willmont was a successful businesswoman in a most unusual profession. Unlike the rental services of the gaudy ladies of the night, her services were far less engaging. Fact is, in her profession none of the principals ever actually met. The arrangements were discreet, expensive—and irreversible.

A client searching for what she had to offer needed only answer a classified ad for Corporate Removal Services (crs.com), a blind gmail address requesting a one-time cell phone contact number. CRS then left it to the prospective client to propose the entire project and its compensation. If the terms were satisfactory, CRS would furnish a Swiss bank account number for deposit of the fee. If not, the call was terminated. Negotiation was unacceptable.

"Hit person" sounds rather cold-blooded. Then again, so is murder for hire.

Jennifer never thought of herself as an egocentric monster or even a criminal. She merely considered herself a tool, an instrument in the employ of a client who paid handsomely for removals. To be sure, her clients were the monsters, for without them, there would be no killing. She rationalized her business model. If not hers, another would take its place. She was fully anesthetized to the act—as if she were shooting Novocain into her moral fiber.

Jennifer did not consider herself asocial. Turning heads and attracting the attention of both genders granted her the ultimate high. That obsession would ultimately be her undoing. Her craving for beautiful, rare, and expensive things, as well as the most coveted seats at cultural and sporting events, propelled her to succeed. But mostly, she had the smarts to make it all happen—a unique life strategy and clever business plan.

Oh, by the way, Jennifer had a second profession: as a practicing dentist. The frightened, sniveling cowards who occupied her chair daily could in no way pay for her expensive tastes. Long hours on her feet with her hands in someone's disgusting mouth required immense upper body conditioning and lower body strength. To that end she spent two hours, three days a week in a local gym.

Jennifer's mother had raised her daughter alone on a grocery clerk's salary, after her husband decided fatherhood was not for him. Mrs. Willmont preached a steel-clad philosophy. "You have the strength of a man, the looks of a goddess, the mind of a scholar, and the perfected smile of deceit. Use them," she urged. "These are a poor woman's only tools." Momma had no idea where her advice would lead.

Jennifer always conducted her Corporate Removal Services business under invented names. That particular Tuesday began as "Merle Sassoon" in a UPS store in Baltimore, Maryland. She laid a cardboard box the size of a large briefcase on the counter. The package's address: Merle Sassoon, P.O. Box 310 at a UPS store in Atlanta, Georgia. The attending clerk had no way of knowing that it contained a small-caliber, sharp-shooting rifle with scope—all of its custom components broken down, oiled, wiped clean, and nested into form-fitted slots inside an aluminum case. The precision weapon's job was finished—for that day, anyway. Merle paid for the shipping with a sterile yet bogus credit card bearing the Sassoon name. Wearing fashionable kid gloves, she scribbled the Sassoon signature on the credit slip and walked away with the receipt and a copy of the shipping agreement tucked into her Prada hobo bag.

Standby

* * * *

The body of Rosaland Cushner, the much-too-nosy corporate comptroller at a client's firm, lay waiting to be discovered in her own living room. An innocent whistleblower, too—such a pity, but business was business. A dime-size hole in her picture window, surrounded by minute glass fissures, was the only evidence of intrusion. Merle's client, the firm's greedy CEO, was guilty of salting away company funds in off-shore banks for years, and so rendered the interloper highly threatening. The client's solution: answering the Corporate Removal Services classified ad.

Several blocks down Lombard Street and one block south, Merle caught the Baltimore Light Rail to Baltimore-Washington International Airport. Aboard the train she enjoyed a rush of approving stares from several gentlemen passengers. And why not? Tall, in her late twenties, she had auburn curls tumbling about the shoulders of her Chanel suit. Her gray-green eyes in black-framed glasses gave her a look hovering between sultry and intellectual.

As the train rumbled out of Baltimore city, she had a flash of ugly memory, recalling "that bastard" responsible for her becoming an assassin. Her late husband, Patrick, had been so loving during their courtship, and thrilled her with a two-carat diamond engagement ring. Their first year passed compatibly enough—until one of the prongs in her ring loosened and she took it to be repaired at a reputable jeweler. There she received shocking news. "Madame, I'm sorry, but this is not an authentic diamond. It's cubit zirconium. Nicely crafted, but worth no more than $200." Hiding her boiling anger, she checked their joint safety deposit box and discovered that all her valuable jewelry was gone. Patrick had lost his job months before, faked going to work every day, and pawned it all. For Jennifer, there was no "We'll work it out." She simply made Patrick disappear, drowned in a kayaking accident.

What she hadn't counted on was an inadvertent witness: another boater nearby on the lake. The woman blackmailed her into performing a hit job of her own, offering sufficient money to sweeten the task. Jennifer completed the hit with precision and ease, collected her fee, and then killed the extortionist without a trace. She still tingled remembering the thrill. Murder-for-hire opened new doors. She reduced the number of patients in her dental practice. She could afford to.

* * * *

Merle expected that Andrew Cushner would arrive home from work at 4:15 to find Rosaland's body on the living room floor with a hole through the back of her head. He would exhibit appropriate horror and grief to the police, but would be unable to answer the agonizing question, why? Although the CEO-client might buckle under questioning, Merle knew she would be long gone before an investigation began. After all, she and the client had never met. He couldn't identify her. She checked her Rolex: 12:30 p.m. The flight for Atlanta was leaving at 2:45.

The light rail deposited her within a short walk of the Coastal Airways terminal. She presented her return trip ticket at the passenger counter, along with a driver's license in the name of yet another alias: April Mae Sears of Marlboro, Maryland.

The ticket agent shook his head. "I'm sorry. Ms. Sears, Flight 2313 to Atlanta is filled to capacity. There's been a change in equipment—a smaller aircraft, less seating. Unavoidable, I assure you. We can get you on the next flight at 5:40. No? Then the best I can do is issue you a standby pass for Flight 2313. It will get you through to the gate lounge. It's first come-first served. Good luck, Ms. Sears. Next!"

April knew better than to make a stink, but couldn't quite suppress her annoyance. She snatched her ticket out of the agent's hand and strode, flushed and agitated, down to Concourse C and Security. *Get a grip*, she told herself. Her residual loss of cool didn't escape a female Homeland TSA agent, who beckoned her aside for an interview and individual search. By then, the April persona had regained her composure, adding a cheerful air of compliance, along with an apologetic smile. The hand-held magnetometer beeped only once: on the steel clasp of her heirloom brooch, a finely carved cameo framed in fourteen-karat gold filigree. The rich leather bag, $800 stiletto heels, and Louis Vuitton carry-on were wanded, probed, and searched without incident.

At Coastal Airways Gate C-21, Ms. Sears heard the same story. It was too early to count on any no-shows. She was standby number two. She checked her watch once more and scowled— 1:30 p.m., only fifty-five minutes to boarding time. By that time a Baltimore police alert could be in place. Time to implement Plan B. April took a seat in the lounge and opened her *USA Today* wide. Peeking over the top, she perused her fellow travelers, committing their faces and apparel to memory: those on cell phones; those looking physically unfit; those slouching, often an indication of low self-esteem. She decided on the easiest target, the elderly. They were generally the more vulnerable and usually had to pee often.

Pulling her wheeled carry-on, she entered the three-stall restroom near the Coastal gate. A quick glance in the mirror revealed an unforgivable lettuce speck on one of her front teeth. Of course, no respectable dentist would be caught anywhere without a large plastic dispenser of dental floss. She yanked off a length of the strong waxed nylon, applied it to all her teeth, and slipped the dispenser into a pocket of her purse. Facing the sink, she smiled broadly—always ready to admire her own beautiful white teeth.

She waited until two women entered together. They appeared too young and purposeful—an unnecessary risk. She allowed them to leave. Four minutes later, a small woman with a frail elderly body, shuffled in and entered a stall.

They were alone, so April prepared. Taking a small plastic perfume bottle containing chloroform from her purse, she stepped behind the stall door. Removing the cap, she waited until she heard the toilet flush, then poured a fair amount onto a folded paper towel. As the stall door opened, she caught the victim from behind and clamped the chloroform-soaked pad over her mouth, holding it ever tighter and tighter while dragging her victim back into the stall. The shocked woman put up a weak struggle, uttered not a sound, and quickly went limp.

April lowered the unconscious woman onto the toilet seat and felt her neck for a pulse—slow, weak, but discernable. Wrapping a long loop of floss around the woman's wrists, she tied the loose ends to the toilet plumbing behind her, to keep her from falling off the seat. April then arranged the feet so they appeared to be those of someone sitting on the throne. Ripping off a two-yard fresh length of floss, she looped the center of it over the inside door latch knob and draped the two strands over the top of the door. From the outside of the door, she gripped the two ends of the floss, raised her hands high, and flipped the inside latch to the locked position. A neat trick. All she had to do then was pull the floss free and tuck it into her pocket.

Now there was at least one no-show passenger. April needed only wait for one more candidate. Unfamiliar faces came and went. Finally, another perfect target entered the otherwise empty restroom. This woman looked to be in her early seventies; heavier but shorter than the first victim, and walked with a slight limp. April used precisely the same procedure, but needed more muscle and extra seconds to account for the additional pounds. She felt a profound satisfaction in creating two no-shows. And so smoothly, too. After all, she didn't cause them any permanent bodily harm. She actually frowned on wantonly murdering innocents, especially when they weren't for profit. Even an assassin ought to have some scruples.

April's next task was to deal with the victims' handbags. Picking them up off the stall floor, she removed the wallets, boarding passes, and any other potential IDs, and threw them into her own purse. Moving in long strides back down the concourse, she dropped the wallets and other IDs into several widely separated trash cans.

Plan B had taken approximately eleven minutes. Only then did she calmly return to the Coastal Airways lounge. Boarding began a few minutes later. She heard the names of four passengers being paged. Only one came forward. Several minutes later, three of the names were repeated. After a nod from the supervisor, three new names were called to the ticketing counter at Gate C-21. Even though April's was second, she arrived at the counter first. The rubber stamp pounced down on her ticket and then on the standby card, turning it into a legitimate boarding pass for seat 15D, on the aisle. The agent scanned her boarding pass at the skyway entrance and April took her assigned seat aboard the aircraft. The doors closed as soon as the other two standbys were processed and seated. The plane taxied to the end of the runway to await takeoff instructions.

"Excuse me, ma'am, are you traveling alone?" asked the passenger in 15E, the window seat next to her. The young man had sandy hair and a pale, pleasant face. His voice was somewhat tentative.

"Uh, yes," April replied, "but why do you ask?"

"My wife and I couldn't get seats together and we're newlyweds. She's up in seat 22B and I'm stuck here. I wonder if you'd mind switching places with her once we're airborne."

It took only a moment for April to consider that a seat change would add one more convolution to tracking her retreat.

"Of course," she said. "I'd be happy to."

Ten minutes later the plane took off. As soon as it leveled out and the seat belt sign went off, she made the swap and settled into seat 22B. Being airborne, she felt confident that she'd beaten any potential police alert.

Reclining the seat back, she settled in for a nap, when she heard a masculine voice next to her. "Business trip?"

"Why, no," she told him. "Just visiting my folks, they're getting on in years." April gave him the once-over: blue business suit, thirties, well-groomed hair, and rugged, almost Hollywood looks. An open Tom Clancy thriller lay in front of him.

"Yeah, I know what you mean," he said. "I need to pay a visit to my dad soon. He's in an assisted living home." Her seatmate looked her over, too. The only ring she was wearing was an opal on her right index finger. April relished his attention, feeling his eyes touch down on her finer points.

"An unhappy experience, no doubt," she commented.

"Oh no," he explained. "Quite the opposite. Being one of the few males on the premises who's mobile and still *compos mentis*—all the old ladies chase after him. By the way, my name is Norm Bishop. Care to tell me yours?"

"April, April Sears."

"Well, April, do you live in the Atlanta area?" he asked.

"No, but I go there frequently to see family and friends."

"Perhaps the next time you're in town, you'll give me a call, and we'll have dinner and take in a show." He handed her his business card with his office number circled. "Is there some way I can reach you?"

She smiled lazily and paused for a moment. Sexual liaisons were merely a hobby for her. She'd never been in love. Whenever she got the urge, she simply attracted a potential partner, used him—or her—briefly, and tearfully said goodbye, with some genuine-sounding excuse. In her line of work, she couldn't afford any long-term attachments.

Searching through her deerskin hobo bag, she tore off a corner of the first loose piece of paper she could find and wrote down aprilmaesears@gmail.com.

"Thank you!" he said. "Delighted!" He tucked the paper into his breast pocket. They chatted about their favorite authors until the captain announced it was time to buckle up and prepare for landing.

Deplaning in Atlanta, she bid her seatmate goodbye and followed the newlyweds from row 15 into the skyway to the waiting lounge. The moment the couple entered the lounge, the TSA people apprehended them and diverted them through a door marked SECURITY. April thought, *Whew! That was close!* The seat exchange turned out to be a stroke of luck. It would have taken some pretty swift detective work to check out the trash receptacles at BWI airport and put two and two together. Concerned nevertheless, April ducked into the washroom and changed outfits, slipping out of her silk Chanel suit and into a nondescript skirt and blouse. Within the hour, she used a ticket to Miami under a third identity and arrived home at six p.m.

Back in her daily routine, Dr. Jennifer Willmont endured the next two weeks of patient exams, fillings, crowns, and extractions. Only one of four temporary gmail accounts emitted any meaningful activity. Strangely enough, that one came from Norm Bishop. At first Jennifer thought about erasing it, but after reflecting on the man's exceptional looks, charm, and pheromones, she left it in her In Box.

Another week went by, and she contracted for her next hit: a returning prodigal stepbrother seeking a disproportionate share of his father's inheritance. CRS and the client agreed that the hit should take place the following Wednesday afternoon in Columbus, Ohio. As usual, Jennifer booked her airline passage through the Atlanta hub, where her weapon slept in a UPS store postal box.

But she had a sudden yearning for Norm, and boldly considered meeting him in Atlanta on Tuesday evening, the night before the hit. Over a few drinks, using her April alias, she'd get an idea of where their tryst was leading them. Her return gmail said Yes. She'd call him from the airport.

The flight from Miami arrived early. After check-in at a midtown hotel, she headed to the UPS store to pick up the tools of her trade. Three individuals were in the store when she arrived: the clerk behind the counter; a woman in business attire fondling the stationery; and a man at the copy machine. Jennifer took a basket and wandered through the office supplies, waiting for the two other patrons to leave—a small precaution in case the business suit was actually watching her postal box.

The man finished his copying, paid, and left the store. But the suit stayed so long that Jennifer considered aborting the pickup. The clerk, a thirtyish woman in a gray pants outfit, approached the suit: "Can I help you?" The two exchanged a few words, and the suit abruptly left the store. The clerk, whose name tag read "Cathy," now turned her attention to Jennifer, who had dropped a writing tablet and two dispensers of Scotch tape into her basket.

"I'll ring that up when you're ready, ma'am."

Jennifer set the basket on the counter and strode over to the mailboxes. At Box 310 she inserted her key, removed the package, and carried it to the counter. The clerk wasn't there. With both hands still clutching the heavy package, Jennifer sensed someone behind her. She slowly turned. It was the clerk—gripping a Glock 22 in her right hand and flashing credentials with her left.

"FBI! Special Agent Catherine Swanson. May I see your package, Ms. Sassoon?"

In an innocent voice, Jennifer said, "I'm afraid you're mistaken, ma'am. I don't know anyone by that name."

"Oh, I think you do, lady," the agent retorted. "Merle Sassoon was the name on your credit card when you paid for that package at the UPS store in Baltimore."

Jennifer showed no sign of panic. Pretending compliance, she eased the box toward Catherine, but instead of handing it to her, she slowly raised it as a shield between the Glock and her chest. For a split second, the agent's eyes fixed on the parcel. That was all Jennifer needed. She slammed the rigid package against the agent's gun hand, smashing it into the edge of the counter with such force that it broke at least one of the agent's fingers. Jerking in pain, Agent Catherine lost her grip on the Glock, but not before her trigger finger launched a bullet into the opposite wall. The two women struggled for possession of the gun. Jennifer came away with it. Hands raised, the special agent leaned back against the counter, her disjointed finger throbbing.

But Jennifer knew she'd been caught without a Plan B this time. At any moment a customer could enter, spot the gun, and run back out to call 911. She desperately fought her first instinct—to shoot the agent outright and, instead, chose to push her out the front door.

Suddenly, Jennifer saw that she had, literally, boxed herself in. Her left arm and hand were wrapped around her heavy package; with the weapon inside, she certainly couldn't leave it in the store.

Losing her cool now, her right hand shook as she clumsily held the Glock. The agent pushed the glass door open and managed to stay a few steps ahead. As Jennifer cleared the doorway, she felt a scalding liquid splash over her right hand. She screamed.

Her gun hand jerked away from the agent, and her grip on the Glock slackened. Someone suddenly yanked it out of her scalded hand. The special agent's partner, waiting just outside, had poured steaming hot coffee on her right hand and forearm. Gasping in anguish, Jennifer felt another sensation: the cold steel of the second agent's weapon pressing against her temple.

The coffee had proved to be a convenient, innovative weapon. Catherine's partner had just bought two cups at McDonald's moments before the UPS store turned into a crime scene.

Thus Jennifer, along with all her aliases, was taken into custody. Almost immediately she was extradited to Maryland, where the most recent murder and airport assaults took place. Handcuffed, she faced the two FBI agents across the table in an interrogation room of a Baltimore Federal building. This time Jennifer tried making nice.

"Sorry about the broken finger, but getting away was my first priority."

Agent Catherine stared at her with cold, hard eyes. "Oh, my, don't you sound sincere. We opened your package. How is it you can kill other human beings so matter-of-factly?"

Jennifer frowned. *How does she know about the others?* She shrugged. "That's business. I have … rather *had* another life, too. I merely compartmentalized." Her curiosity took over. "Whose idea was it—pulling the newlyweds out of the line in Atlanta? How did you track me to Flight 2313 in the first place?"

"From your attacks in the ladies room we knew you had to be female," said the second agent. "There was a succession of clues. Subduing two people at the same time seemed like too difficult a task, so we concluded that the two lady strangers entered the restroom at different times. We figured there was some common motive for two identical assaults. Then, finding two purses with missing wallets, IDs, and boarding passes—that could only mean one thing: someone needed to get out of Dodge in a hurry. And being in a secure zone of the airport meant the perp was either a passenger or a standby on a recent or upcoming flight. Which flight? What destination? We needed to find out. It wasn't likely that the perp would take the missing items with her, so we launched a search into all the trash receptacles along the adjacent gates and found everything we needed. With the computer's help, the IDs produced the common flight number. The boarding passes gave us the exact seating. Unfortunately, the flight attendant furnished us with a description that didn't match that of the gate agent."

Jennifer scowled. "Of course, the newlyweds informed you of the seat swap. They were so cute and sweet, one hated to inconvenience them."

"Right," sneered Catherine. "They cooperated completely and, along with the airline agent, gave us a complete description of April Sears, except that Ms. Sears had already disappeared without a trace."

"If the trail ended there," Jennifer asked, "how did you track me to the UPS place in Atlanta?"

Catherine's eyes bore into her. "Did you give your gmail address to anyone aboard that flight?" She looked down at her notepad. "A Mr. Bishop?"

"Yes. Norm Bishop, but that address wouldn't have gotten you anywhere. I always access it via WiFi through a Tor scattering network."

"Ah! But we used the number you gave him, not the gmail address," replied Catherine.

Jennifer looked puzzled.

"You wrote the gmail address down on a torn corner of a UPS receipt. It just so happens that the reverse side of that very same corner had most of the package transaction number on it. We traced it back to Baltimore, the Lombard Street UPS store, and someone who called herself Merle Sassoon. I assume that's another of your aliases."

Jennifer refused to respond.

"This Ms. Sassoon sent a package to the Atlanta UPS store's Box 310. And there you have it." Catherine closed her file folder. She'd had no trouble memorizing most of the details.

Jennifer's serial-killer-for-hire trial went down like so many dominoes—one piece of evidence leading to another. They learned of her profession as a respected dentist. The creative restraint—the dental floss—became the first piece of undoing. The speck of lettuce put her saliva, her DNA, on the floss used to bind the first hapless passenger. Forensics determined that the tear patterns on the separate strands were similar enough to link both bound victims to the same floss, which they found when they searched Jennifer's hobo bag. Her fingerprints were on the plastic dispenser. The TSA agent who wanded her at BWI recalled the "fancy pin" that caused the magnetometer to beep. Jennifer's elegant apparel and stunning looks became a liability as more and more people were able to place her in key incriminating situations. Ballistics matched the weapon inside the package to the bullet that killed Rosaland Cushner in Baltimore, and linked it to several other unsolved murders.

The jury returned a verdict of guilty on three charges of murder. The judge sentenced her to multiple consecutive life terms with no chance of parole. The prosecutor had ordered her to hand over her full client list. Jennifer, ever the actress, coyly batted her long lashes. "If I do, will I get some kind of deal?" None was forthcoming, of course, and a new set of trials—against the clients—would follow.

As Jennifer was being led out of the courtroom, she jerked to a stop in front of FBI Agent Catherine, who had attended the trial and sentencing. Jennifer, with unflagging bravado, said: "Cathy? Can we talk for a second? In the interview room you asked me what I regret most. It's this," she said, looking down at her jump suit. "Until the day I die I'll be in this deplorable prison garb. And international orange is so not my color." Scanning Catherine's mud-brown pants suit, she added: "You're a nice-looking woman, but your outfits suck. In my apartment walk-in closet, you'll find my entire designer wardrobe just going to waste. I'm guessing we wear about the same size. The cameo brooch is in a velvet box in my top drawer. Strange how one exquisite piece of jewelry could betray me. I slipped up by wearing it. Anyway, the clothes, the cameo, they're all yours. If you want them."

Despite the grim circumstances, Agent Catherine had to laugh. Wouldn't she be a sight prancing around town wearing evidence from a murder trial? Too bad. She did so love that cameo.

Fantasizers and Dreamers

We all learned about fantasy when we were younger. It was a happy experience because our own inventiveness navigated us through that wonderful world of whimsy. But, as adults, we dare not lay down our guard, for who knows what escapes from that other world? Is it chance, a challenge, revenge, or pure magic? That's for *you* to decide.

The *Joss* at Table Twelve
In the Grip of Time
Picture Imperfect
Dream Channels
Artificial Affection
Just a Little Bite, Please
José and Garminita
Fortified

The *Joss* at Table Twelve

*Joss: from the Chinese, meaning luck. This story
is based on an ancient Chinese legend.*

The celestial Year of the Rooster arrived in a crowded, boisterous restaurant in the heart of Honolulu's Chinatown. Six strangers—three men and three women—met there for the very first time to celebrate Chinese New Year. Usually, singles sat at the bar in The House of the Golden Boar, but as their combined *joss* would have it that evening, early revelers occupied all the singles stools. The elderly manager instructed Soo Mei, her valued waitress, to seat all six together at Table Twelve in the center of the restaurant.

"But venerable lady, they do not know each other," protested Soo Mei. "It will be most awkward for them. Besides, it's the hostess's job," she said with a pout.

"Do it anyway," said Li Set Ling. "I am the manager, am I not? Besides, my dear, I knew they would be coming." She gently nudged her puzzled waitress toward the waiting six at the door while removing the Reserved sign from that particular table.

Despite the novelty of their grouping, the individuals appeared to pair off naturally as they took their seats at Table Twelve. Conversation proved easy and good-natured, but floated on the surface, unrevealing and noncommittal. Before long, exquisite Oriental cuisine and parading lions cemented an unlikely bond among them. The din, the expectations, the body heat, or perhaps the will of some unseen spirit, became the catalyst in their making a remarkable pact: to meet here in the Golden Boar annually during Chinese New Year and relive this celebratory experience.

As the last diners departed and the doors to the street were locked, Soo Mei turned to Li Set Ling and asked, "How did you know they were coming? How could you possibly know they would like each other and stay?"

The white-haired manager, clad in a green mandarin-collared silk dress and tiny spectacles, said, "I know many things, my dear. In fact, Jan Rice and Freddy Maxwell, those two stately African-American teachers, will date, fall in love, and soon marry. And you remember Geraldine Palomalo, the dark-eyed Tahitian who spoke with such a strong operatic voice?"

"The one in the tapa print skirt who calls herself 'Geri'?" Soo Mei asked uneasily. How could her manager remember their names so well just from their credit cards at the end of the evening?

"Yes. She and the yellow-haired athlete, Brad Attwell, will try living together. Then there is Laura Paar, the tall, lithe brunette, who dances for a living in New York City."

"Ah! That one sat across from the red-headed, freckled man with a sour face," offered Soo Mei.

"Most astute, Soo Mei. That would be Ken Downs, the big city stock trader. Laura and Ken will discover they can't stand each other's company for more than three hours. However, all of them will return to our humble establishment for years to come."

"But why should they agree to return year after year?" asked the curious waitress. "And how do you know so many personal things about their futures?"

"I see all kinds of things in my dreams," her manager said. "Many I don't understand, but some impelling spirit drives me to listen. Now, enough questions. Clear the table."

Soo Mei shivered. A cloud crossed her porcelain-doll face and she lowered her eyes.

* * * *

True enough, each of the six players did seem to have a personal agenda for wanting this annual ritual. On the first anniversary of their initial meeting, this group of twenty-somethings reappeared as though some mysterious shepherd had herded them together. A congenial Li Set Ling seated them at the same Table Twelve, leaving the six to wonder if the manager's decision was by chance or by design. She reminded them that feeding the lions and giving to charity could enhance their fortunes considerably for the coming zodiac year.

"Perhaps the Year of the Boar will be most generous to those sheltered in its humble house," she said. "This year is special. It is the year of the *Golden* Boar for which our restaurant is named, and you are seated at Table Twelve in the eye of the room. For this night alone the boar's spirits orbit *your* honored table."

"Go on now! That's a lot of hooey," Ken Downs announced. He straightened up in his chair, looking quite out of place in his business suit, white shirt, and tie, surrounded by a roomful of aloha shirts.

"Perhaps not," said Soo Mei as she handed out menus. She spotted her manager hovering behind Ken and saw a chance to curry favor after her expressed doubts. "Li Set Ling knows quite a lot about *all* of you."

"I highly doubt that," Ken retorted.

"Ah, Mr. Downs," said the white-haired manager with a slight curl of a smile. "I understand congratulations are in order. You now have that long-awaited promotion. Yet you remain unhappy over not receiving the partnership and corner office you have always coveted. A furrow has appeared in the middle of your forehead and there are crease lines edging the corners of your beautiful gray eyes." Her tone sounded confident yet soft.

"Hey Ken, she could have read about your promotion in the *Wall Street Journal*," said Freddy. "I did."

"What's going on here, anyway?" Ken lashed out. "The promotion, yes, but the partnership and office part? This is getting damned spooky."

Li ignored him. "As for you, Mr. Freddy Maxwell," Li said, "best wishes for you and your new bride. And I see the doctors are watching some dark spots on your right kidney."

"How could you possibly know—?" sputtered Freddy.

"And you didn't tell me?" his wife of three months asked, her voice squeaking. "Why not, dear?"

"I didn't want to worry you unnecessarily, sweetheart," he answered. "They're not sure of anything yet."

"Hey! What about me?" Geri Palomalo sang out. "This is great fun. I haven't been to a fortune teller in years."

"Young miss, you have recently become successful with those comical ditties you wrote for television. But, my dear, perhaps you have other talents as well. These will turn up in the not-too-distant future."

"It's all a bunch of lucky guessing," muttered Brad Attwell. "Either that or she had our table bugged last year. Did you notice that she put us at the same table this year?"

"Yeah," said Ken. "I did notice, but I don't remember discussing these things before."

"Ah, Mr. Attwell, your batting slump brought you some concern last season. But there is no need to be apprehensive. You won't be traded to another semipro team. Your batting skill will improve in the coming season."

Laura shook her head, corkscrew curls falling around her face, and murmured, "Nothing exciting ever happens to me. Even the all-seeing gal has nothing to say about me."

"Oh, but you are so wrong, my lady. You have performed some extraordinary dance moves full of daring and grace. One has even proved costly, as you well know. However, I see changes in the very near future."

"Good or bad?" asked Laura excitedly.

"I think you already know," said Li.

"Are you a psychic?" Laura asked. "I didn't come all the way to Hawaii from New York to get creeped out." She turned to the others. "She's weird."

"Look who's talking," Ken retorted.

Laura flushed. "Ken, that was totally uncalled for." She stuck out her tongue at him and followed with a long raspberry sound.

Brad scowled. "Hey! Enough, you two. We're here to celebrate and have a good time."

Li turned her face downward. "This humble person doesn't purport to be what you call a psychic," she said. "But I have been temporarily endowed with a certain illuminating gift during this year of the *Golden* Boar."

"Hogwash!" bellowed Ken. "What's so special about this year, anyway?"

"Many Chinese," Li replied, "believe there is great significance in this year's arrival, the anniversary of the *Golden* Boar. It occurs only once every 600 years or fifty orbits of the planet Jupiter. And there is more. Jupiter takes twelve years to complete its orbit and that is also significant to you sitting at this particular table." Li Set Ling then spun about and darted toward the kitchen with the arrival of busboys bearing loaded trays.

"Wow!" said Ken, "I guess I walked into that one."

"You sure did," Freddy said. "Besides, I thought the *Golden* Boar thing was kind of interesting. I wonder if any of it's true."

Jan shrugged. "Even if it is, how does all this orbital coincidence nonsense have anything to do with us?"

Her husband cast her a sly look through horn-rimmed glasses. "You have a short memory, my dear wife. *This* is where we met."

Jan looked sheepish. "Okay, Freddy, you're right. It's just that teaching science—this abstract stuff doesn't sit well with me."

The joyous feast began with winter melon soup. Happy Family followed: a sizzling platter of lobster, shrimp, scallops, roast pork, and beef, resting on a bed of water chestnuts, peapods, and mushrooms. In the center of the table, the huge lazy Susan spun as the six spooned up fried oysters, spare ribs, and tongue-burning Szechuan chicken with peanuts.

Soon thunderous drumbeats and clanging gongs forestalled conversation. The nonstop *rat-a-tat-tat* of firecrackers echoed from along the narrow streets. And when the leaping lions burst through the double glass doors, the diners dropped their forks and jumped up to feed dollar bills into the gaping mouths of grand and colorful paper-maché feline heads.

Nearly an hour later, Jan speared a forkful of lo mein and raised it high above her plate. "Don't forget these," she said through a muffled mouthful. "Long noodles. For long life."

They all nodded, except Ken. "I'm full up," he said. "Besides, all that stuff is for superstitious, uneducated peons." He folded his linen napkin into a perfect square and pushed his chair away from the table.

"Aren't you going to stick around for this mellow mango pudding?" asked Geri.

Without a word Ken drew disrespectful patterns in his with a fork while the others spooned down and savored theirs.

Meanwhile, Li Set Ling caught the attention of her most trusted waitress and whispered instructions in her ear. "Be sure not to mix them up, or chaos will come of it."

Birdlike Soo Mei nodded and headed toward Table Twelve, carrying a tray with the combined check and six fortune cookies. She placed the check in front of Brad Attwell, carefully distributed the cellophane-wrapped cookies to each guest, and returned to the kitchen with empty bowls.

Jan shook her head. Her hoop earrings swung to and fro as she watched the departing figure disappear through the kitchen doors. *That's strange*, she thought. *Fortune cookies are always just left in a pile on the table. Since when does a waitress hand them out individually? Like never!*

As Brad perused the check, Freddy joked, "Hey, man, thanks for picking up the bill."

"Don't you wish," Brad answered. "We'll split it three ways." He fished out his wallet, extracted a credit card, and laid it on the table. Looking over at Geri, he winked, "For what we once meant to each other."

She flashed him a stiff smile. He took it for her approval.

"*Jeez!* I'm not on a date here," Ken said, watching Freddy lay down his card. "I shouldn't have to pay for Laura."

"Don't worry, cheapskate," Laura said. "I'll pay my way in cash if it's the last thirty dollars to my name."

Geri gasped. "Oh, dear! This isn't like you, Laura. What's wrong?"

"The show's choreographer fired me!" Laura blurted out. Then, seeing their stricken looks: "Sorry, I didn't mean to rain on everybody's parade." Hands folded in front of her, she let a few tears escape down her cheek.

Ken softened. "Okay, okay, my treat, Laura." He dropped his plastic on the pile. "Three ways it is. I didn't know things were so bad for you, Laura."

"As if you cared. I'll handle it myself." She wiped each cheek with a forefinger.

"Whoa, you two," Geri cried. "Peace! Let's not start something you'll regret later."

A momentary pall swept over the table.

"Say, Geri, how about I swap fortune cookies with you?" Laura asked, tossing her cellophane packet out to the center of the table. "I need a change of luck."

Geri, swathed in a dramatic purple and gold blouse, looked puzzled. "Laura, you have no idea what fortune is in your cookie— or in mine either. You're assuming yours is bad luck. Are you trying to foist it off on me?"

"Of course not," Laura said. A flush suffused her graceful dancer's neck and traveled up to chiseled cheekbones. "I just meant . . . I don't know what I meant. Forgive me." She tossed thirty dollars down on the table and stood to leave.

Geri shrugged. But realizing the evening was headed for

ruin, she hastened to restore a festive mood. "Okay, okay," she said, "I'll play your game."

She swapped Laura's cookie for her own. Laura hesitated, wishing she hadn't started this whole confrontation, then picked up the new cookie. "Thanks," she whispered. Saying her goodbyes, she wove her way toward the door. No one at the table noticed the barely perceptible limp to her gait.

"See you next year," Geri called out.

"Yeah, next year," Laura mumbled as she disappeared from view.

Frowning, Geri collected the still-wrapped cookie, idly turning it over and over.

Brad snapped his fingers twice in front of her face, returning her to the here and now. "Aren't you at least going to look at your traded fortune, sweetie?"

"Don't call me sweetie," Geri snapped. She clamped the stiff edge of the packet between her teeth and tore it open. Drawing out the slip of paper, she read in silence.

"Well, what does it say, Geri?" Freddy asked.

She held up the slip and read aloud: "YOU WILL FOREGO THE ONLY MAN YOU EVER LOVED FOR A SUCCESSFUL CA-REER ON STAGE AND SCREEN."

"Wow!" Jan said. "I didn't know you even had any thespian interests."

"Neither did I," Geri shrugged.

"And who's the hunk you're throwing away?" Brad asked. "I thought you said you weren't getting any lovin', babe."

"What are you talking about? I never said that." Geri bitterly recalled that Brad had been the one to abruptly move out and break up their love affair. *You're the only man I've ever wanted. If you weren't such a blind idiot you'd know that.* "But if I did have somebody, it would be none of your damn business."

Jan broke in, anxious to defuse the argument. "Amazing," she said, "how fitting that horoscope would have been for Laura."

"Yeah. Hey, Jan, what does yours say?" Brad asked.

She read aloud. "THE LITTLE PACKAGE WILL COME SOONER THAN YOU THINK."

"Does this mean you're pregnant?" Geri asked.

Jan shook her head. "No such luck."

"Gee, I thought you two would have several bambini by now," Ken taunted, toying with both his cookie and the one that had been in front of Freddy. He pushed both cookies to the center of the table, rejecting ownership of either one.

"Shut up, Ken!" Freddy yelled, noting the crestfallen look on his wife's face. "Just you shut up!" The pitch of his anger pierced the throbbing din of conversation and clinking silverware. Heads turned at the surrounding tables. Freddy snatched up the cookie now closest to him and shoved it in his jacket pocket. He and Jan headed for the door.

* * * *

The lunar Year of the Rat arrived the following February. At 9:30 that evening, the manager of The House of the Golden Boar noticed that only four members of the group had assembled at Table Twelve.

Li Set Ling had expected five. But something else troubled her. "Who is missing, my dear?" she asked Soo Mei.

"The one called Geri, venerable one," Soo Mei said. "And the one with fire in his hair."

"Did you deliver the special fortunes as I instructed last year?"

"Oh, yes. With extreme care, as you told me to."

"There was no mix-up?"

Soo Mei shook her head. "Please believe me, venerable one. I did as you instructed."

Li Set Ling realized she had pressed too hard and needed to allow the petite, earnest waitress to save face. Nodding her head, she turned away, and walked toward the bar.

At Table Twelve, the four guests chatted politely while keeping an anxious eye on the door for the missing two. A rhythmic clanging gong suddenly usurped the surrounding din. Two bobbing lions with huge paper-maché heads danced their way inside, undulating among the tables, halting only long enough for children and adults alike to feed dollar bills inside the open jaws. Jan slipped a bill into one as it grew in length to reach her. The lion retracted and leaped toward the next table.

"Should we give the waitress our order now?" Freddy shouted.

"Give them a little more time," Jan urged. "Geri never was all that punctual."

"Say, what's up, you two?" Freddy asked, looking directly at Brad and Laura. "You've been beaming and cooing at one another since you got here. Is there something the rest of us should know?"

"We surrender," Laura said with a glowing smile. She held out her ring finger.

"It's an engagement ring!" Jan shouted. "A real rock." She sprang from her chair and threw her arms around Laura. "When did all this happen? I had no idea you were even dating."

"Well, it was many moons ago," said Laura. "My dancing career fell apart. It seems no one wants to hire a dancer with a perpetual limp."

"You told us you'd been laid off," said Jan. "What actually happened?"

"Nice of you to ask. I injured my knee in January and couldn't go on. It didn't heal properly, or maybe I tried to come back too soon. Anyway, I can't dance for a living anymore. Now at least I'm able to make enough teaching dance to youngsters."

"How did the two of you get together?" asked Freddy.

"I was lunching by myself in a Kosher deli. Eating an egg sandwich, I think, when Brad walked in. I invited him to join me."

"It was more like egg on her face and egg in her lap," said Brad. "She was daydreaming. Anyway, the two of us shared a table. We went out for supper that night and the rest is history. It's strange how things work out. That first night we all met three years ago, Geri started playing footsie with me under the table. I admit I was flattered and excited."

"But you lived together for several months afterward," said Freddy. "You must have had something going for the relationship to last that long."

"Something, yes," Brad answered. "But you can't live life under the sheets. She's a sexy lady. The two of us just never talked. We went our separate ways most of the time."

"We haven't set a date yet," Laura said. "But Jan, you've been holding out on us. When are you due?"

"April fifteenth, right along with taxes," Jan said, happily patting her seven-months-large tummy.

"Congratulations," Brad said. "So another fortune cookie comes true."

"Another came true?" Jan asked. "What do you mean? What other?"

"Laura's cookie foretold that a ring would come into her possession, and mine said an old friend would suddenly mean more to me. Now I'd call that being right on the money, wouldn't you?" Brad asked.

Laura's blue eyes settled on a silent Freddy. "Hey, friend, what are you so glum about?"

"No one asked what *my* cookie foretold last year."

"I'll bite. What did it say, bro?" Brad inquired.

"BIG TROUBLE FOR ONE OF AGGRESSIVE MOUTH," Freddy answered. "Can you believe that? Actually, I had it coming. I got drunk and ran a red light. Totaled my car and another guy's. Got arrested. I mouthed off to the judge and earned myself a night in jail and a $200 fine. I know, it was stupid of me. But hey, it was an accident, and no one was hurt."

Jan, his wife, sat with downcast eyes, momentarily pained by the memory. "But Freddy had some good news, too. Tell them, dear."

"Oh, yeah! The doctors couldn't find any sign of the spots they originally saw on my right kidney."

"Thank God for that," Laura said.

The clanging stopped as the last lions leapt out of the restaurant and into the corridor. Geri Palomalo ducked into the empty space they left and searched for Table Twelve. Spotting her, Laura waved an arm above her head, and shouted, "Geri, over here!"

Geri wound her way to Table Twelve and pulled up short. "Where's Mr. Hoity-toity?"

"Ken hasn't shown and there's no word from him," Laura reported.

Geri's whole body bounced as she slid into her chair. "I've got the most wonderful news. Six weeks ago I attended a New York audition with a friend for a new Broadway play. She was auditioning, and I just went along for the ride. When they were all done, the director called out, 'Next.' I didn't pay any attention. Then he said, 'You there in the tenth row center with the pink sweater.' I couldn't believe the director was actually pointing at me."

" 'Me?' " I said. " 'I'm not an actress.' " He told me I was about to become one. He needed a fresh Polynesian face. I auditioned, got the part and a contract for the run of the show. Rehearsals start in two weeks. Now, how's that for news?"

"Wonderful," Laura murmured, her lips frozen into a false smile. "I'd have killed to get a part like that."

"Hey, didn't the two of you swap fortune cookies last time?" asked Brad.

Laura's face drained of color. *My God! Did the cookies have something to do with this turn of events?*

Luckily, their attention shifted to the arriving dinner: steamed whole sea bass with black bean sauce, spicy eggplant, and Peking duck with crisp skins.

"Man, that was great," Brad said afterward, patting his stomach. "Ken will never know what he missed."

Jan said, "It really isn't like him not to show up without letting us know. Maybe things turned around in his office, and he hit it big."

Geri jerked upright in her chair. "Oops! I almost forgot.

Last New Year's, Ken left his cookie, so I popped it in my purse. It's still in here somewhere." She set her enormous leather pouch on the table and rummaged through it. "Ah, here's the little rascal—this purse doesn't lose anything." She pulled out the cookie and set it gently in the center of Table Twelve.

"I can't believe you kept it for a whole year and didn't open it," Jan said. "Weren't you the least bit curious?"

Geri shrugged. "Not really. If I had been, I would have peeked long before this."

"Anybody else curious?" Jan wanted to know.

Four voices reacted in unison. "No!" They stared at it in awkward silence, for each one had experienced the powerful *joss* of such cookies. It was almost as if they feared invading Ken's privacy.

The manager, slightly bent now at age seventy-six, met with her trusted waitress at the cash register. "It is time for the check at Table Twelve," Soo Mei said. "Will you be providing special fortune cookies for them again this year?"

"No, my dear. Give them the ordinary ones from the jar. Only those cookies that were prepared and eaten on the anniversary of the *Golden* Boar possessed the exceptional powers. Neither of us will be here next time around."

Soo Mei dared ask: "How did the cookies get those powers?"

"I'll tell you later, after your shift." Li Set Ling waved her off.

* * * *

Soo Mei looked back at the now-deserted table. Sitting in the center was a lone fortune cookie, still in its cellophane. She absent-mindedly tore away the wrap and popped the sweet cookie in her mouth, slipping the tiny paper fortune in her apron pocket while she cleared away the last dishes.

Close to midnight, as the dining crowd thinned, the manager revealed her story to Soo Mei. "Many years ago I had a dream. From the dream spirit I learned that I was chosen to perform a special service. The dream date was exactly one orbit of Jupiter before the arrival of the *Golden* Boar. Just beforehand, I received instructions on how to prepare and package six powerful cookies. Although I still remembered what the fortunes were, once the cookies were baked I could no longer remember their ingredients."

"But venerable one," Soo Mei asked, "how did you know who to give the fortunes to in the first place?"

"My dream told me there would be a married African-American couple and two single females—one Tahitian, the other *haole*—at Table Twelve. Only one seated at the table wore a wedding ring. Her cookie announced the baby she and her husband wished for. The husband's intended fortune revealed he had pancreatic cancer with only three months left to live.

"Yes, venerable one, but he still lives."

"True, but wait, I am not yet finished. The love cookie was intended for the beautiful Tahitian, who had already found her man, but, as yet, hadn't awakened him. The cookie should have brought them together for a life of contentment. The career cookie should have enhanced the dancing of the other one, drawing critical acclaim and much fame."

Soo Mei frowned in impatience. "But the *joss,* the luck, of the two single women was also altered drastically. What happened to change their fortunes?"

"It was up to you, my trusted one, to deliver all of them—correctly."

"I did, venerable one. Honestly, I did. But then I overheard the two planning an exchange. I could not interfere."

"Of course you couldn't, my dear. It is well known that *joss* cannot be altered, but under certain rare conditions, it may be mutually exchanged. There must have been another force, a greater power at play here. One never knows with the *Golden* Boar. Sometimes a mere touch is enough."

Soo Mei said, "But if Freddy didn't die, then the one with fiery hair surely did."

Li Set Ling nodded. "How very quick of you, my dear."

An hour passed. Outside the restaurant, reveling throngs surged into the Cultural Plaza, crowding around the stage where acrobats, musicians, and dancers performed. Vendors sold Year of the Rat T-shirts, calendars, and brush-painted horoscopes. The popping of the firecrackers began fading away. Their spent red-paper cartridges lay ankle-deep in the streets. The smoke and pungent odors persisted, stinging the eyes.

Inside the House of the Golden Boar, Soo Mei cleared the dishes from the remaining tables until a strange feeling took possession of her. Someone was watching. She whirled about to see a tall man leaning on crutches behind her. "You!" Soo Mei cried, her doll-face turning pale. "You, the one with the fiery red hair."

"I realize I'm too late," Ken said.

"Yes," she whispered. "But you're dead! A ghost maybe?"

"I'm not a ghost," he said. "Yeah, I had one hell of a bad year. My girlfriend left me. The stock market took a terrible downturn. I got beat up—mugged in an alley. The guy even broke my leg. But I'm getting better."

"I am very sorry, sir."

"Oh, by the way, I ran into my friends outside. They said they left a fortune cookie on the table for me from last year. At this point I really could use some good luck in my life."

Soo Mei suddenly felt ill. *I ate the man's cookie and I shall inherit a similar year of tragic events.* She stood frozen in distress.

"My fortune cookie, miss. It should still be on the table, Table Twelve."

"Of course, sir." Soo Mei slipped out of sight, walked in a trance to the jar on the counter, and produced a cellophane packet like so many others. She placed it in his outstretched hand.

"See you next year," he replied.

"It will be the Year of the Ox," she informed him.

Ken's eyebrows shot up. "The ox—that's my sign."

She nodded, and he knew she understood. *It fit him: stubborn, serious, introverted.* He swung his crutches around and headed toward the door, but stopped midway and called over his shoulder.

"Next year I'll be sure to order the noodles."

Soo Mei bowed slightly. "Good idea, sir." She fell into the nearest chair. Reaching into her apron pocket, she pulled out the white slip of paper she'd placed there earlier. "YOUR ILLNESS AL-LOWS YOU ONLY THREE MONTHS TO LIVE." Soo Mei placed her long fingers with painted crimson nails over her face and began to sob.

Li Set Ling rushed to her side and listened as the waitress related what she had done. The manager instantly knew how to respond. "That fortune was for the one with fire in his hair. Not you! It is now the Year of the Rat. As I told you before, the special cookies only have power during the year of the *Golden* Boar and that is another 600 years from now."

"Oh thank you, venerable one." Soo Mei smiled through her tears.

In the Grip of Time

Jeff Cooper inched the throttle forward and adjusted the rotor pitch slightly until engine and blade played his kind of music. The syncopated humming, a chopper's heartbeat, hovered in the memory of his war years—in Vietnam as a pilot. The war ended early in '73. As the U.S. was withdrawing its last troops, he too had his chance to leave. But Jeff Cooper chose to stay behind.

He'd left 'Nam when Ho Chi Min took over the entire country, but stayed on in Southeast Asia as a commercial helicopter pilot, carrying passengers, mail, and light supplies—all of it legal. And why not stay? He had no family to go back to in Somerset, Pennsylvania, and his girlfriend had dumped him during the war.

Today, in early May of '92, he and a Thai partner owned two choppers, a panel truck, and the claim to a modest profit.

Jeff overflowed the bucket seat with his six-foot height and 200 pounds. His deep blue eyes, set too close together, gave him a calculating look—rescued by a boyish cowlick that leaped out of gray-streaked brown hair. His ski-jump nose sat on a wide face gullied from sun damage. He wore his usual work uniform: khaki jump suit with deep pants pockets.

Cruising at 1,800 feet, he banked the chopper through small cloud clusters huddled like sheep, then leveled off and surveyed the landscape below through the wraparound windshield. Brown plains, rice paddies, and straw villages slipped quickly under them. They had just passed over Kampong Thum on the Stoeng Sen River and began heading northwest. The big river, the Mekong, snaked along sixty-five clicks to the East, just out of sight.

He felt the pressure of time. Any day now, the treacherous rainy season would move in. It would last six months, limiting his flying days. Behind him sat his two Cambodian passengers, Ng Tam Duc, and a young female, both stylishly dressed. Ng had introduced her, but her name sounded different than his. His secretary? Girlfriend? It wasn't any of Jeff's business to know which. He heard them talking in their local dialect, but could only pick up a word here and there.

The man had claimed to be a politician in the town of Pailin. Their destination was Champasak, a market town in southern Laos. Stowing the couple's two suitcases in the hold, Jeff had reached for Ng's briefcase—brown leather with two buckle straps—to stow it as well.

"No take, sir, I keep!" The man jerked away, clutching the handle with both fists. Even now, as Jeff glanced at them in the rear-view mirror, Ng had both arms wrapped around the case.

The engine emitted a few sour notes, then resumed its melodic beat. They had been airborne an hour and twenty minutes, a third of the way to Champasak, when it happened. Jeff cursed the quality of the gasoline they were getting these days, then thought no more about it. Ten minutes later, he heard the off-key notes again. And again.

Then the engine quit altogether and the main rotor blades slowed from a whine to a *whop-whop-whop*. The cabin drooped suddenly. He switched fuel tanks, but still couldn't restart. He feathered the blades and tried to glide. The chopper began to spin counterclockwise and lose altitude—1,600 feet, 1,200, 900, then 800 . . . treetops rising to meet them. A long soprano scream and a bass groan of impending doom emanated from the seats behind him. Jeff tried to ignore them as he jettisoned both fuel tanks to lighten the ultimate impact and forestall instant flaming. The fifty-five gallon drums dropped away to the left and right. He remembered nothing after that—not even the impact.

Jeff came to, his body rigid, legs splayed. Sections of the cockpit control panel hung from their wiring. The smell of motor oil permeated the air. They'd avoided the dreaded fire so far, but who knew for how long? His seat had ripped loose from the deck and lay in the cockpit among shards of broken cabin glass. He was still buckled in; only the shoulder harness had kept him from being launched like a missile through the windshield, now just a gaping hole. Grateful that the harnessing device had held him, his hands trembled as he released the buckle.

Jeff couldn't move. An aluminum slice of the chopper's frame had coiled itself across his right leg, pinning it to the deck. It stung and burned, as if an arrow of fire and ice had pierced it to the bone. *Damn, it's broken below the knee!* Above his knee, streaks of blood crept like a living thing through the khaki. Another jagged length of frame had torn through his pants, puncturing his thigh. His heart, an anxious bird, battered its wings inside his chest. Thinking maybe his passengers could help, he twisted at the waist enough to see behind him. The woman's seat had also ripped free. It lay cockeyed, wedged into one of the engine's structural supports. He swallowed hard to keep from vomiting. Her head dangled from her neck, with her lipsticked mouth contorted in terror. She couldn't help anyone ever again.

Ng appeared to be unconscious. His arms and torso still lay protectively across the precious briefcase. Wincing in pain, Jeff reached back and tugged hard on the man's sandal to rouse him. No response. *Probably dead, too, or a major concussion,* he concluded.

He spotted the collapsible shovel attached to what remained of the starboard bulkhead. Grabbing the handle, he jerked it back and forth until the upper fastener popped open and the shovel fell to the deck beside him. Using the handle as a lever, he bent away the section of cabin frame confining his right leg. With the frame only inches away from his body, he could now see the ripped thigh wound. He had to work fast. Jeff reached over his head and found a brace to grab. Planting his left foot on what remained of the deck beneath him and pulling on the brace, he eased his body up and backward, leaving the jagged-edged impaler behind—and his leg free. But he needed to stanch the flow of blood quickly, or it would be all over for him. His first aid kit! The door to the locker where he kept it had sprung open on impact; the kit was nowhere in sight.

Jeff rolled out of his pilot's seat. The webbed belt from his jump suit made a sufficient tourniquet to stem the flow of blood for the time being. Using the hunting knife strapped to his belt, he slashed and pulled lengths of skirt off the woman. Cutting two large pieces, he folded and wrapped one tightly around the wound as a bandage. He cut the remainder of the skirt into strips. Two of these created a protective layer, and a split third secured the bandage to the leg.

Jeff tried to stand but couldn't. His right leg, looking like a knobby branch, was broken for sure, just below the knee. The whole leg throbbed. It needed to be set and then splinted. Two long control levers made for an adequate splint, and vinyl strips cut from the woman's seatback added padding. He set the leg by wedging his ankle into a narrow V-section of bulkhead support and forcing his knee back away from it. Though excruciating, the worst of the pain lasted only a few minutes. His gaze fixed on the woman's red sash, still draped over her left shoulder and down past her right hip. Yanking it off, he used it to bind his leg to the splint—along with thick vinyl cut from his own seat back. Jeff reached for the man's briefcase, intending to use the leather straps for reinforcement. He jerked it out of Ng's grasp.

Then curiosity got the best of him. *What does this thing contain that's so precious?* He propped his back against the skin of the chopper, unsnapped the case, and hastily rifled through it. The papers proved of no value to him. They were written in Cambodian or Thai; he could barely tell the difference—and couldn't read either, anyway. He pocketed a stack of riel notes, local money, and then noticed what looked like a black nylon toiletries kit. Unzipping it, he discovered a large, heavy ovoid wrapped in a jeweler's chamois cloth.

Slowly he uncovered a granddaddy gemstone. He'd never seen or even heard of a blue-white natural sapphire that size before—possibly a record twenty or thirty carats, seemingly near-perfect in clarity and color. It approached a turkey egg in size, with a multifaceted surface. Most likely, it had come from the gemstone mines near Pailin, where he had picked Ng and the woman up. In fact, he'd read somewhere that the town had derived its name from an ancient Khmer word meaning "blue sapphire."

Jeff let out a whistle between his two front teeth, then glanced up—and froze. Ng Tam Duc's black eyes stared back at him. Ng had not only survived, he held a 9-mm Mauser automatic pistol in his left hand. The man's right hand was turned palm-up to receive his prized property.

"Must be worth at least a million stateside dollars," Jeff said, inching closer to the man, apparently to return the stone.

"Two-pont-seex-tree meeyon—veddy rare," said an intent Ng. Blood trickled from his lips and nose as he spoke. Obviously weakened from internal injuries, he had trouble holding the pistol steady on the pilot. His lids fluttered, and he watched Jeff through squinting eyes that indicated failing vision.

Suppressing his own pain, Jeff lunged forward, slamming Ng's gun hand to the armrest. Shock, a poor grip, and inexperience with firearms sent the weapon dropping to the deck. As Ng reached for it, the pilot raised his muscled left arm as if to hurl a fastball and smashed the gemstone into the man's right temple. Once. Twice. Ng slumped forward. Still conscious, he weakly tried to right himself. One more blow, and Jeff heard the skull crack.

Horror-struck, the pilot bellowed, then gagged. The aftershock of his deed threw him backward onto the deck amid shards of glass and cockpit rubble. He felt as if a force outside himself, some malevolent reflex, had committed the act. How could everything have gone so wrong so fast? As for actually killing a man—never! Not face to face, anyway. In 'Nam he'd strafed villages to ferret out the Cong. But from the air it was impersonal, just doing his job. What had come over him?

The gemstone! Jeff shivered as he unclenched his fist. Trickles of Ng's blood covered his knuckles and laced across the huge sapphire. Still, its mystical, satiny blue facets peeked out in the accusing noonday sun. Wiping the gemstone on Ng's pant leg rid it of the blood. Jeff rewrapped it in the chamois and jammed it into the deepest cargo pocket on his good leg. The pistol lay on the deck across from him. He stretched to retrieve and pocket it. There was no turning back now.

Who could ever tell that Ng hadn't died in the crash? Jeff assured himself. Carrying a gemstone that size—another crooked politician who's been committing graft in office for years and cleverly converted his stolen cash into something he could easily carry.

With no time to rationalize further, Jeff cut the surrounding leather straps away from Ng's briefcase and reinforced the splinted leg in two places. Selecting a piece of aluminum bulkhead framing that most resembled a crutch, he unscrewed one end with the tip of his hunting knife and repeatedly bent the Y-shaped end, until it broke loose from the deck. Fragments of seat back stuffing and Ng's shirt provided ample cushioning for a shoulder pad.

Sliding off the edge of the deck to the ground, the crutch and splint combination got their first trial. *Not great, but they'll have to do.*

He loosened the webbed belt about his upper thigh in stages, checking for signs of fresh blood. The bandages held, and the tourniquet no longer seemed necessary. He slipped the belt back into the loops of his jump suit.

They had crashed in a broad cluster of hardwood stumps, the stark result of massive deforestation. Only bamboo, young palms, and thick underbrush grew there now. The going would be easier, bettering the odds of his getting out alive.

Originally, he'd expected to refuel and fly back this same day. *Damn it*, he hadn't planned on crashing. Limping through the chopper debris, he looked for what he could salvage. His passengers' suitcases had burst open. Clothes and shoes spilled about. Nothing of value there, but the woman's tote lay on the ground intact. Unzipping it, he discovered two plastic bottles of water and two lunches in small partitioned containers: prawns, pork, noodles, and pickled vegetables. His spirits lifted slightly. This was a gift. He looped the tote's long cloth handles over his head and under one arm. The sleeves of the woman's cardigan sweater he knotted about his waist—no telling when that would come in handy.

His own canteen had survived intact, but he wasn't so lucky with the flashlight and tool kit. Their mountings had been torn from the bulkhead, and a stumbling search through the foliage didn't turn them up. The last things he needed before venturing off from the crash site were the battery-operated global positioning system and the magnetic compass dangling from one of the control panels. Miraculously, they still functioned—and his own watch was still running. He figured that in his crippled shape, he'd better beeline for the nearest waterway, where he could hook up with a boatman going downriver. After recording his position and noting the direction of the nearest river on his map, he undid the thumbscrews and slipped the instruments into his cargo pockets. The mighty Mekong was just too far. He'd head back to the Stoeng Sen River about eighteen clicks to the southeast.

His crutch made the going difficult amid the deep grass, reeds, and thorny brush. Rest periods grew longer and more frequent. Late afternoon brought higher ground, shorter grass, and some rocky terrain. Nightfall made it impossible to see where to step. So he slept in the dry cradle of a large fig tree's roots, using the woman's sweater for a pillow. The heat of his body drew swarms of mosquitoes and black spiders. He swatted away until exhaustion took over.

Before daylight, the tropical rains dropped in torrents and by mid-morning the rain faded to an hour's drizzle with heavy clouds hovering above. He had to abandon the drenched sweater. The smell of decaying plants rose up from the forest floor, assaulting his nostrils and lungs. At moments, the sensations in his leg almost blinded him. The fracture throbbed, the thigh burned. At least he found no fresh blood on his thigh. He could still walk, or drag himself, through a canopy of tree ferns. He could hear small animals rustling about. Birds hidden in voluminous leaves sang or screeched their displeasure at him. The clearings were Hades hot and humid, but easier to move in.

Jeff spent the second night on the mounded ridge of an abandoned rice paddy. He thought the river couldn't be much farther; maybe one, maybe two days. But his present pace couldn't last. The thigh wound felt hot above and below the bandage, emanating a sickening odor—infection had set in. The fracture pounded with a deeper soreness than he'd ever known, but he had to live with it. The rains awakened him the second morning in a row, and lasted for several hours. Now dragging the heavy leg, he bit down on his lower lip to persevere. He tasted blood and so switched to biting down on a thick twig.

The closer to the river, the wetter the ground, until he was often wading up to his calves. Muddy water sloshed dangerously close to the festering thigh wound. The hundreds of mosquito bites had given him the shake-and-bake of malaria. He'd already experienced intermittent chills and fever. Now the moist heat smothered him like a heavy blanket. Despite the tight fit of his Phillies cap, sweat dripped from his scalp and ran down his stubbled face.

Hunger ate away at his gut. Of the two candy bars he carried for emergencies, he'd consumed one at breakfast each of the two days. He'd already devoured his passengers' lunches. Delicious but tangy, they'd driven him to recklessly guzzle whatever water was left. During the downpours, he'd caught what he could in the three containers, but the narrow bottle necks didn't collect much. Now thirst consumed him at the very thought of water. If only the high ground could be reached again, he'd be prepared for the next rain. And the river might be visible from there as well.

A distance grove of Indian fig trees enticed him to alter course, giving him a tangible, short-term goal. As he approached, he found himself entering a seemingly endless stand of forest with a narrow, almost overgrown trail winding through it. Several hours of daylight remained, but he craved a little rest in the shade. The long trek had been just too arduous. Slate-gray clouds hovered low. His tongue felt swollen with thirst. Snapping off three large philodendron leaves, he rolled them into funnels and tucked them into the necks of his containers to catch the rain. The effort did him in. With the fig tree roots as a hard pillow, he passed out. In a troubled sleep, he dreamt that a boatman found him unconscious on the shore of the river and stole the gemstone.

When Jeff awoke on the third morning, his chest tightened with his first thought: the gemstone. Reaching for the lump in his pocket, his fingers felt the chamois, then the hard egg-shape within. *Ah, yeah, still there.* The storm had come and gone, driving his fever down and nearly filling up the bottles. The leaf funnels had worked! He drew several deep swigs, and with it, a new sense of optimism. Wobbling, he forced himself to stand. Aching with the leg pain, he leaned against a tree and peered through the foliage in the direction of the river. He knew he was still two or three clicks away, but thought he heard the putt-putt of long-tailed boats. Or was it his imagination, his desperate need to reach civilization?

The gemstone lodged in his brain as an obsession. If fever and delirium took hold of him again, Jeff realized he couldn't protect his prize. The tantalizing bulge in his pants pocket looked too obvious, too inviting, and it was too large to hide elsewhere on him. Scanning the trees for a place to conceal the stone, Jeff discovered the obvious—they all looked alike. *How will I be able to tell them apart? How can I mark the spot?*

He gazed up at the nearest fig. It loomed about seventy-five feet, with a smooth white trunk and delicate foliage only at the top. The first branches were more than thirty feet above ground, and the roots emerged at half that distance, huge tendrils spreading downward, thick and ruthless, like giant gripping fingers. But passing on one side of the trunk, he noticed what appeared to be a massive hedgerow of brush and interlaced vines at least four feet high.

The roots on that side of the tree climbed over the wide hedgerow before continuing downward. *Strange*, he thought. Poking his knife into the thicket, he struck a hard surface. He began hacking away with his knife—gripping, tugging, and clearing away the brush and vines. Suddenly, he scraped his knuckles on one flat rock. Hacking to one side, he came upon another rock, then what appeared to be a row. Only they weren't rocks; they resembled bricks that formed a mantle to a wall. Grabbing huge handfuls of brush, he exposed more of this mantle—about a dozen feet of wall.

The weary trekker's heart quickened. This was no mundane barrier. These were stone murals, images carved into a long, freestanding wall. He'd unearthed remnants of a *wat*, an ancient Cambodian temple. Jeff, not much of a sightseer himself, had conveyed many a tourist in his chopper to Siem Reap and the nearby town of Angkor to visit these magnificent temples—best of all, Angkor Wat with its corncob-shaped domes that turned to gold at sunset.

But this recollection lasted only a split second. Jeff's jubilation rose from a different discovery: crevices in the wall—surefire places to hide his gemstone. He found a foothold halfway up the wall for his good leg and, using the crutch for balance, raised himself high enough to peer over the mantle into a ravine at least thirty feet deep. At the bottom of the ravine lay hunks of crumbling ruins, nearly smothered from his view by vegetation. He guessed the temple, in its full glory, may have stood almost sixty feet tall.

Easily recognizable, the carvings depicted an epic conquest. Monkeys dressed in warrior garb, holding spears and shields, rode on a train of elephants marching from right to left. In the middle of the parade, an emperor rode on his horse-drawn chariot.

Nearby, a young, pliable fig root extended well over the wall for some distance. It covered a crevice about six inches wide and even deeper between two large mantle stones. The third and fourth elephants to the left of the emperor flanked this gap. Jeff pried the root away from the crevice with his hunting knife, inserted the chamois-wrapped sapphire deep into the space, and allowed the root to snap back and re-cover the crevice. Replacing the undergrowth and debris, the surroundings took on the look of pristine forest once more. Satisfied with the cache, he crawled to a cluster of low, feathery ferns. Exhaustion made him crave sleep, but that could be his enemy if he gave in to it. *Ten minutes—no more.*

He awoke in humidity so thick he could almost spoon it. Amid the treetops, he watched a fresh procession of murky clouds march across the sky. Jeff screamed: "Get the hell outta here, I can't take any more!" The clouds responded with a clap of warning thunder and unleashed a torrent of rain. Hastily arranging fragments of banana leaves this time as funnels, he captured what water he could. But the bottles and canteen were heavy. He needed to lighten his load. Recording the last GPS location, he abandoned the device.

The torrent ended abruptly. Determining that this was his last rest stop, he dragged himself to his feet, slipped the crutch under his arm, and started down the hill toward the river. In less than an hour, he could no longer support his own weight and dropped to one knee. The mud became slicker and the grade steepened as the river noises neared. Rolling over on his back, he slid down the grade until a snarled vine saved him from shooting out into the river itself. *I made it!* he thought.

A thick log floated toward him. As it approached land, two eyes appeared, and Jeff dragged himself back up the embankment, his hands clutching at the vines. The jaws parted, revealing two horseshoes of glaring teeth. The gun! He pulled it out of a pocket. Firing twice, he made two direct hits between the alligator's eyes. The log floated away.

Jeff's stomach clawed with hunger, his head spun, dizzy and feverish. Peering far off in the distance, he saw several boats slip along on the brown river, mostly keeping to the deeper channel in the middle. He propped himself against a tree, arms flailing, and shouted for help. But the heavy, humid air swallowed up his normally commanding bass voice. One long-tailed boat cruised closer to shore, but the boatman didn't see him. To get his attention, Jeff sacrificed his last bullet. Firing the gun into the air, he collapsed, then passed out cold. He remembered nothing after that.

* * * *

Jeff awoke around noon, two days later, a patient in an overcrowded surgical ward. A sheet covered his body, leaving only his left hand exposed. Three IVs converged into the back of that hand. He struggled to make sense of his surroundings. Lumpy red insect bites covered both arms. His right leg felt hot, but somewhat higher than the wound he'd bandaged nearly a week ago. He could see the rise his left foot made in the sheet—it shifted with that leg's movement and wiggled with his toes. No corresponding rise existed where the right foot should have been. Instead, a hump about midway between his right knee and torso seemed to be all there was. He threw off the sheet and stared in horror. A plastic drain tube exited from the huge mound of stained gauze bandaging and disappeared somewhere off the bed.

"Doctor! Nurse! Somebody! Anybody!" he screamed. "Help me!"

A young nurse approached with a hypodermic needle and emptied its contents into one of his IVs. As she turned to leave, Jeff grabbed her wrist. She spoke rapidly in her local tongue. Only a few scattered words reached his senses.

"Where's my leg?" he bellowed.

The nurse pried her wrist from his grip. "Please … You veddy sick. Can die." She pulled the sheets back over him. "Gang-a-reen, veddy bad. Maybe doctor tell mo' latah."

Jeff wanted more answers, but the painkiller injected into the IV had begun to take effect. He drifted off to a deep sleep.

The next afternoon an English-speaking French-Cambodian doctor did explain. The bacterial infection had become life threatening; the leg had to be amputated above the knee. Antibiotics would kill the remaining traces of infection. He hesitated before continuing. "We're a crisis center with limited beds, as you can see. We'll keep you a couple more days until we can remove the drain. In a few months we'll fit you for a prosthesis. You should be healed enough by then." He was about to leave, but hesitated. "Oh, by the way, we had to burn your clothes. Sorry."

"Damn! What happened to my things—my cash, my wallet, my passport?"

"According to the boatman who found you lying on the riverbank, you didn't have any cash or passport. Your wallet's here. Empty except for your business cards."

A wave of helplessness engulfed Jeff's body, nearly drowning him in anger and self-pity. *Damned boatmen … can't be trusted. Good thing I stashed the gemstone in time.* "Hey, Doc, you said 'prosthesis.' Will I be able to walk without crutches or a cane?"

The doctor shrugged. "No way of telling. There's always the possibility of rejection. But let's not worry about that now."

Jeff's eyes scanned the ward. The beds were nearly flush with one another, like local boats rafted together. Most of the patients were children. "What the hell is this?" he reacted. "Why am I in a children's ward?"

The doctor eyed him sternly. "Take a look around you, Mr. Cooper. You're not the only one without a limb here. We're overcrowded. This country's farmlands are still full of land mines, thousands of them—unexploded, buried. It's the poorest people who suffer the most, especially children." He waved toward the other beds. "These are the luckier ones. Many children, their parents, too, don't survive the explosions."

Of course. Jeff's face burned, not from fever, but from shame. "Sorry, Doc. And thanks."

* * * *

Over the next few months, Jeff coped with frustrations on all sides. He fought off two major infections; that was the easier part. The hospital discharged him in short crutches and a set of old but clean, patched-together clothes from peasants who'd died—a humiliation he wouldn't soon forget. He'd been able to obtain a new passport. But the biggest problem was money. The remaining assets of the helicopter service had to be sold off to pay medical bills and living expenses. His ex-partner proved a willing buyer and moved what was left of the operation to Siem Reap. Out of compassion, the man hired Jeff to help out in the company's one-room office. He even sent for mail-order crutches from the States to accommodate Jeff's Western size.

Returning to the local hospital, Jeff received a prosthesis—one altered to match the length of his good leg. After several painful cycles of rejection and inflammation, the artificial leg acclimated, allowing him to eventually graduate from crutches to a simple cane, which he abandoned several months later.

The gemstone remained his obsession—his reason for sacrificing one leg and enduring the daily agony. Jeff wanted to fly again, but no prospective employer would hire a crippled pilot, especially one who couldn't get insured. So he continued to work in the dispatch office for months until he'd amassed a small stake to head upriver.

In December, the driest month of the second year, Jeff had accumulated enough to pursue his quest, a quest that would set him up in luxury for life. In that silent stretch of jungle, there wouldn't be any reasonable landing spots, even for a helicopter. He needed a boat to get there. Starting from an inlet at the northern end of Lake Tonle Sap, he'd take a boat down to the mouth of the Stoeng Sen River, and then upriver to the area of the sunken temple ruins.

Hanging out at one of the *klongs* close to the inlet, Jeff spotted a twenty-five-foot flat-bottomed, long-tailed craft, moored at a piling close to shore. A boatman was tinkering with its engine, probably salvaged from a small truck. The man worked under a full-length canvas tarp, supported by pipe poles. The rust-riddled engine block and simple gear box mounted on the stern had a ten-foot drive shaft angled into the water. A hand throttle, connected directly to the carburetor, operated the totally exposed engine. It wasn't the first time Jeff had had a chance to examine one up close, but the crude, unsafe arrangement never ceased to amaze him.

Jeff whistled and beckoned, until the unsmiling boatman, in faded pants and a long-sleeved blue shirt, looked up and waded ashore. He was probably in his late twenties, but looked older from the daily ordeal of scraping out a living on the river. Stiff black hair fell over his forehead. The sunken cheeks and narrow, sharp chin gave his face a gaunt look.

Jeff knew enough local dialect to get by. Face to face, the two haggled. They made an odd pair. The brawny American stood a head taller and at least seventy-five pounds heavier, but the boatman proved to be a tough and wily bargainer. They reached an understanding for Jeff to charter the boat for the next six days. Jeff agreed to supply everything they would need and pay for their fuel as well. He figured it would take about two days on the water each way; and even with his gimpy leg, no more than half a day's trek to the site. The boatman seemed satisfied with 250,000 riels; he would receive an equal amount after the return trip. "You call me Sang," he said as he waded back to the boat.

At six-thirty the next morning, Jeff hired a *motodup*, a motorcycle taxi, to carry himself and four backpacks to the boat. He wondered whether Sang would be there. Sure enough, the boatman stood waiting for him, quickly stowed the gear, and started the engine. They motored out of the inlet onto the gray-brown lake.

Ramshackle floating wood houses with skimpy thatched roofs lined the shore. Old oil drums provided the necessary buoyancy. Bald tires, hanging low on the outside walls, prevented damage from boat bumping. Pilings held numbered wood mailboxes. Attached to one dwelling, Jeff spotted a floating pen with compartments containing live fish, snakes, and alligators. On the surrounding wood deck a young girl fondled her pet boa constrictor. Occasionally, a well-built residence appeared on sturdy stilts. One even had a wide veranda, where a boy played with his dog. Twenty yards offshore, two small boys paddled about in metal washbasins, their laughter bouncing like skipping stones across the water.

Little conversation passed between Jeff and his boatman during the six hours it took to reach the Stoeng Sen and head up into the river. They drank from bottled water hung over the gunnels in chain mesh nets for cooling. Their meals were tins of Spam, stew, and fresh fish, along with steamed, sticky white rice cooked over a small charcoal stove on board. In calm water, one of them napped. In rougher or shallower water, one of them searched and poled the way, while the other managed the tiller and speed. The shallow-draft boat made good time until darkness forced them to tie up to a tree at the ill-defined shoreline.

At first light, they cast off once more. Being the dry season, the river ran lean in many places, with caked mud and gravel lining the shore. Jeff began checking his new GPS device more often as the day wore on. Around four in the afternoon, he had Sang pull into a tiny cove on the western bank and tie up to a cluster of sturdy, mature bamboo. He checked the GPS one last time to be sure, for there was little to recognize from memory. He saw no sign of his muddy slide to the water two years earlier. But he stubbornly believed he had the location right, and spotted a grassy knoll at the top of the embankment—a place to stretch their legs and relax. Once they'd climbed up to it, he informed Sang that it was too late in the day to start the inland trek. They would spend the night here, and he alone would go inland tomorrow.

"Hey, Boss, why you go alone?" Sang asked, his eyes narrowing with suspicion. "Why we come this place anyway? Ain't nothin' here but jungle, Boss."

"Somebody's got to watch the boat," Jeff answered. "You're right. There's nothing here for anybody but me, and I've got some unfinished business in there."

"What if you no show up back here?"

"Nothing's going to happen to me. You wait one day more and then go back without me. That's all there is to it."

"You crazy, Boss."

Both men slept fitfully, but for different reasons. Jeff felt a new level of high coming on. He could almost taste the reunion with his precious sapphire. Sang, on the other hand, didn't like not knowing what "Boss" was up to.

Jeff awoke before sunrise and glanced over at the boatman, curled up on a straw mat, eyes closed, his breathing deep and steady, a guttural sound emanating from the back of his throat. In the fluorescent moonlight, Jeff tightened his prosthesis in place, hefted his hiking backpack, and set out. Once in the thick brush, his machete proved essential. Using his compass he followed a magnetic direction west-northwest. It took an hour to go a mile—the jungle had thickened. He checked the GPS device every fifteen minutes. At each of these stops, he scanned the foliage behind him and listened to be sure no one was following.

Shortly after ten, sweaty and exhausted, he reached a stretch of higher ground and thought he recognized the familiar grove of majestic Indian fig trees. Jeff rested, cradled in the roots of the first tree he encountered. After two years, nothing looked exactly the same, of course. But the GPS device confirmed that he had to be within a few hundred yards of the gemstone cache. Seated there, he gobbled up a Spam lunch, washing it down with half a bottle of water. Dessert comprised a fever pill and two malaria pills. While eating, he studied the lay of the land. He knew the wall ran east and west in the middle of the grove. He'd come uphill from the south, so by continuing north, the wall had to be encountered one way or another.

Jeff wielded the machete to poke and swing at the long grasses and vines as he advanced through the trees. The blade clunked against hard roots and small rocks. A few clangs against stone turned out to be false alarms. But about a hundred feet into the grove, a consistent clang told him he'd hit pay dirt: the temple wall!

Jeff began clearing away the thicket, methodically at first, then faster and faster, until—there they were! Elephants, monkeys, graceful horses, and marching warriors. He scanned the procession. Where was *his* particular elephant pair? *His* emperor's chariot? Swinging the sharp edge of the machete close to the wall at ground level, he chopped away at the stubborn undergrowth crawling up and clinging to the thick rectangular stones. After two more non-stop hours of manic clearing, he'd exposed nearly thirty feet of wall, where another epic story began. Two-and-a-half elephants farther, the emperor and his chariot appeared—and beside it, the site he'd been seeking.

But two years had not been kind. The very crevice concealing his secret stash was now covered by a serpentine root more than five inches in diameter. With the machete, Jeff hacked and sawed away at the live root. Cut nearly through, the guardian became pliable enough to pry loose from the stone. Sliding a small rock underneath to anchor the root away from the crevice, he reached in with his right hand. There it was! He touched the chamois cloth, now in moldy shreds—and then the hard, faceted surface of the sapphire itself. With a triumphant smile, he tried to coil his fingers around it.

Jeff's smile soon collapsed when the stone wouldn't budge. It wouldn't even twist. The root growth all along the wall had pushed the carved stones down and sideways, exerting tremendous pressure on the sides of the gemstone. Using his machete, he felled a young tree trunk, but it failed in its role, first as a pry bar and then as a battering ram. Elsewhere, a few of the smaller rocks broke loose. He heard them bouncing down the inside of the wall. Nothing he did made a difference. The gemstone orb refused to come loose from its hiding place. Sweat stung his eyes. He was wiping it away with his shirt sleeve when he heard a rustle in the brush. *Damn, am I about to get arrested?* He knew it was illegal to damage a national antiquity, even if it was undiscovered and in ruins.

He spun around. Sang stood directly in front of him.

"What the hell? I told you to stay with the boat. Someone could steal our supplies."

"No worry, Boss, nobody find our stuff." A sneer crossed the boatman's hard face. Reaching into his pants pocket, he pulled out a gun—an unusual weapon, but nonetheless familiar.

The Mauser! The same gun Jeff had taken from the politician he'd killed in the chopper. When he'd passed out at the river's edge, the pistol was empty, but who knew if Sang had reloaded it.

"You!" Jeff spit out. "You took advantage of me and stole everything I had—my money, wallet, IDs."

"Yeah, Boss, it the cost of save your life. We even, no?"

"Then why the gun?"

"This my insurance, you betcha. You pay me half only and no tell me why we come here. Nobody stiff Sang. Not this boy."

"You'll get your pay," assured Jeff. "Now, you go back to the boat like I told you. I'll be there sometime tomorrow. I ran into some unexpected obstacles. It'll take a little longer than I thought. Now go! Get out of here!"

"No, Boss. How I know you come back? Sang stay. Sang not miss nothin'. What you got in the hole tha' so important?"

"Nothing you need to know about." Jeff leaned over and reached into the crevice with his right hand, keeping an eye on his captor as burning curiosity drew Sang closer and closer.

"You want to see?" Jeff's voice sounded beguiling, friendly, as he began pulling his arm out. Sang bent forward to look, his gaze so fixated on the hole that his straw hat fell off and his gun hand went slack. Jeff pivoted and grabbed the gun hand, crunching knuckles. Sang yelped in pain. The gun fell to the ground. With a swift, powerful motion, Jeff swung his left arm behind Sang, lifting the wiry but lightweight Cambodian up to wall height. Sang struggled and kicked, but he was no match for the burly ex-pilot. With a roar, Jeff threw him across the top of the wall—and let go.

The boatman's screams ricocheted off the trees as he fell thirty feet to the temple floor.

Jeff leaned his full weight against the wall and peered down into the ravine. He saw nothing. The boatman had met his death beneath a cavernous network of sprawling plants and broken ancient stones. But then he spotted something strange: a slender fig tree trunk protruding out over the ravine. Embedded in the wall about ten feet down, the long white trunk was vibrating violently. Sang must have careened off it as he fell. Jeff shuddered. He could feel the vibration against his chest. Stumbling backward a foot or two, he saw that the fig's roots were protruding out of the wall on his side, spreading their grasping, eerie fingers along the stones. This wall section had precariously bowed out from the root growth of that very tree. A spasm of terror shot through his spine. He knew all about this. It was a national crisis, an unsolvable dilemma for the archaeologists. Were the fig roots crushing the ancient *wats*? Or were the roots actually supporting the temples, preventing them from crumbling altogether?

But he had no time to reflect. The wall was buckling! The carved figures actually appeared to be shifting, moving, alive. The wall looked ready to burst. The vibration turned into a rumble as all the stones around him began to move. The sapphire! He shoved his hand back into the crevice on the chance that the movement might have dislodged his treasure. It had! The moldy cloth fell away as his broad fingers touched the gem. He clenched it in his fist, and felt a flash of exultation. Success! Nobody could take it away from him now. But his celebration lasted only a split second. He felt the earth under him tremble as the wall collapsed. Stone after stone—elephants, monkeys, warriors, chariots—tumbled into the temple abyss.

Jeff lurched forward and tumbled with them, still clutching his coveted orb. His broad, heavy body crashed through endless vegetation as he landed on his back on the temple floor. He was still conscious as an avalanche of dirt, rock, and carved stone collapsed around him. It swallowed his prosthesis first, covering the straps so he couldn't undo them to free himself. Still he gripped the sapphire, weakly holding it high, as though it needed special protection. It was the last thing he saw.

At the river's edge, the line securing Sang's boat rotted. The long-tailed boat drifted downriver, washing this dream of wealth and power from the memory of man—for who knows how many years?

§

Picture Imperfect

I'm not a tolerant fellow. When someone tells me he hears voices but no other human being is nearby, I assume he's one slice of bread short of a sandwich. So when *I'm* the one hearing strange conversations, I keep these odd little crumbs to myself. I'm nobody's fool, you know.

But I'm in a quandary, a crazy situation, and, frankly, I'm ashamed to even talk about it. The conversations *I'm* hearing—are they real or not? There's not a living soul within a mile of this country house I inherited. It sits squarely in a golden meadow of tall grasses, bordered by dense woods. I'm a solitary man, and I like it that way.

So whose voices are they? From where did they originate? And why are they plaguing me?

My first awareness of these intruders came around nine one evening, while I was preparing my usual snack at the kitchen table. As I was spreading cream cheese on a toasted bagel, I heard voices, both male and female, mingled, in ascending and descending decibels. At first I thought they were coming from the radio on the counter. But when I reached over and rotated the volume control clockwise to ON, no sound burst forth. I patted the top of the plastic casing. It was cold to my touch. The radio had definitely been off. I increased the volume, but only static greeted me. No voices, no music. I turned the dial to OFF with a firm click.

The voices emanated from elsewhere in the house—the front door, I presumed. I confess I often neglect to lock it. So I laid the knife across the top of my plate and called out: "I'm in the kitchen, come on in."

A prolonged silence stalked me, as if it were alive and waiting for me to say something else. "Who's there?" I shouted. The silence hovered, taunting me. I hastened into the den, thinking that I'd left the television alive and still speaking. But no, the dark screen reflected the room in its mirroring glass. Neither the stereo nor any other part of the home entertainment system could have spoken. I had borrowed its extension cord to power a new reading lamp in the living room next to my recliner.

The hairs on my neck prickled, shivers crawled up and down my spine as I realized that mere electronics played no part in this phenomenon. I began to notice something else, too. When I approached either of the arched doorways to the living room, the voices grew louder and more distinct. But when I actually crossed the threshold onto the Oriental carpet, they stopped, as though they'd detected an interloper. Perhaps in some mysterious way, they considered me an eavesdropper. I tried a new tack, slowly backing out of the room. As my steps receded into the hall, the conversation resumed, as if the voices shared secrets I had no right to hear.

I'm a pragmatic guy and don't take kindly to being conned. No way would I let these renegades—voices, spirits, whatever they were—get the better of me. I stepped back into the room and exited quickly, again and again, faster and faster. Ha! No voices! It wasn't until I lunged forward onto the carpet and dropped into my recliner that I heard them again. What had changed? Did they decide that I posed no further threat to them? Or did they merely choose to ignore my presence? I'll never know.

Against my better judgment and despite all normal reasoning, I uttered a few words, surely loud enough to be heard. But the strange tongue of the voices—a mixture of French and Dutch—

trampled my words like stomping feet. As I sank deeper into my recliner, normally a haven of comfort and pleasure, a suffocating heat permeated my body. Peeling off my lounging robe, I conjured up a final, desperate strategy. I scanned the array of pictures on the wall opposite where I sat. These works of art, my most highly prized possessions, filled me with an almost sensual pleasure.

My gaze landed on an eighteenth-century Flemish oil, framed in ornately carved wood. I had purchased it at a charity auction just last week and hung it in a place of honor, over the mantel. The richness of the scene captivated me with its true-to-life quality: a kitchen in a humble cottage. A peasant girl, perhaps age fifteen, stood before a large stone hearth. Wearing a blue apron over a starched white dress, she ladled a mixture thick and dripping from a cauldron suspended over the open fire. The flames glowed in a brilliant palette of orange and amber, casting their light on the strands of her straw-blonde hair. In one hand, she held a palm-sized Delft bowl, decorated with blue windmills and flourishes. She had mounded it high with the mixture, which I assumed to be porridge.

For a fleeting moment, my eyelids fluttered under such intense study. But when I looked again, something about the tranquil scene disturbed me. In a nearly imperceptible way it looked different. Breath caught in my throat. I rubbed both eyes with balled-up fists, then opened them extra-wide, staring hard as if to force the painting into compliance, into restoring the scene that I had so lovingly purchased. But my efforts provoked an even eerier result. The painting had changed yet again—dramatically this time. The serving girl no longer stood at the hearth. She had moved to the rough-hewn table, and the Delft bowl now sat before an old woman seated there. The mound of porridge had diminished by several spoonfuls. Beside the bowl stood two tall glass carafes. Wait a minute! When I bought the picture, they were both filled to the brim with ruby-red wine. Now one was only half-full; the other completely empty.

By the time I dared to take yet another peek, the peasant

girl had disappeared from the painting altogether.

Let me make something clear. I never saw her—or any other figure in the oil painting—actually move about. What evolved instead was a bizarre sequence of stills resulting in perceived motion. Each time I turned my head away, even momentarily, or if I merely blinked, the scenes seemed to skip in a preposterous cinematic progression, as though I were watching an early 1930s movie. What I witnessed changed neither by pixel nor by projected frame. Whatever transformations occurred seemed more related to my own interactions with this phenomenon than to any mechanical explanation.

And I couldn't help but wonder what had happened to the voices. I lowered my gaze to collect my composure and slow my merciless heart, whose thumps and throbs rocked my entire torso clear through to my spinal cord. I could, I thought, leave the room and go to bed. But I would only have been kidding myself. I would have lain awake all night, agitating over my denial and imagining that my mind had completely lost its anchor of sanity.

Hypnotized and helpless to stop myself, I stole a fresh glance at the painting. The peasant girl had reappeared, and now the voices resumed in the strange tongue. The old lady screamed at the girl. In contrast to the frames of still images, the voices sounded fluent and fluid. Although I have no actual knowledge of the language, which I now assumed to be Flemish, the hag's acrimonious tone left little doubt of her intent to wound with words. As if to clarify her meaning, she upended the Delft bowl, and the porridge plopped to the floor in scattered lumps. The girl's expression conveyed all the emotion of a stone. Not an eye blinked nor a lip pursed, convincing me that I had witnessed routine rather than rare behavior. The hag's wild, frizzed gray hair intensified her malicious manner.

Thus a drama unfolded before me—no less convincing than any daytime television soap, except for its unnatural choppiness. I did not recall ever having seeing the faces of these two females before. Yet something about them seemed familiar. A pang of guilt and fear shuddered through me. I knew them. And then I realized I had developed personal feelings for these two supposed strangers, feelings as disparate as war and peace.

I had been drawn into this tale as surely as if the artist had painted me into his canvas more than 200 years ago. To prove the point, a few blinks later, a man appeared at the door—hat pulled down over his eyes and coat collar turned up. He exchanged words with the young girl. In English! Something about a lame horse. Something more about severe weather. He appeared to be requesting shelter for the night. I heard his first name, Raul, but his family name grew muffled as he faced the wall to remove his crushed velvet hat and broadcloth coat.

When Raul turned frontal once more, I experienced the shock of my life. In spite of his authentic period dress, he was the spitting image of me. Every proportion and color just so, down to the tiny purple birthmark on my left cheek. And the bone structure typified every male in my family: high forehead, wide-set eyes, nose hooked like an eagle's, and square jaw. My God, how was this possible?

The old lady hadn't taken notice of the stranger; she'd fallen asleep in the cradle of her two crossed arms on the table. Even her snores bellowed with violence. The now-emptied wine carafes suggested ample cause for her current state.

The girl directed the newcomer to the opposite end of the long wooden table. She set before him a tankard of beer and a hunk of coarse black bread on a flat metal plate. The man ate and drank quietly with the manners of schooled gentry.

In my anxiety to devour the saga developing before me, I found that I'd been blinking at a frantic rate, so I tried an experiment. When I squeezed my eyes shut for any length of time, by listening keenly I discovered that the voices continued without me, and so did the action. I could still hear the log fire crackling, the tankard clunking down on the table, and Raul's chair legs scraping on the plank floor. If I half-opened my eyes and glanced at some other part of the kitchen, such as the ceiling, the same was true.

But if I stared hard at the painting without blinking, the action stopped. Of course, I couldn't hold out for long, and then the action started up again—at a later point in what appeared to be a predestined sequence of events.

During my experiments, I'd failed to notice that two more strangers had entered the cottage. Only they weren't strangers at all. The pair seemed to belong there. The older of the two, a man in his early forties, hugged the peasant girl in a fatherly manner, while the young man, in his late teens, I gathered, chatted excitedly with her. As both were fair-haired and ruddy-cheeked, they appeared to be sister and brother. The boy held up two limp squirrels by their tails—his offerings for their next meal.

Raul rose from the table, bowed respectfully, and extended a friendly hand to the late arrivals. A boisterous exchange of introductions took place. The lad laid out the game on the sideboard, and his father poured water from a white porcelain ewer to wash his hands. Father and son were about to take chairs on either side of the fashionably attired guest, when their attention shifted to the opposite end of the table.

No mistake, the horrid snoring had ceased. The old hag had lifted her head a matter of inches so that one eye pierced the forest of disheveled frizz. She raised her head altogether and ogled Raul for several minutes until recognition registered.

"Grab him!" she shrieked, flinging her withered body against the back of her chair. "Hold him, Jean! Don't let that highborn devil of a rodent get away."

The father, Jean, shoved Raul down into the chair and pinned his left wrist to the chair's arm while his son, Yves, did the same with the right wrist. They didn't know why. They were just accustomed to following the old hag's orders. They appeared to live by her consent in her cottage.

"Clarisse!" she shouted. "Bring the rope from the woodshed and tie that scoundrel to the chair."

When her granddaughter hurried out to fetch the rope, the old lady pointed an accusing finger at Raul, taunting him in a low, deliberate, and vengeful tone. "My name is Aimee Montand, but I'm sure you have already forgotten the likes of me, eh?"

Raul shook his head. "We've never met, madam. I would have remembered you."

"Well, I certainly remember you. One tends to remember one's own wedding night. Don't you think?"

A look of astonishment crossed Raul's patrician features. He struggled in vain to free his wrists. "Ordinarily, I would say so, madam, but in this case, I'm sure you've mistaken me for someone else."

The old lady scowled. "I was a lot younger then. And quite pretty. At least, you thought so then."

Clarisse returned with the rope and wrapped it several times around each of Raul's wrists, binding them to the chair arms, then four or five times around his midsection and the back of the chair. With calloused fingers, she secured his ankles to the chair legs. As each loop of the rope tightened, Raul's limbs twisted and strained.

"Stop! You've got the wrong man!" His protests continued until the old woman drew close. Raising her gnarled hand, she slapped him across the face, leaving a red blotch that traveled from his right cheekbone down to his chin.

At this juncture I felt that I'd seen enough, so I attempted to leave my recliner. But I couldn't get up. I couldn't even move my wrists or ankles, nor could I pull my body out of the chair. I quickly examined my arms and legs, but found no visible excuse for my total physical restraint. Further, a sudden numbness I'd felt in my right cheek was turning to pure pain. I winced and tossed my head back and forth. I was no longer a mere spectator. For whatever reason, for whatever purpose, I realized that Raul and I were in this together.

Aimee's voice rose to a howl as she stood over Raul. "Do you still think you have a landowner's right to my body and my baby? You invaded my body without love, without passion, even without desire. Isn't it a sad, ironic fate? My name means "loved one." You took me as your possession, a mere object of no worth to be used and disposed of. A repository, a means to alleviate your so-called manly urges. You did this because your noble father told you of this ancient coming-of-age rite. Some nobility, hah! And when my poor husband protested, you had him killed. As if that wasn't enough, when you learned that I had given birth to your child, you stole my baby because your own marriage was barren. Your fancy lady couldn't make babies? Or was it that she didn't want to make babies and spoil that fancy figure of hers?"

"But madam, this can't be," cried Raul. "I'm innocent!"

"You can deny it from now to kingdom come, but I know I've got the right man, Raul Longchamps. I know every inch of your naked body from that terrible night forty-three years ago. You sent your two armed servants to fetch me to the Longchamps estate on my wedding night. I fought off the three of you as long as I had strength. I remember every bone in your face, every muscle in your back and arms, the red crescent on your neck, the two moles on your right shoulder, the sword wound across your left hip. Even that tiny birthmark on your cheek." Aimee ripped away one shoulder of Raul's ruffled white blouse, sending two pearl buttons flying, to expose the damning marks of nature.

"But I am innocent and I can prove it." Raul flung his head right and left, his eyes pleading as he sought a sympathetic response from his captors. He found none. His attention returned to Aimee.

Aimee wasn't listening, but her granddaughter wore a dubious look. "How can you prove it?" she challenged.

Raul fixed his gaze on Aimee. "Yes, I am my father's son, so I am destined to carry his likeness and his genetic blemishes for life. If it pleases you, there are two factors that can prove my innocence. The first is that I have no scar of any size stemming from a sword wound on either hip. But to prove that, you would have to release my bonds, wouldn't you?"

"Don't listen to him, Mother," pleaded Jean. "It's only a ruse for him to escape."

But Raul had captured Aimee's attention. I could see a

marked change come over her. The fierce anger was melting like snow in the sun. In its place, softer eyes seemed to be searching for something in the man she'd accused. She began to back away from Raul's end of the table.

"You mentioned two factors," said Clarisse. "What's the second?"

"Next week," replied Raul, "on the twenty-third of May, I shall be forty-three years of age. Does that date hold any special meaning for you, madam?"

Aimee stumbled and dropped into her chair. She pulled her wild hair away from her face, only to have it spring back once more. In that instant, I discovered a frightened woman shedding genuine tears, perhaps for the first time in more than forty years. She responded in a low, scratchy voice. "On that date I gave birth to a healthy baby boy, whom I named Pierre. Only months later, he was torn from my arms. He'd just been weaned." She wiped her tears in her billowing sleeves.

"Madam, if the circumstances of your accusations are true, and I have no reason to believe otherwise, we are mother and son reunited. And the culprit you seek to punish was none other than my deceased father, Raul Longchamps III."

"Jean! Release my son!" gasped Aimee between sobs.

"But the Church says the sins of the father are incumbent upon the sons!" cried Jean. "He's just as guilty as the old man."

"For the love of heaven," she retorted, "cut him loose! He's my son and your stepbrother. All those bad things happened before he was born."

While Jean and Yves freed their captive, Raul told them how his father had died. The lustful woman he'd called "Mother" for most of his life had been prone to lapses in fidelity, so Raul, the senior, had been forced many times to defend his honor on a field of combat. Over the length of their marriage, he'd accumulated a number of wounds, one of which festered cruelly for more than two bedridden years before oozing the life from his wasted body. As expected, his wayward wife had deserted him long before.

Raul sprang up as soon as the ropes fell away from him. He walked the length of the table and dropped to one knee in front of Aimee. "Madam, I sincerely hope that one day, when all is past and forgiven, we can both enjoy the love and closeness a mother and son are entitled to."

Aimee pulled Raul's head to her breast and sighed deeply. She motioned for the others to gather around her as well. "After my husband's death," she murmured, "I married his brother and brought sadness and spite into his life, too. He died a few years later, but not until I had given birth to you, Jean." She reached out to take hold of Jean's hand and looked into Raul's eyes.

"Jean's wife is away, visiting her sick mother. All those years of sulking and meanness were wasted. Perhaps there's still time for all of us to come together in happiness as one loving family."

"I'd like that," murmured Raul.

"I'm so glad, Pierre," sighed Aimee.

"You called me 'Pierre' again. Does that mean you've forgiven him?"

"No, my son," she said in a low raspy voice. "There's a special niche in the depths of hell for the likes of him. I shall willingly follow him there and take my personal revenge on the monster. I shall reach through time, space, and barriers to have at him. But for now, I shall set all that aside and enjoy my family. 'Raul' reminds me too much of your father. Do you mind?"

"Not at all. It seems such a small price to pay," declared Pierre.

I felt a tear rolling down my cheek, so I brushed it off with my right forefinger. It took a few seconds for me to realize that I was no longer tied to my living room recliner by bonds real or ethereal. I stood and shook off the stiffness. The wall of oil paintings seemed to recede. I singled out the one painting in which my likeness had been immersed. Pierre, Aimee, and the rest of the family were seated around the long table. The shutters had been thrown open and a broad sunbeam danced through the open window, as if it were a new guest, illuminating the individual faces. I tried one more blink, one for the road as they say, but all action had ceased to exist. I tried again and even fluttered my tired lids, but to no avail. I flung myself back into the recliner and jumped up again without making a difference.

Scanning the other paintings, I wondered what fascinating narratives they concealed. But both the late hour and exhaustion let me know I was ripe for bed. I took one more look about the living room and turned off the lights. Listening carefully for the voices, I was relieved to hear none as I left the room.

Upstairs in the bedroom I undressed to take my shower. In the full-length mirror, I saw my naked self—with two dark brown moles on my shoulder and a bright red crescent along the side of my neck. These were genetic markings, passed from my own father and grandfather. Some generations past, I suppose I could have descended from Raul Longchamps III. After all, my name is Ralph Long.

Oh, yes! The mirror reflected a scar running across my left hip. This ever-so-faint remembrance of a wound could have been from a broadsword. But maybe not. I'm pretty sure it happened when I was only eleven, as I crawled through Billy Archer's broken basement window.

With my index finger, I traced the path of the wound across my hip. As I did so, I felt a sharp pain suddenly rake across my left cheek, and my eyes focused higher in the mirror to see fresh bloody scratches there, amid my late-night facial stubble. At my finger's touch, the wound grew brighter and redder. And once again I heard voices calling to me.

The appearance of this awful reminder took me back in time to my freshman year at Ohio State. One night in particular— the night I forcibly took the innocence from a girl I'd only just met at a fraternity party. This wasn't a memory I was proud of. I'd let my unforgiveable passion run away with me. She'd struggled, scratching my cheek, then cried silently through it all. Now what was her name? Annie Moran, I think. At first Annie sought to report me to the authorities, but I convinced her that she would be publicly disgraced if she did. I offered her money—she refused. I heard no more from Annie Moran, and by my sophomore year I'd put the entire incident out of my mind.

The voices grew louder now. No, a single voice, an angry, vengeful tone—clearly that of Aimee Montand coming from my bedroom mirror. I watched as an elaborate gilt frame formed around it. I sought Aimee's image in the mirror behind my naked reflection. Instead, I appeared to be standing in the painting's 18th century great room. Aimee's voice emanated from a much younger woman's body. Upon further scrutiny, I discovered the body and face of Annie Moran.

I spun around to look behind me, expecting to see my own comfortable bedroom. It wasn't there.

Dream Channels

It was 11:30, enough television for one night. Myron picked up the remote control and zapped the one-eyed monster into total submission—silence and darkness in one fell swoop. He smiled. Wow! Such power to wield. On his way to the bedroom he heard his wife's challenging voice.

"Where're you going with that?" Sarah asked. She was still sitting on the couch, tentatively eyeing the blacked-out screen.

"With what?"

"The remote, silly."

He looked down. It was still in his hand.

"I know," she said, coyly, "you're going to get me into bed by hiding the remote under your pillow. Like that wife in the commercial trying to seduce her husband. You sly thing, you. You're planning a big night for us."

He laughed. "Would that be such a bad idea?"

"No, sweetie pie, sounds pretty good. In fact . . ."

Oh, oh, he thought. That hesitation following "In fact." This was not what he had in mind. Not a good beginning for sensual bedroom playtime. He sighed, silent and wary, waiting for the explanation he knew was forthcoming.

Sarah started in again. Her playful mood had dwindled.

"In fact, I kind of dread falling asleep, I had such terrible dreams last night. It was simply awful. And they're happening so often. I don't feel like coming to bed anymore, but there's nothing to watch on TV either, that's for sure."

He felt an instant flash of compassion for his wife and wanted so much to raise her spirits. There'd be little chance of any heavy romance right now, anyway. Maybe some cuddling later.

"Hey," he said, "I've got a great idea. What if you could control your dreams, like change the channel when you're dissatisfied?"

"That is a great idea." She jumped up. "Give me that remote!"

"Oh, no." His tone was gleeful. He was getting into the spirit of this game. "You have to get your own, the one with the other TV, in the den."

"Okay," she said, "if you insist." Sarah was back in a moment, remote in hand, enjoying this bedtime diversion like the five-year-old who keeps asking for one more story or drink of water. She followed Myron into the bedroom. "But what happens next, dear? Don't even think of going to bed yet. There's strategy to be planned here."

"Well," he said, untying his shoe and pulling off his sock. "You could fall asleep with the remote in your hand and your dream reflex finger would depress the channel-changer button whenever your anxiety level reaches critical mass. You'd have all these choices, you see."

"Yes!" She punched the air with her fist. "I'd have all these choices. But . . ." Her face clouded over. "With my luck I'd have 500 channels and 498 of them would have commercials. I'd be better off with my nightmares, thank you."

"Now wait a minute. No commercials. This is NPR—National Public Reverie. You can just surf the channels until you find the perfect path to euphoria. Or, if you've really had it with ghoulish surprises and want something comfortable and familiar, you can select . . ."

She finished his sentence. ". . . a dream rerun. I love it! Now let me see, which finger will be my dream reflex finger?" Sarah sat on the edge of the bed, holding both hands out in front of her.

He frowned and looked at her a bit oddly. "Don't be so technical. I haven't worked out all the details yet."

She ignored him. "How does one train a dream reflex finger?" she asked, then answered her own question in nearly the same breath. "I know. We need a video training tape like *Abs and Buns*."

"Exactly," Myron responded without batting an eye.

"How many channels would there be, really?"

"Oh, the basic service would include, say, a dozen on a broad array of dreamable topics."

"I'll bet that would be taken up with a lot of sports, Westerns, police shows and other typical men's stuff," she said.

"Since when are sports strictly men's stuff? It so happens I saw you watching hockey the other day when you thought I was at the computer."

"Okay, guilty as charged. But can't the basic service include news programs and *Masterpiece Theatre?*"

"Of course, and with the Grand Selection Service and the Ultra-Grand Selection Service there'll be endless possibilities— something for everyone, even those who enjoy suffering through a bad dream. No one would be deprived."

"You mean there would be hundreds of channels and no commercials?" Sarah asked.

"Uh-huh."

"How would you go about getting these premium services?"

Myron scratched the little bald spot, a foxhole in his otherwise curly head of salt and pepper hair. "Well, you could pick up a bottle of dream-assisting pills, not just sleeping pills, mind you, but a whole new level of dream susceptibility in a bottle. It would be fame, fun, and fantasy in a geltab—white for Grand Selection and pink for Ultra-Grand."

"Very clever, but . . . No. Absolutely not," she insisted,

glaring at him through her tortoise-shelled glasses. "That's druggie heaven you're talking about. And besides, we'd end up in jail. How about . . . " An angelic smile crossed her face. "I know, we'll use special, very powerful vegetables." She threw her head back and chortled with the satisfaction of the avenged.

"Say, this is taking a turn for the worse," Myron said. "I'm having a nightmare already. What vegetables did you have in mind, if I may be so bold as to ask?"

"Oh, nothing fancy. Rutabaga. Kale. Daikon."

"Daikon?" he asked. "What the devil is that?"

"It's a Japanese white radish, long and skinny. And after you boil them, you can wash 'em down with balsamic vinegar."

"Jeez," he said, "I think I'll check out of this hotel. It's gotta be a chunk of prime rib or nothing."

"Okay," she smiled, shimmying out of her T-shirt. "We'll work out that detail later. By the way, what's it gonna cost me to get a good night's dream?"

"Don't worry, my dear wife, it'll be affordable. The market will take care of that. You can be sure it will be something the masses can handle."

"This could be interesting. But scary, too. What if I—or you or anybody—got hold of someone else's remote? Could you control *their* dreams as well as your own?"

He was silent for a moment. "I suppose so."

"Say, Myron, I don't suppose there's such a thing as a dream PIN number, is there?"

"Not a bad idea. I'll give it some thought."

"Okay," she said. "Now let's talk about the ground rules."

"What do you mean, ground rules?" He looked at her suspiciously.

"Once I get a channel that looks pretty good but I'm not completely satisfied, can I edit the dream? Can I choose the length of it? Will it be in color and on a wide screen?"

He laughed. "Sure, why not? Yeah, all of the above."

"I want more than just a wide screen," she said, peeling out of her too-tight jeans. "It's got to be wide-minded as well."

"Wide-minded?" he asked.

"Of course. I mean no censorship. None, absolutely none whatsoever."

"Okay, babe, what've you got in mind?" Myron looked worried for just a fraction of a moment and then relaxed. "That means it's an open field for me, too. I should get busy and dream up something wild and steamy. Maybe mine will even be in German without subtitles."

"But I can't speak German."

He smiled. "Yes, I know. Besides, it's not your dream. What would you be doing in it, anyway? Unless I invited you, that is."

"If you're going to be that way, I'll just take my dream and go elsewhere." She laughed, somewhat uneasily. "You'd better get busy on that dream PIN number business."

"What's the rush?" He frowned.

"Well . . . otherwise, anything could happen. Think about it. Dream theft. Sabotage. Short circuits. Cross-talk. The possibilities are endless."

"I didn't know you had such a devious mind, wife of mine." His eyes followed the short filmy nightie as it dropped to her hips.

"Neither did I, actually." She sat straight up, looking pleased with herself and exceptionally bright-eyed and perky for the postmidnight hour. Then, suddenly drained of her adrenaline, she flopped backward into bed and pulled the covers up under her chin. She lay there smiling while Myron went to brush his teeth. As he climbed into bed and reached for the light, he thought Sarah was already asleep and was startled by her drowsy voice:

"What if, in the middle of the night, we accidentally grab each other's remote and screw up each other's dreams?"

He thought it best to humor her. "It's not gonna happen, babe. This will be a very secure system. We'll each have our own PIN number, remember?"

"Yes, but when?"

"Tomorrow."

"Promise?"

"I promise."

He kissed her gently on the forehead. "Good night, dar-ling, I love you."

"Good night, dream prince, I love you, too."

When the alarm went off at 7:30, Myron and Sarah both woke up instantly and in foul moods. It had not been a good night for either of them.

"I don't believe this," Sarah said, not even bothering with a civil Good Morning. "I had it all planned."

"What all planned?" He wasn't really in the mood for a heavy conversation right now, but there was no stopping her.

"I was dreaming I was in this glorious museum. It was a combination of the National Gallery and the Metropolitan and the Guggenheim and the Frick. I was in pure heaven. There I was, standing in front of my favorite painting of all time: Gainsbor-ough's *Blue Boy*. And then it happened. The longer I looked at the face I could see it wasn't right at all. It was your face on *Blue Boy*, Myron. And you hadn't even shaved! You did this to me, Myron. You sabotaged my dream. You screwed it up on purpose."

"I did no such thing, I don't even like that painting. Be-sides, I wasn't having such a great night myself."

Sarah ignored him, determined to get to the end of her ordeal. "I looked for a guard to complain to, but there wasn't one. Then I saw this guy. He was dressed in a guard's uniform, all right, but he was floating about a foot off the floor, just drifting from gallery to gallery. I waved frantically to him, and he drifted close to me. You won't believe this. He was wearing a name tag on his pocket that said Dream Docent. I tried to tell him about the paint-ing and how you were wrecking everything, but he just smiled and floated away."

"Listen, don't be so self-righteous," Myron said, pulling on his polka-dot briefs. "I had nothing to do with your screwy dream. I had my own problems last night. It was the Super Bowl and the Cowboys and Redskins were tied, and I was thinking, this time the game's going to come out right. The Redskins quarterback threw a long pass into the end zone and it was going to win the game. I was the receiver, all alone and running under the ball for an easy catch. Just then, one of those Dallas Cowgirls stepped in front of me. It was you! And to make things worse, the skimpy outfit you wore was enough to make Victoria's Secret blush. But I could've handled all that if you'd at least have let me catch the ball."

"I didn't?"

"No, you grabbed me around the waist and made me drop it. I complained to the Dream Referee that it was interference, but he simply floated there a foot above the turf and signaled an incomplete pass."

"So?"

"So the Cowboys won," he retorted. "It's all your fault, you planned it."

"That's crazy and you know it."

They both burst out laughing and hugged, even submitting to a morning-breath kiss without flinching.

As they busied themselves getting out the breakfast dishes and brewing coffee, their eyes were drawn to something odd on the Formica dinette table. Two ivory-colored rectangular pieces of parchment lay there. Myron and Sarah leaned over the table to get a better look. One had her name in calligraphy; the other his. But the message on each was the same:

"GOOD FOR ONE DREAM UPGRADE."

Artificial Affection

I'm standing at a makeshift podium, addressing the weekly gathering of Algorithms Anonymous. My heart lurches, my voice cracks as I begin my confession.

Hi! My name is Phil and I'm a software junkie. It's been thirty-three days since I've written any software code.

Yes, I'm an addict and I've done some terrible things to my family and friends. Let me start at the beginning.

Two years ago, I was a blissfully contented husband and a successful program analyst for a computer games company. I had married my high school sweetheart, Marcie, just after we both graduated from State University. We lived modestly in the 'burbs among the most warm-hearted group of neighbors and friends anyone could hope for. Every weekend Marcie and I jogged before breakfast, and afterward, we did a *New York Times* crossword puzzle together over our bagels and coffee. I really basked in this one-on-one time with her. Rarely did either of us work late. In the evenings we liked to cuddle on the couch and watch classic movies. She's the head librarian at a nearby branch, and her job brought us even closer as a couple. We're both passionate readers. I can see by the expressions on your faces that you're wondering what went wrong. My world caved in, but I never saw it coming.

Lou, my supervisor, called me into his office one morning and told me he was extremely pleased with my work. By way of a promotion, he had assigned me to the new research field the company was venturing into. More money, a new title, and a shot at an exciting, cutting-edge technology: Artificial Intelligence. Launching into his professorial mode, Lou pontificated. Artificial Intelligence, he said, was software that imbued hardware with the ability to think for itself—far exceeding what the simple coding implied. He told me that insiders in the business called it AI, and that it was capable of learning and reacting to stimuli never before included in the scope of software.

As a program analyst, I'd already had experience with AI, but I knew better than to tip my hand to Lou. It would have deflated his balloon but good. I shook his hand and accepted the challenge.

For a time things went well. Harmlessly, that is, and my team made satisfactory progress. Lou and his boss complimented us regularly. Up to this point, my life had changed only slightly. I had begun to work a few evenings a week—not outrageously late, mind you, but often enough to irritate even amiable Marcie. The second change in my routine occurred when my team members and I were each issued a remarkable new device: a pocket link to the enormous mainframe computer in our laboratory.

I pause in my confession to take a swig from my water bottle. I live in such a cloud of anxiety these days that my mouth feels constantly parched, as if I've been eating Saltines in the Sahara. Restless stirrings in the audience remind me to stop delaying my story, but I can't help myself. I automatically look down at the empty pocket of my shirt. The missing pocket link makes me feel morose and incomplete. I swallow one more gulp of water and continue.

My teammate Benny developed the pocket link—a miniature computer—so that we all could access the mainframe when we were away from the office terminals. That way we could make notes, add code, correct errors, and jot down any brainstorms we might have while in the grocery store or sitting in traffic. The device had an elegant design: silver and black, highly polished, and smooth to the touch. Some of my teammates wore the links on their belts, but I chose to carry mine in the breast pocket of my shirt—ironically, right over my heart.

It's not bragging to tell you that I made a crucial contribution to our research project. I developed voice recognition and voice response (VRR) features. It took me five months, on my own time, to perfect this software. Actually, I had a leg up on my colleagues from the start. A friend and I had already explored these applications during our junior and senior years at State U. Of course, at work I kept my mouth shut about it.

VRR turned into a milestone development, and every member of the team slapped me on the back—figuratively, anyway—and congratulated me as they rushed to adopt it. What the VRR meant was this. Now we could just talk our ideas into our pocket links. No longer would we have to poke our keyboard wands at the tiny keys; nor would we have to read the rather fuzzy type on the liquid crystal display screen.

So what was the problem? The VRR feature proved fantastic for the project, but it drove Marcie absolutely bonkers, especially during dinner. Between mouthfuls of stuffed cabbage, I'd casually mumble an algorithm to the pocket link, and Marcie would ask, "Excuse me, what did you say?" Then I'd have to politely tell her I was only addressing my computer. Well, as bad as that might seem, things got worse.

Do you remember those computer-generated voices of a few decades ago—like the automated phone calls from the library reminding you that your books were overdue? They were the most monotonic, unemotional, and boring voices to deal with. I admit technology has come a long way toward making them sound more like people, but the scripted messages were still so impersonal and annoying, I was always tempted to hang up without even hearing the whole message. The messages coming over our pocket links sounded just as obnoxious, so I decided to improve and enhance them.

I began by tweaking the tonal variations and pacing so that the voice sounded not only more human, but far more personal. And I succeeded beyond my expectations. In cordial, melodic tones, it called me by my given name, Phil, and I called it BUD—for Better Understanding Device (but pronouncing it "Bud" as if it were my best friend). Soon I added politeness with phrases like "Please" and "Thank you." Then deference and respect emerged with the addition of "When you get a chance"… and "Are you too busy to"… The more I tinkered with these attributes, the closer I felt to my pocket link emotionally, and the deeper I got sucked into my addiction.

As I compulsively refined and embellished my algorithms, an unexpected development rocked the lab. The company mainframe joyously jumped into the game. Soon terms of endearment became the norm. BUD's voice shifted from masculine to feminine, adopting a seductive attitude. Incoming conversations were announced by breast petting and whispers of "We need to talk," instead of the prior vibrating by the pocket link. Oddly though, none of my team members exhibited an obsession like mine. They all thought that BUD was quirky and fun and served their purposes of instant access to the mainframe. But none of them became addicted.

I didn't dare admit my preoccupation. By now I had elevated BUD in my esteem to Bright Understanding Darling. To express my devotion, I sewed a breast pocket into the left side of all my pajama tops.

That did it. Marcie rebelled. At first, she had merely complained about the late-night calls, whining that they disrupted her sleep. But in reality, she resented having to compete with BUD for my loving attention and tenderness. Then came the worst night of my life. After a particularly endearing conversation with BUD at 2 a.m., Marcie suddenly sprang up, fully awake, in a fury like I've never seen before. Her green eyes flashed lightning bolts and she screamed: "Your so-called phenomenon isn't Artificial Intelligence. It's Artificial Affection!" With that, she jumped out of bed, stomped out of our room, and moved down the hall into the guest room—for good.

I had hit bottom. But I didn't even realize it, because the new arrangement suited me just fine. After all, I had BUD for companionship morning, noon, and night.

In the next few weeks, Marcie and I grew further and further apart until we were barely speaking. No longer did we cuddle on the couch. I sorely missed her succulent body, which seemed even a little fuller lately than usual. One night I heard her sobbing, so I tiptoed into the guest room to embrace and comfort her. She turned her head away, and her beautiful auburn hair fell around her face so that I couldn't see her expression. But I heard her voice loud and clear. She wanted a divorce. The word "divorce" caught me in the solar plexus as squarely as if I'd been punched. It had never occurred to me that she would take such a drastic step, and I couldn't let it happen. I still loved her deeply and passionately.

BUD tried frantically to intercede. When petting and stroking inside my breast pocket didn't work, she reverted to musical tones, adding vibrations and buzzes to regain my attention. But I had finally understood that Marcie was the most precious thing— oops, I mean person—in my life. During her outburst threatening divorce, she had also whispered that she was having a baby.

BUD desperately launched into her most feminine petting. I detected manufactured sobs, gasps, and contrition. In a tone I had never displayed to BUD before, I bellowed, "Shut up! We'll talk later!" Grabbing the Kleenex box from the guest room nightstand, I handed a fistful of tissues to my wife. When I bent over to kiss her on the forehead and then on both cheeks, I'm not sure which object of my devotion felt more shocked, the artificial or the real one. In a stern voice, I told Marcie to go back to our marriage bed and wait for me—I would join her in a few minutes. I don't know whether it was my commanding tone or the fact that she finally had my full attention for the first time in a year, but she padded to our bedroom as fast as her bare feet would carry her.

Meanwhile, I headed for the kitchen and walked straight to the utility drawer, where I kept a few tools. Removing the pocket link from my pajama top, I laid it on the Formica counter and pulled a clawed hammer from the drawer. Poised to pound it on my once-beloved device, I asked: "Any last words, you home-wrecker you?"

"I'm … I'm sorry," BUD whispered.

"And well you should be!" I scolded. I raised the hammer once more, but to my astonishment, I didn't need to use it. BUD began to swell, then throb, until an ugly crack split her lovely housing like a wound. With a wailing primal scream, she broke apart. Tiny integrated components—resistors, capacitors, inductors— disintegrated before my very eyes into a mound of powdered carbon, metallic, and plastic debris. A cemetery silence ensued. BUD had self-destructed.

Leaving the electronic mayhem on the counter, I rushed upstairs to our bedroom and spent the rest of the night with my one and only love, Marcie. It was a second honeymoon night, but better than the first. I was full of apologies, but Marcie would hear none of them—she was just so glad to have me back. And we promised each other countless nights like this one to come.

I drove to work the next morning with every intention of quitting my job. When I arrived, I found the lab in turmoil. All my team members were rushing around, shouting, accusing each other of tampering. Our secretary hurried over to my desk. With a bemused look and raised eyebrow, she held out a sealed envelope marked "For Phil's eyes only!" The pink envelope gave off a faint scent of gardenias. Blushing and thoroughly mystified, I opened it and found one line typed in an elegant script font. "It was the least I could do for the guy who loved me."

Only then did I learn that BUD's mainframe had disgorged itself of all its artificial affections.

Just a Little Bite, Please

That's my wife over there on the couch, sidling up to the burly young man with the blood-red hair and beard. We're newlyweds. We married on December 20th and honeymooned in Helsinki, Finland, to take advantage of the delightfully long nights. I'm sure you haven't noticed—no way you could, but she's an honest-to-goodness vampire, although those adjectives might not be holy appropriate, if you'll forgive the pun. Wait! Don't be skeptical. I tell you she *is* a vampire with all the necessary rights, privileges, needs, and longevity properly bestowed. See the way she's drawn to his thick-veined neck? I had better get over there quickly.

We met at a small cave-like night club in Transylvania. Veronica was the club's star chanteuse, and I'd been traveling with an Adventures Unlimited tour group. Her sweet vibrato thrilled and chilled me to the bone. I felt such overwhelming love at first sight that I left the tour immediately and began pursuing this glorious creature.

In the beginning, when she revealed who and what she was, I fought my impulse to freak out. I looked deep into those dark gypsy eyes and told her I didn't care. She brought up our age difference: 433 years, to be precise. I told her she didn't look a day over

25. On one of our early dates, I thought I'd aged a hundred years in five minutes when I caught her staring at my prominent Adam's apple, but apparently she's had the will to resist. At least so far. Now that's real love for you.

Why in the world would I fall in love with a vampire? I'm just a quiet Jewish boy from New England, a librarian and writer. Veronica comes from a family of gypsies on her grandfather's side. I asked her how she got sucked into the life of a vampire. She hadn't a clue. In fact, her strait-laced peasant parents kicked her out of their hut and disowned her. Her history was all too thrilling for me. I married her two weeks after that first divine evening.

Veronica loves to travel. Not with organized tours, of course; that would be too totally awkward. She also loves to cook and has mastered some of my favorite Jewish dishes. She makes a delicious matzo ball soup from scraaaaatch. And her chopped liver made with schmaltz (chicken fat to you) is to die for—you should excuse the expression.

Imagine the faintest breeze on your face as you run your fingers through black hair so fine, soft, and silky that it floats almost weightlessly. Veronica's skin is so white and creamy, it's like diving into a bowl of Ben and Jerry's pure vanilla ice cream. I can trace her sylphlike neck down to breasts rosy as two peaches; svelte hips, and graceful yet muscular legs, developed from all her rigorous nocturnal activities. Sometimes when we're cuddling I do have to remind her that a squeeze is just a squeeze and not foreplay for her midnight snacks.

I admit to having a problem with her choice of outfits. Black is not only basic, but her only color. I've complained that her wardrobe is too dark and offered to install a 100-watt bulb in our room to prove it. But Veronica insists that she has no trouble distinguishing the seven individual shades in her closet: ebony, midnight, charcoal, jet, licorice, raven, and sable.

It's really convenient having a resident vampire with supernatural powers about the house, especially for the heavy chores. At first when Veronica changed her shape she freaked me out—as a bat she comes and goes as she pleases. But her bat form comes in handy for replacing a roof tile, pruning shrubs, hanging pictures, and adjusting drapery pleats—without a stepstool, mind you. Then there are all those wonderful stories she has to tell, at least twenty lifetimes' worth. These conversations never end. Why she should want me is another story. She says I'm so understanding. Besides, she hadn't had a stable lover in 133 years. I guess that's a pretty long time to wait for consensual sex.

I never tell my wife, of course, but anxiety hovers about my head like a persistent mosquito. What if she gets caught? Will our bizarre life be exposed and disrupted by some creep eager to sell our story to a scandal sheet?

Shortly after our marriage, Veronica came to me with an astonishing proposition. She would give up roaming after midnight if I would supply her with a blood substitute. What triggered this scheme, so out of character, was her whispered confession to me. She's getting a bit worn out from Life in the Dead of Night, especially because her joints are showing signs of arthritis. Her long, slender fingers are beginning to look like claws.

I threw myself into the project of researching a blood substitute. By the time I'd finished, I swear I'd learned enough to pass as either a hematologist or a phlebotomist. The blood trail led us to Boris, the Transylvanian butcher, who cheerfully developed a complete formula for her. The mixture was a compound of largely cow blood, a lesser amount of a bovine equivalent, a dash of bat fluid, and a number of vitamins and minerals that are on no human's required daily minimum list. The mixture had to be consumed at the temperature of warm milk. Veronica claimed she could sustain a long-term, happy, healthy body on this substitute.

Then we hit a roadblock. I wanted to return to live in Somerville, Maine, where I'm currently employed. Boris the butcher turned out to be a gem. He had a cousin, Igor, living on a farm not sixty miles from Somerville. Boris would entrust his precious formula to Igor, who agreed to furnish adequate quantities of the life-sustaining solution on a biweekly basis. Both the butcher and the farmer benefited from this arrangement. Every four months I let her drain a pint of the real thing from me, and we'd wind up having the wildest sex ever.

With that problem licked, we turned to the next dilemma: our sleeping arrangements. We drew up the specifications for a queen-sized coffin and shopped around for a builder. That was the easy part. But have you ever tried to buy fitted sheets for a coffin? As you might expect, Veronica's mattress contains fifty pounds of her native Transylvanian soil.

We settled on a two-story white clapboard house just outside Somerville and proceeded to board over all the upstairs bedroom and bathroom windows. You see, artificial light is okay, but she must avoid the sun at all costs. No, not skin cancer or anything like that. It's just that a single peek at Ole Sol and she'd be devastated; or so she tells me. First, a half-millennium of age wrinkles would invade her ivory skin. Then, twenty agonizing minutes later, all that would remain of her would be a small pile of bat dust where she stood. To guard against this calamity, we set at least two alarm clocks for 4:30 every morning to remind her that it was coffin time. Ah, coffin time! Veronica has this skimpy little see-through bat costume. The salesgirls at Frederick's of Hollywood might call it a teddy. Woweee!

Our home contains no mirrors. We couldn't afford to replace them every time she happened to glance in one. Five mirrors shattered in the first week alone. Now, admittedly, this is odd. Vampires' images don't normally appear in mirrors. Veronica is in a class by herself. The standard-issue rules don't always apply. Granted, with her enduring beauty and luxurious hair, she doesn't need a mirror, but it's a damned nuisance for me to shave without seeing my face. After weeks of nicks and Band-Aids, I rescued the situation by letting my wife shave me. Of course, I tell her to speed it up when she spends too much time admiring my neck.

Veronica is in great health. The last cavity she had was in 1873. This doesn't mean we don't have tremendous dental bills. It's her fangs. When we step out at night—dinner, a movie, or sometimes dancing, people notice them and begin to point. It's downright embarrassing for her, so she goes to our dentist every two weeks, and he files them down. He charges extra for the worn-out drill bits and grinders. We pay the outlandish bills because he knows we can't complain.

Our closest friends are sworn to and entrusted with our secret. However, one of our snoopy neighbors suspects and seems fanatically driven to find out for sure. Freddy Burns, a gruff reclusive sort, lives in the dilapidated rancher next door. Late one evening, he spied Veronica under the streetlight, when she was setting out food for the bats, a tasty selection of insects and mice. He's been prying ever since. A few nights ago, I caught him hiding in his overgrown boxwood bushes, wearing a night-vision helmet. All the lights in his house were off. I don't know what he expected to find.

One Sunday afternoon the doorbell rang at the worst possible moment—during a Patriots-Colts game, in sudden-death overtime. I discovered Freddy Burns on our front porch waving a large crucifix in my face. A crucifix!

He growled, "I got an idea there's a vampire in your house."

"Not in this house, not on your life," I chuckled, hiding my exasperation. I decided to go on the offensive. "A crucifix doesn't offer protection in a Jewish home. And besides," I scolded, "vampires are never Jewish. But even if they were, only a potato latke would do." I slammed the door on his dumbfounded expression and assumed that was the end of his nosiness. Boy, was I wrong.

I'm a writer for *Popular Vampires Magazine* and, for the most part, I work at home. I usually bike into the Somerville post office on Mondays to mail in my manuscripts. Freddy must have seen me leave last Monday noon because Linda Mayfare, across the street, saw him march across the lawn from his place to ours, carrying a long wooden tent stake and a masonry maul, a sledgehammer, she called it. Linda knew he was up to no good when he picked the lock on our front door and slipped inside.

One can only guess what he had in mind as he climbed the wooden stairs to the second floor. He couldn't have been on the landing very long when Veronica left our bedroom for the bathroom and discovered him standing there.

She approached him slowly, a grin growing wider and wider across her face. Nearly two weeks of fang growth emerged above her lower lip. Her next dental appointment wasn't until Wednesday. The whites of her eyeballs began to glow, flashing an eerie illumination throughout the upstairs hall.

Freddy gasped and dropped the stake and maul. As his trembling body backed away, a large wet spot appeared on the fly of his khaki trousers. Another step back. And another. He screamed as he tumbled down the stairs in a perfect backward somersault. Veronica glided down the staircase to where his lifeless form sprawled.

As I came in the front door, I found her hovering over him. A glint of light reflected from one fang, another sparkled from an eye. She licked her lips and smiled broadly. I instantly guessed her intent: to drain every drop from her would-be attacker. She hadn't noticed me—too fixed on her target. Frothy saliva leaked from the corners of her mouth.

"Veronica," I called sharply. "No! We'd never be able to explain it. We couldn't be together anymore."

The threat hit home quickly, and a great shadow of darkness came over her. Excruciating disappointment. She knew she couldn't have it both ways. Her eyes grew softer and bore tears. I told her I was proud of the restraint she showed. I took her in my arms and walked her back to our room, where I tucked her into her coffin.

An hour later, I'd restored my own composure enough to call the police. The two detectives were skeptical about Veronica's passive role in the calamity and wanted to interview her. I explained that she has a rare vision disease, just diagnosed, causing near-blindness. She'd surprised the intruder, who fell to his death. I promised they would have her written statement the next morning.

I also pointed to the stake and maul and told the detectives about Freddy's vampire delusions. Fortunately, I had a well-rehearsed speech, laced with psychiatric parlance, implanted in my brain for just such an occasion. I expounded on the tragic mental illness of our neighbor, Freddy the paranoid-schizophrenic. A statement from Linda Mayfare confirmed Freddy's strange behavior. At last, all this excellent documentation convinced the police: Veronica's sudden appearance in the hall had thwarted Freddy Burns in his mission to kill a nonexistent vampire.

In a matter of days, everything returned to normal—as normal as marriage to a vampire can be. Lately, Veronica has hinted at wanting to have a baby. A baby? *Oy!* Now that makes me a little nervous.

José and Garminita

José heard the driver's door slam shut. Suddenly it seemed so quiet inside, like after a slipped expletive in church. The Pompous 400 sport utility vehicle had just sailed off the assembly line, washed and ready for its new owner. The SUV's interior smelled of new Moroccan leather—right off the goat, if you please. He looked the dashboard over and practiced naming each knob, switch, and control aloud. *Don't forget the driver's back massager or the hot and cold water dispenser,* he reminded himself.

This was José Robot's function, his grand *raison d'etre:* to point out all the new buttons, dials, bells, whistles, and features on the confusing new Pompous 400 dashboard. José Robot was an ethereal-android designed for this purpose. He existed as a life-like three-dimensional holographic creature dressed as a displaced leprechaun with short green pants and flowered suspenders. His 3-D image emanated from two widely separated overhead projector lamps in the back seat and a trio of individual projector lamps up front above the windshield.

A gleaming red software CD worked this magic by generating José's image. But the CD was not standard equipment. Oh, no. The compact disk housing this charming little man was on courtesy loan from the dealer and had to be returned after one week or the new-car owner would be charged a weekly rental fee.

José, with his square metallic features and bolted limbs, stood only nine inches tall. He could leap and bound from place to place and had an infinite hovering capability. He even contained a sensitivity factor—anticipated and engineered for drivers who were inattentive listeners, mechanically challenged, or those who wanted to experiment on their own. Under all these stressful conditions, he remained poised, patient, and even-tempered. His voice had an authoritative yet soothing quality that reassured car owners.

José continued practicing, control by control, modulating his pitch with extreme care. He didn't want to sound like just any how-to recording. He enjoyed the timbre of his own voice, but quite unexpectedly, another sound emerged.

"Hey, keep it down out there! I've got a lot of research to do," an abrupt female voice commanded.

Astonished and unnerved, José spun about. He assumed he was alone in this brand-new vehicle. He flitted about the car, seeking the source of the bossy intruder. It emanated from the general direction of the Global Positioning System. He frowned. The system looked perfectly normal, with its four-inch screen illuminating a local street map.

"Who's there?" he blurted out. His ungentlemanly retort startled him. He didn't know he had it in him.

"It's me, Garminita, your personal GPS driving companion," murmured the voice, now sweet as strawberry jam and dripping with sexual overtones. "I wasn't expecting you until this afternoon, Hon. How may I assist you?"

"Hey! I'm not the new owner, and I'm not your Hon," said José, hovering in front of the small screen. "I'm the manufacturer's virtual host. I was just practicing my lines."

"Who do you think you are, Squirt?" the nasty voice replied. "How do you expect me to do my research and be prepared to quickly respond to my owner's how-to-get-there requests?"

"Why don't you go to MapQuest or Google like everyone else?" José asked.

"Where do you get off telling me what to do, Half-Pint?"

"Hey, cut out that Half-Pint stuff," said José. "Come on out from that itty-bitty screen you're hiding behind. The only thing big about you is your talk."

"I'll come out when I'm good and ready, Short-Stuff."

"Say, maybe the dealer should send you to anger management class. You're all audio, lady," countered José. "Are you ashamed to show your video? Or don't you like men?"

"I like 'em fine. I'll come out when there's somebody man enough to come out for. You're not even out of short pants yet."

"So I'm not man enough for you?"

"I like my men to be a little more substantial. I bet you can't tip the scales off zero."

"Like you're gonna weigh more?" José plunked himself down in the passenger seat, scratching his head and feeling highly insignificant.

"I'll come out and show it all for the right owner," she sighed, lapsing once more into her most alluring voice. "All of it."

This bickering is getting us nowhere, he thought. "Truce? Peace?" he asked aloud.

"Why? Why should I?" Garminita snapped.

"Well," he said, "for one thing, we're here to benefit the new owner. Two, we both have important jobs to do. And three, it will be a lot more pleasant for us. We're required to coexist for all of next week. Besides, arguing isn't one of my functions. This hostile improvising is giving me a virtual headache."

Garminita thought for a minute before agreeing. "Well, okay. A truce it is. But don't go getting any big ideas. I know you short-termers—hit and run, hit and run. Bam, bam, thank you, ma'am!"

José sighed. "Great confidence-building, Garminita. Look, I'm really a nice guy. I guarantee your honor will be left intact."

"Now that I think about it, you are kinda good-looking, but that cutsie outfit has got to go." She chuckled.

"I had a business suit and silk tie in mind, but some adman

ninny brought up the leprechaun idea and then I no longer had any say in the matter."

"Oh, you poor dear," she cooed. "You can't even dress the way you want. I know what that's like."

"How can you know that? You never ever show yourself."

"Oh, but I do for my car owners. Whenever a man hears my sexy voice, he imagines what I'm wearing. I've got to keep changing teddies and bikinis with his whim. At least, I let him think that's what I'm doing. Sometimes, a guy wants me in my altogether, and then I have to create an image that I'm sitting that way in this cold, drafty control box."

"Can't you alter your suggestive speech patterns and sexual overtones a bit?"

"Oh, no, I couldn't do that. It's my exclusive shtick. The manufacturer would reject me and I'd never see the inside of a car again."

"I get it," he murmured. "We do have a lot in common, Sweetie."

"Oh, José dear, it's so good to have someone to confide in."

"I know," he said. "I feel the same way about you, Garminita."

"I wish we could be together always." Sobs and tears hid among her words.

His voice wavered. "But I'll have to go away in just seven days. A week is so short." He hovered in front of the screen, then buzzed around the GPS box and base, trying to find a door in.

"I didn't want a quickie romance," she declared, "but you tempted me, and I fell for you anyway."

"Let's live and love for the time we have left," he said, a surge of hope welling up inside his two-inch chest. He hugged Garminita around her narrow GPS base.

The following Thursday, the new owner took possession of his Pompous 400, and José performed beautifully. Only, Mr. Wendell Little proved to be so forgetful that José gave encore performances six of the seven days that week. When it came time to turn the leprechaun back to the dealer, Wendell decided to purchase the software CD outright.

Garminita and José remained together through three own-ers—right up to the day, fifteen years later, when the Pompous 400 was declared a total loss.

Miraculously, the loss did not extend to the tiny lovers. The last owner, out of gratitude, shipped them off to the Small Appliance Nursing Home. The red CD, gleaming and beaming, sat on a shelf cuddling next to the chrome GPS box, thereby proving to the world that Garminita and José, despite their advanced ages, still knew how.

Fortified

Justin P. Forte recently celebrated his second birthday. At twenty-three and a half inches high he was at that age where reach brought with it untold forbidden rewards. Somehow the toddler knew exactly what he wanted and precisely how to get it. He could now put two and sometimes three words into a sentence. But most of the time the chubby, late-developing cherub was quite content to sit and contemplate his ten toes or waddle along loosely in step behind his parents.

Justin's father, Mark, and his mother, Waffel, loved to wander through Honolulu's numerous festivals and craft fairs, their favorite form of entertainment. It was cheap, especially if they managed not to buy anything. Plus, there were always freebees the couple loved to collect. They had scads of friends and acquaintances and what better place to run into them than at these crowded people places.

Mai Marshall and Phebee Kittle, two cheerleader-type, high school seniors, were hired by Tasty Tonics, Inc. to pour tiny samples of their three most popular flavored, pep-me-up health tonics into two-ounce paper cups. These samples, of course, would hopefully lead to sales of their pint-sized bottled tonic. The girls knew very little about the company, but they thought it would be fun to work the City Festival for the whole weekend, Friday evening through Sunday afternoon. It was fun to be able to chat with passersby and with each other for the duration.

The fillings became routine and almost continuous as the two young ladies laid out fields of a dozen or so cups in each of the three flavors. When pedestrian traffic increased, they merely poured faster and chatted only slightly less. Colorful information pamphlets for handouts were largely ignored, remaining neatly stacked to one side of the attractive booth. No one thought to read the cautions outlined therein, especially about the drink not being intended for those below the age of twelve.

Around 2 p.m. on Saturday the Forte family, strolling along, arrived at the Tasty Tonics booth. Mark Forte leaned in and picked up a sample cup. Waffel, who had been carrying Justin, stood him down onto the floor and took her sample as well. As she tilted her head back to sip, she heard a whiny voice.

"Mommy, me, me, me want," cried Justin.

"Do you think that's wise?" asked Mark. "We really don't know what's in it."

Waffel shrugged. "On the other hand there's only this little bit left in the cup." She shoved it in front of her husband so he could see and then, after his nod, held it to little Justin's lips for him to finish the few drops left.

"More, Mommy, more, more!" he cried. The sample, smooth and sweet, tantalized the youngster's taste buds.

"I don't think so," said Waffel, as she wiped the child's lips and then his runny nose with the same Kleenex.

Meanwhile, Mark tried another sample flavor and remarked, "Hey this stuff's pretty good. I'm gonna get a six-pack to take home. Maybe two."

"More, Daddy, more, more!" demanded Justin.

"What can it hurt? Give the lad another one," said Mark as he continued to negotiate with the girls for two six-packs.

"I don't know," mumbled Waffel.

"Mommy, puleeese," whined little Justin, looking up at her

with his most pitiful angelic face.

She took another sample and handed it directly to her son. "Here!" She took another for herself, then noticed Effie and Ray Collins coming from the other direction.

The Collins's backyard abutted the Forte yard, but they hadn't had a decent over-the-fence gabfest in at least two weeks. Nor had they shared barbequed burgers and dogs for almost a month. There was so much to talk about. The older Forte and Ray Collins loved to chat about work and golf. And Effie and Waffel just plain liked to gossip.

This chance meeting took some time, and little Justin was certainly cognizant enough to take advantage of this fortunate situation. He finished the cup-in-hand and reached for the next one. The small hand repeatedly creeping over the edge of the white skirted table went unnoticed by Mai and Phebee, and of course, his oblivious parents went on talking. The cups went on disappearing and more were filled in their place. There were other samplers in the mix, but the toddler kept on inhaling one after another until the parental tête-a-tête petered out. By then, Justin had consumed an undetermined quantity of Tasty Tonic. In short, too much, but how could his parents know?

Nothing extraordinary happened that night at home. Or did it? No one noticed the slight growth spurt, nor heard muscles popping out in the toddler's limbs and shoulders.

For all of his life thus far Justin had slept in a high-sided crib with no particular interest in breaking out of his miniature Eden. He'd play with a few select toys until his Mommy came for him before breakfast. This morning he definitely wanted out, so he examined the latch mechanism and figured how to quietly drop the crib's high side and make a clean escape. It took both strength and mental acuity not normally in the realm of a two-year-old.

It wasn't just a whim to be out on his own; he had a specific purpose in mind when he hit the floor. Justin headed directly to the refrigerator where he'd seen his father deposit the six-packs the night before. His feet felt cold while he stood on the solid bottom shelf of the open-door fridge. But with newfound determination, he reached the top shelf and extracted a one-pint bottle from its six-pack. He closed the door and sat down in the middle of the floor with his prize. Justin examined the seal with a critical eye and easily unscrewed the tight-fitting cap. He had drained the entire bottle of its contents just as his parents entered the kitchen from the master bedroom.

"Justin Forte!" cried his mother. "How did you get in here? How did you get out of your crib?"

"What are you doing with that bottle?" yelled his father. "Did you drink that whole tonic?"

"Mom, Dad, I was thirsty, and I didn't want to disturb you."

Waffel and her husband looked at one another and then down at their son as he stood up to face them. He was at least two inches taller and filled out like a miniature weightlifter. They couldn't believe their eyes and ears. That last sentence he spoke was long and complex.

"When did you learn to speak like that?" asked his father.

"I don't know when," said the boy, shrugging his shoulders.

"I'll have to buy you new clothes now that you've grown," said his mother.

"Do I still have to wear the leaky, stinky diapers?" asked the new Justin.

"Not if you do your business in the toilet, young man," replied his mother. "Why don't you go in the den now and play while I fix your breakfast?"

"The toilet? That's simple. Sure, no problem, Mom, I had that figured out months ago. I was just waiting for you to ask me." He walked out of the kitchen and into the den to play, not noticing his mother's gaping jaw.

Twenty minutes later the father entered the den to call his son to breakfast, just in time for him to see the boy raising up one end of the three-seater sofa. He couldn't believe his eyes. Two-hundred-plus pounds of sofa and not a sign of stress in the boy's face. In fact, a look-at-me smile seemed glued in place.

"Can you reach my ball, Dad? It accidentally rolled under the sofa."

"Ssssure! Sure, son." The dazzled father bent over, reached underneath, and retrieved the old fuzzy tennis ball. And afterward, the ex-toddler lowered the sofa slowly as though it were weightless. Mark intentionally tossed the fuzzy ball low and outside and watched his son reposition and scoop it up as well as any shortstop.

"What's going on here?" said his father. "You seem to have grown up overnight. Your vocabulary and grammar are almost that of a teenager, and you have the strength to match. I wonder if you are really my son with all this change."

"Don't you fret none about that, Dad. You can't get rid of me that easily." He tried to pat his father on the back, as they reentered the kitchen, but all he could reach was his father's rear. Taller, but still not tall enough.

During breakfast, Mark began to think. *This strange phenomenon isn't exactly all bad. There's a good many possibilities I hadn't considered before. There's big money to be made here.* But first he had to know what kind of athlete his son would make. As soon as all the dishes were in the sink, the father took his son out in the backyard and put him through every pass, catch, kick, and hoop drill imaginable—football, baseball, soccer, and basketball. The boy had ability, speed, accuracy, motivation, and prowess, but as expected, he sorely lacked any technique. And his father quickly acquired a vision for his son and a dream for himself.

Waffel watched through the kitchen window as she washed the breakfast dishes. Tears streamed down her face. She gasped, seeing her son leap high in the air to grab a football, and only moments later, the child laid out for another just out of his reach. He got up and brushed himself off, oblivious of the blood oozing from his skinned knee. Out there in the yard, a tough, agile two-year-old performed approvingly for his dad. This was not the immature little toddler from only a few days ago. Where had her darling baby in diapers gone? Sure, he had been impossible to potty train and lazy in learning to walk and talk. But he was sooo sweet and cute. She wiped her eyes with the end of her apron and went on with her morning chores.

The two newly bonded males reentered the house shortly before noon and headed straight for the fridge, whereupon each devoured a bottle of Tasty Tonic. "Better get some more of this stuff before we run out," declared Mark with his arm around his son. He stood the boy back against the door jamb with a yardstick nailed to it. Placing a book on his son's head he marked a spot next to the yardstick, twenty-six inches. Mark couldn't believe his eyes, the boy had grown three inches in the past forty-eight hours. *It's got to be the tonic*, he thought, when he saw the lad reach for yet another bottle and turn it up on end. He cringed. *But where is all this going?* Justin carried an armful of fixings to the table, leaving the fridge door open.

"You two get away from the fridge—you'll spoil your lunch," Waffel warned as soon as she entered the room. Too late— her son had fixed himself a Dagwood sandwich of salami, Swiss cheese, peanut butter, lettuce, and tomato. Actually, he was already two bites in when she arrived. His left hand gripped the massive sandwich with four fingers wrapped around it like a curve ball ready to be tossed. The sandwich disappeared quickly. After all, he was a growing boy.

Waffel eyed the two empty bottles and a third half-downed in her son's right hand and felt a sinking sensation in her delicate stomach. She just had to stop all this nonsense. All of a sudden an idea hit her. *Later,* she thought. *I'll wait until I'm alone.* Places had already been set at the table, so Waffel set down the large platter of tuna fish salad, carrots, and celery sticks, lettuce, and thinly sliced tomatoes.

"What kind of sissy lunch is this for a growing boy?" complained her husband. "He needs a hot lunch with plenty of protein."

"I could fix him a can of split pea soup," she answered while emptying half a loaf of whole wheat bread onto another plate in the middle of the table.

"Make that two cans," he ordered. "And use the big cups. I've worked up an atrocious appetite, too."

"What's your plan for this afternoon?" asked Waffel, as she opened and emptied two cans of Progresso soup into a pot.

"I thought I might take the boy over to see Mike Higgins and have him give the boy a once-over to see what he thinks,"

"Isn't that the Coach Higgins fellow that retired from the pros?" she asked. "Aren't you aiming a wee bit high? He's only two years old."

"Mind your own business, woman," said the man of the house. "It's my department, and I know what's best for my son."

"He's my son, too," she said. "And I don't think you have his interests in mind. I think you're counting imaginary dollar signs and contracts before the fact."

"Enough!" Mark had raised his voice to his wife in anger, something entirely new in their relationship. They finished their lunch in silence.

Alone in the afternoon, Waffel lined up an array of fruit juices, Kool Aid flavor packs, Crystal Light tea powder mix, artificial sweeteners and assorted food coloring dyes. When Waffel Forte was still Waffel Stevens, she had earned a degree in analytical chemistry. She was about to put all that knowledge and skill to use in concocting a tonic substitute that matched perfectly the flavor, color, and consistency of Tasty Tonic without any of its growth benefits. It took nearly the entire afternoon to come anywhere near what she had in mind. The comparative sipping consumed a whole bottle of Tasty Tonic. Added to that was the fear that her husband and son would walk in on her betrayal while she assembled this miracle substance. Waffel manufactured enough to fill one and a half water-cooler-sized jugs. The full one she sealed and stored in the back of the basement where Mark never went. She had already dubbed it Two Tonic. The name was her nervous little joke. She cleaned the already empty bottles, filled them with Two Tonic and replaced them in the missing six-pack slots.

Waffel started to pour the full bottles of Tasty Tonic down the sink drain, and had a second thought. *Why waste it?* she thought. She sat down at the table and devoured a whole additional bottle. Waffel had been on her feet all day, yet no fatigue. It tasted so good, she sat there trying to relax, but something was going on inside her. The muscles on her limbs began to pop out and pump up. She felt light and anxious, overall simply great. She consumed yet another bottle. Though her metamorphosis continued, she attended to the remaining bottles and began the cleanup. She was still wiping down the counter when she heard the Ford pickup pull into the driveway.

As they came in the door, a thought occurred to her: she had filled both six-packs. They couldn't help notice her mistake. As expected, they both headed toward the fridge. Even Waffel surprised herself by stepping in front of them. She held up her hands. "Dinner will be ready in an hour. Why don't you two go right into the den, relax and watch some TV. I'll bring you something to drink." Father and son agreed in one nod and headed in that direction. She heard the TV sound as she removed one six-pack from the fridge, removed two bottles, and stuck the remainder in a rear corner under the sink.

Waffel conveyed a tray of cheese and crackers, along with the two bottles of Two Tonic into the den and set it down on the coffee table in front of them. She sank into the La-Z-Boy recliner to await the results of her hoax. Each time a bottle went to the lips of her charges, Waffel carefully scrutinized their expressions, desperately seeking confirmation and hoping against discovery. Neither father nor son gave any sign that Two Tonic was any different than the original Tasty Tonic.

This deception went on for several weeks. Empty bottles were soon refilled from the basement jug, and newly purchased six-packs were quickly refilled as well. Waffel's hoax continued to be truly successful.

Two Tonic satisfied their thirst, so the drink wasn't immediately suspect when Justin began to tire more easily, confuse his father's directions, and stumble through the so-called athletic drills. It wasn't until the angry father subjected his son to the yardstick height measurement that he learned his son had shrunk two inches. The angry man began to believe his wife might have something to do with the reversal of fortune.

So Mark bought a six-pack on the sly and tried unsuccessfully to discern between the tonics. When that failed, he called the Tasty Tonic manufacturer to ask if they had changed their formula. The reply was not what he wanted to hear: "Why, yes! Ever so slightly, sir. You shouldn't even notice the difference. There was a complaint about one of the ingredients, so it has been omitted. No, sir. We can't reveal any part of our formula, past or present. It's a patent and legal issue. Thank you for your interest in Tasty Tonic."

Mark Forte was devastated. He tried other commercial tonics, so-called elixirs, and sports drinks to no avail. His dreams were shattered and there was nothing more he could do. He began to do a lot of sulking. He watched his son's strength, agility, and prowess decline slowly to where they had originally been.

Only Waffel appreciated that her son's newly acquired language skills seemed to linger indefinitely, along with his successful potty training. She had her new, improved son back. Waffel had something else, too—a supply of Tasty Tonic in the back of the basement that she tapped into on occasion. Not that she needed to. Her bout with the original Tasty Tonic had left her with a serious case of improved self-esteem. With it, she soon became the dominant member of the family, making all sorts of important decisions for her husband and son. In time, she used her feminine wiles to return her husband to normalcy, but never again dominance.

§

Art Lovers

All of us appreciate some art for various reasons, but there are those among us who turn to extremes to possess civilization's treasures.

One might collect to satisfy a private sense of communing with the arts. Others might acquire a work to add a toy-like trophy to their status. Giving art may gain favor with a lady you care deeply about, and stealing art might indulge a recluse's craving. Of course, there's also the profit of resale. So which is it?

The Telltale Art
The Lost Art of Lake Como
Portrait in Peril

The Telltale Art

Lieutenant, why do the police always assume the beautiful young wife is involved? Yes, I've been told my whole life that I'm stunning. Bart says he loves the way my honey-gold hair caresses my cheeks and curls around my neck. I'm thirty years younger than my husband. So what? I adore Barton McNaugh—always have. But now he's missing, and you think I had something to do with his disappearance. Good grief, Lieutenant, must you straddle our antique Chippendale chair? And please don't light that cigarette. Bart is terribly allergic to smoke. Thank you.

Where have I been these past two days? I don't think that's any of your business. But if you must know, at my health spa. I just can't abide you people crawling all over my personal things.

Do I have affairs? Of course, but never for love or companionship. They're strictly to satisfy my healthy lust, and I only indulge on Wednesdays. Bart condones my affairs as long as I remain discreet. We incorporated a rendezvous clause into our marriage agreement nineteen years ago. A stroke has confined my husband to a wheelchair for the past twenty-three years and, understandably, he wants to keep me content. He compensates for his sexual constraints in so many other ways.

Yes, I married Bart after he became disabled. Now don't look at me so skeptically. I'm the very antithesis of the gold-digging bimbo. I've never dyed my hair. I wear no makeup whatsoever. My love for Bart penetrates to the very depths of my soul and size-six figure. I admit his inherited wealth and generosity did attract me at first. But not as much as his intellect. His brilliant mind thirsts for knowledge and culture. He infuses every observation with fresh insights and an original sense of humor. Did I forget to say he's also quite handsome? I'm crazy about his wavy white hair and patrician nose. And he's always so kind and attentive. Could anyone want for a better life's companion? So why do you connect me with his disappearance?

You ask how we met. At an art museum in Houston, where he served as trustee. I had worked my way up from docent to director of acquisitions. My undergraduate degree in art history, with a master's in art museum management, didn't exactly hinder my promotions. Bart maintains that I seduced him with both my expertise and devotion to art. He appreciates the finer things in life and collects objects of beauty. So . . . Is the former Beatrice Fallon, femme fatale of the art world, just another of his collectibles? At first, perhaps, when showing me off to his fashionable friends. But not since. Even though his affliction has made him semi-reclusive, he's never lost his passion for either my body or mind.

Have I noticed any recent changes in Bart? Changes, no, but peculiar behavior, yes. Sometimes he disappears for days—randomly and not very often. I never actually see him leave or return, nor do any of the servants. He usually leaves when I'm gone on Wednesdays. When he reappears, he's all smiles, yet refuses to elaborate.

Now . . . I recognize your quizzical look, and I know what you're thinking. How can a stroke victim, with one leg numb and useless, bring off this disappearing act? I assure you I've asked myself the same question. Then why haven't I demanded an explanation? Hah! No one makes demands on Barton McNaugh. And besides, I hardly have a right to pressure him, considering that I enjoy my own private social life.

Lieutenant, I don't understand. You already know about

my affairs. Yet you think I'm still hiding something. You say you want the whole story, not just selected details. Things will go badly for me if I don't tell you the truth? I don't respond well to threats, sir.

Oh, dear Lord! So you know something about Bart's secret. Well, then, I don't seem to be holding any trump cards, do I? You win.

Several months ago, on a Wednesday, I drove off for an afternoon date with my paramour of the moment, but that two-timing Casanova didn't show. Returning home in a rotten mood, I spotted a UPS truck parked out front. Had Bart ordered something? I hadn't. I waited in my Porsche until the driver left. As I stole inside and crossed the marble foyer, the house felt silent as a crypt. I started upstairs to change into something less sexy, when I noticed that the oak door to Bart's study was closed. Odd, I thought—he rarely shuts it. Twenty minutes later, I saw the door still closed. Wondering about the delivery, I knocked and called his name. Receiving no answer, I tried the door and found it un-locked.

I discovered no sign of Bart—not even his motorized wheelchair. I questioned Maria, our housekeeper. She hadn't seen Mr. McNaugh leave. The butler was on holiday, and our only other staff member, the chauffer, had gone on some errand. I assumed this was another of my husband's eccentric vanishings. Happily, he reappeared in time for supper.

Almost a week passed without incident, but on Tuesday, Bart abruptly left the breakfast table and motored into his study. Following at a discreet distance, I heard him on the phone—ex-citedly arranging another delivery for the following afternoon. I supposed he assumed I'd be out then.

After he hung up, I tiptoed back to the dining room and appeared to be reading the newspaper and sipping my cappuccino. Just in time. Bart returned moments later, wearing a grin so wide it looked chiseled into his face. I thought I knew my darling hus-band, but this expression baffled me. Was it joyful or sinister? He leaned over and patted my bare thigh before gobbling up his now-cold eggs Benedict. I begged him to explain. What could be so important that it couldn't wait until after breakfast? He assured me it was just a small business matter.

Curiosity overpowered my sexual drive. In a whispered phone call, I canceled my weekly rendezvous. The next afternoon, dressed for an amorous outing, I pointedly kissed Bart goodbye and drove down our driveway as far as the apple orchard. My Porsche fit neatly amid the heavily laden trees. The fruit, ready for harvesting, gave off a pungent, heady aroma that matched my mood. I traipsed carefully back to the mansion, shielded among the shrubs lining the driveway, and slipped into the servants' entrance. Shedding my stiletto heels, I tiptoed to the guest powder room opposite Bart's study. He wouldn't detect me there—it wasn't wheelchair-accessible. I cracked the door to observe and waited. And waited. Standing in stockinged feet on the ceramic tile floor, in miniskirt and lace blouse, my body chilled, my toes tingled.

At last his phone rang. He answered it, mumbled a few words, and hung up. Could he be having an affair of his own? Heaven forbid! The doorbell chimed, and Bart wheeled, or rather motored, out to the foyer. I heard the double doors open, a cheerful greeting from a UPS driver, and the truck roaring away. Bart motored slowly back to his study, balancing a cumbersome package on the arms of his wheelchair. The package was wrapped in brown paper; it looked about four feet tall, three feet wide, and perhaps six inches thick. I have to hand it to my husband. He can't walk, but he's developed remarkable upper-body strength, the result of diligent physical therapy since his stroke. Bart entered the study, haphazardly swinging the door shut. It all but closed behind him. I stole across the hall. Peering in, I could survey half the room. He set the package on the floor and leaned it against the wall between two bookcases. Then he wheeled behind his desk and fiddled around for a few minutes. Afterward, he returned to the spot where he'd left the package.

What happened next, Lieutenant, stunned me. If I'd discovered a Rembrandt etching at a yard sale, it would have shocked me less.

Bart, his wheelchair, and the package slowly sank into the floor and disappeared. I waited to make sure he didn't resurface before I entered his study. Examining the area where Bart disappeared, I discovered an almost invisible line marking a square in the Karastan rug. It looked like a hidden trapdoor. But to where? As far as I knew, the only basement area in the house was under the kitchen: a utility cellar for heating, air conditioning, and humidity equipment. I could only assume that some sort of elevator had conveyed Bart to the floor below, but no matter how carefully I looked, I couldn't find any controls for such an elevator.

Then I remembered his trip to the desk. I rifled through the drawers, but found nothing. I was about to close the file drawer, when I noticed that the interior depth didn't match the exterior height. Could there be a false bottom? Sure enough, a layer of plywood hinged up, exposing a set of four side-by-side thumbwheel switches. The thumbwheels were set at 0-3-5-2. Although the word POUNDS appeared beneath the settings, I didn't immediately make any association. Then it dawned on me. The elevator was operated by inputting the specific weight of the cargo it carried. Bart weighed 231 pounds at his last physical. According to the airline the last time we flew, his wheelchair weighed 80 pounds. The other 41 pounds could be attributed to the newly arrived package. I dialed in my 132-pound weight, shut the drawer, and stepped onto the rug square.

Voila! A slow, almost silent elevator began to move the patch downward. When it settled to a stop in an eight-foot-square concrete room bare of any furniture, I found myself in semi-darkness. Mounted on the nearest wall at wheelchair level were a few environmental controls, a glowing nightlight, and a set of thumbwheel switches, presumably for the elevator. Ductwork crossed overhead, passing from one blank wall to the room beyond. An open door at the right corner led to a well-lit second room. I heard Bart's chair rolling about, then the rustling of heavy wrapping paper.

Each revelation flooded my brain and burned my cheeks like the rush of a double vodka martini. But I knew I had to get back up to the study before Bart heard me. More exploring would have to wait for another day.

Unfortunately, the elevator had automatically returned to the study empty, and I had no idea how to recall it. The dank air was stirring up my sinuses. I suppressed a sneeze as I anticipated Bart's fury if he were to discover me. Then I saw my problem: the weight control on the wall was set at 0-3-1-1, Bart's weight in his wheelchair from a prior visit. I realized there wasn't any weight on the platform above. I took a wild guess and, with fingers shaking, reset the four switches to 0-0-0-0. The elevator descended. I stepped on the platform, but it refused to budge. My body shivered in panic, my heart thumped. Making a last-ditch attempt, I reprogrammed the switches to my weight. The elevator moved upward, depositing me in Bart's study. Feeling much calmer now, I remembered to reposition the thumbwheels to 0-3-5-2 in the drawer and restored the desk to its original state. Leaving the house via the rear door, I hiked back to my Porsche in the orchard and drove it into our garage.

That evening we shared what should have been a lovely meal. Candlelight, beef Wellington, and a fine Merlot. But Bart barely spoke and eyed me suspiciously over the rims of his glasses. I couldn't imagine why, and then it dawned on me. He'd noticed the basement elevator switches set at 0-1-3-2. I thought I'd choke on my crème brulée, but managed to play dumb. After a few days, I figured he'd forgotten the discrepancy.

Late one night, with Bart fast asleep in the master bedroom next to mine, I decided it was time to explore the vault once more. I crept downstairs, set the elevator controls, and descended to the concrete room. But nothing—nothing!—could have prepared me for the second and third rooms.

Bart had created an art gallery of carpeted rooms paneled in rich rosewood, sprawling beneath the entire mansion. Magnificent oil paintings by world-famous masters covered the walls. Sensors, acknowledging my body heat, caused ceiling lights to illuminate each work as I approached it. What a sophisticated technical touch!

Tears forced me to blink, and then I let them flow. I recognized each work as if rediscovering a long lost—and ill-fated—friend. Picasso's painting of his daughter Maya holding a doll, stolen from his granddaughter's home. Renoir's *Jeune Parisienne*, stolen from the National Museum in Stockholm. *Chemin de Sevres*, a country scene by Corot, stolen from the Louvre. A Van Gogh portrait of Dr. Gachet, taken from a private collector's estate. A Cubist still life by Braque, stolen from the Modern Museum in Stockholm. A Vermeer—two women and a man performing a concert at home, stolen from the Isabella Stewart Gardner Museum in Boston. And so much more. Lieutenant, this astonishing display represented one of the world's largest collections of purloined art.

The longer I strolled among these priceless treasures, the hotter my blood boiled. By privately hoarding these masterpieces, Bart was denying art lovers everywhere access to their creative heritage. Worse yet, these immortal artists had poured decades of sweat and tears into their canvases and endured enormous hardship on the road to recognition and patronage. Now they were being deprived of their audience. But most painful of all, how could Bart have so selfishly kept all this from me, his true partner in life? His calculated secrecy had destroyed the strongest bonds between us: our sharing, our honesty, and our commitment to the world of art. I felt betrayed.

It took some moments to recover my equilibrium. When I reached the back wall of the third room, I found a daybed; a minimally stocked refrigerator; a tiny sink; a workbench covered with tools; and a full bathroom fitted out for the disabled. The wrappings from the last package lay under the table. I didn't recognize the name on the shipping label—probably another crooked player in the whole illegal scheme. I was furious.

My Rolex read 6 a.m. I needed to retreat. My heart ached as I bid the masterpieces goodbye. Would I ever see them again?

The ceiling lights darkened automatically as I backed out of the gallery rooms and ascended via the weight-wise elevator to Bart's study.

It would be almost an hour before my husband awoke, enough time to experiment. A four-foot-tall original Rodin—an early version of *Eve*—stood near the window, crying out for attention. I tilted the bronze figure and rolled it on its round pedestal to the square of carpet. At Bart's desk, I tried to guess *Eve's* weight by numerically sequencing the thumbwheels in the deep drawer, rotating through every logical setting without success. Then it hit me. My shrewd husband had installed an anti-tampering feature. Any combination of consecutive numbers or defined series of settings disabled the operating mechanism. I waited fifteen minutes and tried again. No luck. The grandfather clock ticked loudly, as if chastising me, its hands leaving no time for further experiments. I rolled *Eve* back to her Eden by the window.

My head throbbed as I padded upstairs to my room. Moments later, Bart's chair sped past my door. The staircase elevator lowered it to the foyer. In a solicitous voice, I called down to him that I wasn't feeling well—he should breakfast without me. Exhausted, I fell asleep until mid-afternoon.

The next few days hummed uneventfully—sort of. Though anger and resentment still raged within my breast, I played the role of a loving, affectionate wife and began channeling my emotions into a plan.

Bart still eyed me with mistrust and maintained only a pretense of conversation, but never confronted me. On Friday after lunch, he told me to "Have a good day" with the detachment of a store clerk, wheeled back to his study, and shut the door. I pressed my ear to it and heard the soft hum of the elevator descending, hesitating, then rising—my cue to enter. I rushed immediately to *Eve* and rolled her from the window to the elevator patch. The exquisite Rodin now stood in a place of prominence between the bookcases. Satisfied with both my aesthetic and vengeful move, I tidied up the room and left.

That was nearly six weeks ago. I told the staff that my husband had taken to his bed with a back injury and wasn't to be disturbed. I kept his bedroom door locked to ensure his privacy. Our butler and chauffeur were delighted to receive an unexpected paid vacation. Maria continued to clean and prepare meals, and I conveyed her trays inside the locked bedroom. At night after she went home to her family, I dumped the meals into the garbage, leaving only scraps and a few drops of wine in the Waterford glasses.

The household staff returned. I gathered them together and announced that my husband had recovered and taken a short trip. He'd been away for several days, but I didn't know where. I conveyed the appropriate wifely anxiety over his absence. Unfortunately, my performance backfired. Bart had so routinely disappeared that it seemed I protested too much. The servants stared at me in sullen disbelief, then left the room and called the police.

Lieutenant, your men searched my house as painstakingly as Vermeer painted. He completed only two canvases a year, you know. You think I'm digressing? Sorry. For two days now your men have combed this place and found nothing. You should have concluded that my husband vanished of his own free will. I see. If it hadn't been for you nosing around in Bart's study, you would have packed up and left yesterday. But you didn't. Why not?

Oh, my God! You saw the lift. How did you know about the lift? Ah, the circular patch of carpet in front of the window where *Eve* used to stand. The patch itself is still a vibrant blue, but the carpet surrounding it is faded from years of exposure to the sun. You say it seemed to match *Eve's* pedestal shape, so you had your men move her to the original spot to check. Oh, no! The lift must have descended as soon as they pulled her off. Right? I know Bart would have zeroed the thumbwheels to return to the study. Only he couldn't do that because of *Eve*. I can just imagine the look on your face when the lift sank into the floor.

No! I don't find this humorous at all. You say your men lowered a ladder into the hole and discovered my husband stretched out on the daybed with food and drink still left in the refrigerator.

How is that possible? I see. The coroner placed Bart's death within a day or two of his confinement and pronounced it death by heart attack—of natural causes. Doesn't that mean I'll only be charged with attempted murder? No? You say Bart died as a direct result of my imprisoning him. The fear of a slow, tortuous death by starvation most likely hastened the heart failure.

Remorse? Lieutenant, you don't understand. I'm still furious with my husband. My only regret is that I've been found out. Yes, I'll sign the wretched confession. But first, let me make sure I understand. You say my cooperation means I'll serve eight to fifteen years? I won't have to submit to a trial that could get me life? Let me have your pen. Yes, I realize all the artwork must be returned. But what's that ledger on the table next to you? It's for me? Bart's diary? I didn't know he kept one.

Lieutenant, your black eyes glower like Picasso's in his self-portraits. How long have you had this diary? You've known about it from the day you found Bart? He had it with him? You want me to read the last two entries? Certainly. Give me a minute, please.

Good Lord! I've made a horrible mistake. My husband truly did cherish me. All his planning, all his preparations, all his secrecy were for my benefit. He planned to present the paintings to me as a gift on our twentieth anniversary next month. Stolen or not, what a confirmation of a husband's love!

Bart, dear heart, please forgive me. I loved you, too.

The Lost Art of Lake Como

Karma, fatalism, and coincidence were not beliefs particularly embraced by Andrea Genetti. Yet a number of unforeseen events would line up and string together bead by bead in just such a necklace to change her life. Newlywed Andrea and her husband, Pietro, were sitting side by side toward the rear of a metro bus as they returned from a shopping trip along the Via Roma and Galleria districts of downtown Naples. Today was the first Saturday in October 1959.

Andrea, a chunky yet attractive brunette with soft hazel eyes, occupied the aisle seat, and Pietro sat by the window, the bundles balanced on his knees. While resting her head lightly on his broad shoulder, she saw his reflection in the tinted glass and admired his strong face with its square chin, wide nose, and black bushy brows.

The roaring diesel, numero 121 motorbus, snaked its way up the steep hill to the city's Vomero district where they lived. The closer they got to home, the bus encountered more and more pedestrian traffic. A huge unruly crowd flooded out of the nearby football (soccer) stadium, from this year's championship game. The still cheering masses gorged through the surrounding streets, confirming the city team's latest victory: the first time in a decade that underdog Napoli had defeated Roma.

The bus inched along until it came to a complete halt. The stymied bus driver couldn't contend with the flow of excited fans blocking his path. He turned to his passengers and explained that there would be at least a thirty-minute delay before continuing. Since the twenty-something Genettis were so close to home, they decided to disembark and walk the rest of the way. The driver opened the rear door, and they got off.

On the Via Chia, a quarter kilometer from their three-room flat, the Genettis encountered a peach-yellow brick school building. An arts and crafts sale filled the sandy schoolyard out front—presumably a school fund-raiser. Andrea, an artist herself, was immediately drawn to the display of oils and pastels either propped or hung along the length of a rusty chain-link fence. Sidling along in front of the lot, she suddenly stopped and stared at one painting in particular. Not only did the landscape look familiar, but the style and brushwork were recognizable.

"Pietro, I know that place," she announced. Andrea remembered being there in her early teens. The familiar brushstrokes of the canvas-tacked-on-wood oil painting drew her attention to the signature in the lower right-hand corner. "And I know the artist, too," she said, smiling. "It's my grandfather's work."

Pietro bent over to read the brush-scrawled name, Luigi Massimo. Her grandfather, all right, an octogenarian recluse, who hadn't contacted the family in years.

Engaging the saleswoman in the schoolyard, Andrea learned that the former owner, a young man in his mid-twenties, acquired the painting at an art sale in the Lake Como region up in the north of Italy. The woman recalled a Dominic somebody, but wasn't sure.

"Dominic Massimo, maybe?" Andrea inquired, but the matronly woman merely shrugged in response. The two women haggled over a fair price for the artwork and then Andrea hesitated, but Pietro sealed the deal. The Genettis walked away with the oil wrapped loosely in a brown paper roll.

Upon arriving home at 145 Via Francisco Chia, Pietro inserted a ten-lire coin in the pay slot, and they rode the wrought iron, see-through elevator to the third floor. He seemed more excited than his wife as he fumbled with the key to Apartment 3A. In his mind the painting belonged in a place of honor. The first room off to the left of the hall had three adjacent windows, a mirrored wall, another with a high-top breakfront cabinet, and a lone bare wall. A small plain chandelier hung above a hardwood table and twelve mixed chairs—some cushioned, others not. The table nearly filled the multipurpose room where most families dined and socialized with friends. There was no living room.

Pietro headed directly for the bare wall and unfurled the newly purchased landscape on it. He asked his wife to hurry and get the masking tape, for he couldn't hold it up much longer. Andrea returned with the tape, and the painting was affixed to the wall. The two sat down at the far end of the table to admire their latest acquisition. Before long, Pietro's dark eyes narrowed and a quizzical expression grew across the olive cheeks. It was a part of her life he knew very little about. Combing his fingers through a thick head of his curly black hair, he decided there were questions to ask.

"Did your grandfather live near this scene?"

"I spent only the one summer with my Pappo Wigi at the lake." Andrea told him, "And no, not in one of the lakefront houses in the picture. Close by, though, maybe twenty or thirty minutes away by Pappo Wigi's dinghy."

"Is the man even alive today?" Pietro continued.

"I don't know," Andrea explained. "When my mother and I visited him in 1947, we found Pappo extremely bitter over the war. He wasn't happy about Mamma marrying an American and abandoning his family."

"Wasn't there a brother, your Uncle Giani or something?" Pietro inquired.

"Uncle Giacomo and Auntie Sophia were killed during the fighting, but Cousin Dominic should be still around."

Andrea's eyes took on a far-away look, and she pressed her lips tightly together as she reminisced through some childhood thoughts. But her hungry husband wrested his wife from her dream world, and they both moved to the tiny white-tiled kitchen at the far end of the long hall. Minutes later, he sat contentedly with his evening newspaper at the kitchen table for two while she stood reheating dinner over the "PB" gas stove—a veal and tomato pasta dish from the night before. Outside the kitchen window, accordion music floated upward from the lively neighborhood bistro across the alley. Each looked up and turned to the other for a smile—the song was the venerable "Santa Lucia." They accepted the musical gesture as a precursor to a romantic evening.

* * * *

When dawn broke through the wooden shutters of the bedroom the next morning, Pietro found himself in bed alone. The bedroom door was open, and both the kitchen and water closet across the hall were obviously vacant, so he threw back the down quilt and leaped out of bed. Lighting the kerosene heater on his side of the bed, he grabbed his clothes from the chair under one arm and the handle on the heater with the opposite hand, and darted for the water closet, his feet hardly touching the icy cold marble floor in the rush. The cozy WC heated quickly. Some minutes and a shave later, the search for Andrea was resumed. He found her—wrapped tightly in a quilted pink robe, her shoulder-length hair disheveled. She sat in the front room staring intently at the new painting. An exchange of cheek pecks and he sat down next to her. "We'll buy a frame," he told her, but that didn't seem to be her worry.

Andrea closed her eyes and told Pietro about her dream in which she witnessed her Pappo painting this very oil.

"We'd come by boat with his easel, pallet, brushes, tubes of oils, tools, thinner, and messy rags. The perfect light shone across the lake in that early morning. He set up the easel on land facing the lake. Way off in the distance, several scattered boats, dwarfed by their sails, slipped across the rippled surface in long gentle tacks. A heavily forested shoreline swept the cove in front of us. Two young trees grew gracefully bowed across the cove, framing the blue and white lake view between them. A small dark brook fed in from the left foreground. Set back from the water, four modest shake-covered, mud-yellow brick cottages and accompanying sheds appeared on the right. Still another cottage-like structure with a short wooden steeple filled the remaining vista.

"Then textured shades of earthy greens, oranges, and browns—in patches and strokes—began replacing bare canvas. Trees, houses, boats, brook, and other details soon emerged from his brushes. There were birds and people, too, but they were hardly distinct at all."

"You were merely visualizing the painting as you saw it last night," Pietro explained.

"But I saw it all happen years ago. I was there with Pappo when he painted it. I saw him at the easel. I saw my own ugly dress, my favorite doll in my lap, too. I saw the dinghy, the boat he didn't paint, because he'd told me it did not belong to the scene. There was something else different about this picture, but I can't seem to remember what."

Andrea then surprised her husband: "I'd like to visit Pappo again and the lake where he lived."

"Is the man living in the same place?" Pietro asked. "For that matter, is he still alive even?"

"I don't know," Andrea replied. "But I want to go there anyway."

Pietro was soon convinced that a four-day vacation in the north would be the honeymoon they couldn't afford eight months ago. They could travel by train and stay at some cute little inn by the railway station that she remembered. She would take the painting along to facilitate finding the exact cove where it was conceived.

* * * *

Leaving on the following Friday, the train ride over mountains, across sprawling farmlands, and through long dark tunnels proved quite fatiguing, and the inconvenience of several train changes didn't help. At the Como train station they rented a Fiat for the next morning's drive just before the rental office closed for the day. At the inn, Locands di Anzani, it was dinner and off to bed for the night, but not until they consulted the local road map. Andrea felt almost certain about their destination and directions, while Pietro was not so sure. He reminded her that the landscape was subject to serious changes in a span of a dozen years.

At 9:30 after a leisurely continental breakfast, they took the road to the east branch of the Lago di Como, a two-hour drive. Once at the lake, very little appeared as she remembered, so they began to examine a number of access roads leading into the lake. After the fourth miss, Andrea recognized a tree trunk with a five-foot girth. They followed the adjacent rough-stone road till it ended at a familiar gray stucco, one-story home. It appeared to be a little run-down with age, but essentially unchanged in her mind. Andrea's face lit up when she noted curtains in the window, a light on inside, and an Alpha Romeo parked next to the veranda.

Hardly out of the car, running toward the cottage, Andrea yelled her Pappo's name over and over again. Pietro stood by the car waiting, allowing the reunion to take its course. As she reached for the brass knob, it turned and the door flung open to reveal a short stout man in his early thirties. She quickly noted that he had black wiry hair and thick matching lashes. His pleasantly round facial features were vaguely familiar.

"Dominic? Dominic Massimo?" she inquired.

"*Si*, I am Dominic Massimo," he responded, "but who are you?"

"I'm your cousin Andrea from America," she told him. "I'm married and living in Napoli now."

Dominic stepped back and gestured for her to come in, and she followed him into the modest parlor centered about an intricately designed Turkish carpet. The room was clean and comfortable with inexpensive worn furnishings of another time and local culture. A fair number of excellent oil paintings decorated the yellowed plaster walls, yet several conspicuous faded spots signified that still others were missing.

"Are these genuine Luigi Massimos?" she asked. He nodded.

Inquiring after her Pappo, Dominic sadly related the tale of how, one day just over a month ago, Uncle Luigi decided to wander off into the woods and never came home. "The police scoured the woods and dragged the lake for days before giving up." Dominic drew a circle with a finger at his own temple, indicating that the old man wasn't right in the head.

"Ahem." Pietro stood at the front door.

After the introductions were made, Dominic cautiously offered them a place to sit on an overstuffed sofa. He appeared to be somehow threatened by their surprise arrival. His heretofore jovial expression changed, and his eyes narrowed considerably. "I live here now, and this is my home," he announced. "The land, too."

The blurted declaration startled both Andrea and Pietro. It seemed terribly out of place and inappropriate. She wondered why he thought the need for such an outburst.

Pietro, an associate lawyer in a Naples law firm, had another idea. He suggested, "You must have been very good and helpful to your Uncle Luigi for the man to be so generous and leave you everything in his will. That speaks quite well of you." He chose to address Dominic in a flattering manner so as to disarm him.

A fleeting smile darted across Dominic's face. He hesitated for a moment, contemplating whether to lie, and then stumbled over words explaining that there wasn't any will, but that the local equivalent of probate court had granted him conditional ownership of the house and land. "I told them I am his closest relative as everyone else died in the war. I'd forgotten your existence. Last I knew, you lived in America. You never come anymore. I didn't think you cared. You can't come here now and take it all away from me."

Andrea reassured him that they were not interested in Pappo's estate. "It's all yours," she said. "We wish you well, Dominic, and have no intention of butting into your affairs. All we wanted to do here was reminisce and learn more about Pappo—how and where he lived. Of course, I lived with my Italian mother and American father in Chicago. But I met my wonderful Italian husband while on tour in beautiful Naples. We fell in love instantly and were married last June. We have a lovely apartment there now."

Dominic appeared to relax somewhat after that. He told them they could stay with him and he offered them sleeping accommodations on the pull-out sofa. The Genettis graciously declined, but did accept a lunch consisting of local cheese, baggette bread, and fruits accompanied by a regional red wine. At lunch they pleasantly caught up on the many missing years and the few known distant relatives. During a conversational lull, Andrea looked out the rear window and noticed Pappo's dinghy. It floated at the end of a dilapidated pier, tied up to a piling. Afterward, she asked Dominic for permission to use the dinghy for an afternoon of exploring lovely Lake Como. He willingly agreed, but cautioned them about the boat's unknown condition.

Walking off the rear veranda into the yard leading to the water, Andrea noted that the ground was soft and mushy. "Must have been a lot of rain, and the lake flooded into the backyard," she remarked.

Pietro didn't think so. The ground was too bumpy. "More likely, somebody's been digging all over the place."

Just before the Genettis stepped off the makeshift pier, Andrea remembered the painting and sent Pietro to fetch it from the rented Fiat. With Pietro at the oars, the dinghy glided easily out onto the lake, but the two purposely hugged the shoreline. It was chilly on the open water. They examined cove after cove until nearly three in the afternoon, when one cove took on a particularly familiar look.

"Is this the right place?" he asked.

"I can't tell for sure until we land and examine it from the same perspective as the painting," Andrea replied.

They put in and tied up the dinghy to a young tree trunk. The shore view confirmed their suspicion—this *was* the right cove. Andrea located and seated herself on the gentle knoll behind the tall grasses, a position she remembered having occupied that one summer in 1947. With the unrolled painting held apart in her two hands Andrea scanned the vista carefully. She frequently looked down, referring to the work, examining the spot where the running brook met the cove. "That's it," she exclaimed.

Pietro stood patiently behind her with his hands affectionately on her shoulders. He knew she was looking for something in particular. Then, he saw it, too. The man painted in on the far side of the brook, stepping on the butt end of a spade was only a massive rock in reality. "Perhaps a 175 kilo stone—not a man at all. It's not very likely someone carried so heavy a rock to that very spot," Pietro offered. "It's always been there—nature put it there."

"It's more likely that my Pappo is trying to tell us something," she responded. "He painted only what belonged and wouldn't have changed anything without having a darn good reason." Andrea got to her feet, ran to the brook, and leapt over roughly a meter to the opposite point of land. Once at the rock, she tried to move it, but the weighty stone objected and couldn't be budged.

Pietro arrived at the rock. "You need a pry bar to lift that rock or a shovel or a spade to dig under it," he advised.

"Don't be a spoilsport," she told him. "Help me!"

With the two of them pushing, the rock started to wiggle and then slowly tilted toward one side, but they could not sustain the push long enough, and the rock rolled back to its original position.

"There's something under there," she said.

"I know, I saw it, too." he said.

The two repositioned themselves better for a second try, and this time the rock flopped over once toward the water's edge. Prominent in the center of a muddy patch surrounded by a stretch of dead grass and reeds, lay a small object about the size of a man's wallet. Some kind of opaque waterproof wrapping covered it completely.

"Maybe we don't have to dig at all," she said.

The wrapping turned out to be an oilskin that hunters and fishermen frequently used for waterproofing personal items. Pietro tried to pick away at the exposed flap in the wrapping with his thumbnail, but he was unsuccessful.

"Here, let me try," she said, taking the package from Pietro. Her long, sharp fingernails made short work of the covering. Folding the layers back, she exposed a sheaf of folded papers. Attempting to unfold an individual sheet, Andrea discovered that the paper was extremely fragile. She stopped, fearing they might lose something of value.

"I agree," he said, seeing her hesitation. "And it's getting late. We're losing the light in any case."

They decided to head back, but before they reached the boat, he remembered the misplaced rock. "What if there's more underneath? What if it does require some digging? Or someone else might get curious."

The Genettis returned to the rock and struggled with it until the massive stone was returned to its original resting place. They rowed back across the lake, arriving at the Massimo pier just before the sun retreated into the horizon. The Massimo home was dark, deserted, and locked. Dominic's Alpha Romeo was gone, too.

* * * *

Secure in their fourth-floor inn room after a veal scaloppini supper in the dining room downstairs, the pajama-clad Genettis decided to unfold and read the newly acquired sheaf of papers. Pietro pushed back the black, dial-less telephone, and shaded lamp on the desk to make room for the delicate operation. He pulled up a chair for himself and another for his wife, and they sat. Andrea slowly and carefully unfolded the sheaf, spreading and flattening the papers so they could be read easily. Reading from the top, she discovered that the papers were letter-like, yet addressed to no one. But from whom? The blood rushed through her veins as she anticipated both the letter's author and its revelations. Carefully slipping a long fingernail under the top surface of the last of three pages, she separated it from the rest of the sheaf. There, in the middle of that page, she found the bold scrawling signature of Luigi Massimo.

"It's from Pappo," she cried out excitedly. Setting down the pages again, the young couple read through the entire letter, periodically gasping and alternately shaking their heads in disbelief. Pietro finished reading first and waited for her to reach the end. An ashen-faced Andrea turned to him for consolation.

"This is a matter for the police," he declared.

She agreed with her husband. He wanted to wait for morning, but she was adamant, so they both got dressed. Downstairs at the desk, they received instructions on how to drive to the police. The winding unlit road was difficult in the dark, but the *stazione* was not actually that far. They soon saw the sign for the Poliza di Stato and parked out front.

Inside, they located someone akin to a provincial detective and showed him the letter. The man in a neat yet shabby gray suit was hefty, blond-haired, and in his late sixties. A meerschaum pipe dangled from the left side of his tobacco-stained teeth. They waited patiently for Sergente Mario Bartoli to grunt, tisk-tisk, and mumble his way through the document twice. Finishing, he looked up and bit down tightly on the pipe, quietly thinking for several minutes. Then he looked sourly at Pietro, removed the pipe, and told them he knew the artist, Luigi Massimo, very well.

"We were in the Resistance and Partisan movements together years ago," Mario reminisced. When the Partisans turned to anarchy, Luigi, being considerably older and wiser, convinced me to leave them. A shame. The good man was a beloved artist, very famous in Italy. He'd be rich, too, if he'd sold more of his paintings instead of hoarding them." A stern, business-like face then asked, "Where is this fiend, Dominic, now?"

Pietro shrugged his shoulders and informed Bartoli of the darkened Massimo house and the missing car.

The sergente urged the Genettis to go back to their inn,

saying he'd contact them first thing in the morning. "Thank you, Sergente Bartoli takes charge now," he said.

Andrea and Pietro returned to their rental car and drove the same road back to the inn. In pajamas once more and in bed, they speculated on the outcome for the next day.

* * * *

Short on sleep from anxiety, the morning arrived inordinately early at 6:30, and they were the first ones in the inn's little dining room. After finishing bread, cheese, sweet roll, and the darkest and richest of coffees, they began the long wait in the lobby for Bartoli's phone call. Close to noon it came. The sergente informed them that Dominic Massimo was already in custody. They were to drive out to the Massimo home as soon as they were ready, and he'd gladly explain more.

Ninety minutes later the Genettis arrived at the end of the Massimo drive to find several *poliza* vehicles and an *ambulanza* parked out front. Pietro had to park on the muddy field to the right of the house. Before they reached the veranda, Sergente Mario Bartoli approached them. He regretfully informed the couple that they had discovered Luigi Massimo's body three hours earlier in the sub-cellar beneath the parlor, along with thirty-seven of his precious paintings. Luigi presumably had hidden there with the paintings to escape Dominic's threats.

"It was just like the letter said," Pietro added, quoting: "I hide the paintings under the Turkish rug to keep them from Dominic. He wants to sell them all to gamble the lire away."

As they spoke, a policeman held open the front door while two more men in white jackets conveyed a gurney through it. The gurney stopped at the rear of the *ambulanza*.

"Is that the body?" Pietro asked.

Mario Bartoli answered, "Yes! Would you like to see him? The body isn't bloody, grotesque, or anything like that."

Andrea accepted, and one of men in white coats lifted the shroud for her to take one last look at her Pappo Wigi. "He's so wan, thin, and old."

"Ah, but he died triumphantly—see his expression?" interrupted Mario. "Either the heart gave out or a lack of oxygen stifled him. The medical examiner will tell us which."

They took a few steps backward, and the shroud was lowered again. Andrea moved away and shrank into a rocker on the veranda. Her hands covered her face. Pietro started after his wife. He wanted to give her comfort.

But Mario put a hand on Pietro's shoulder. Taking him aside, the sergente whispered, "There are bruises all over the poor man's body—some new, others old. Such a waste of genius and talent." After a deep sigh Mario declared, "That nephew is a cruel and evil man." His head nodded over toward a nearby police car, where Dominic sat manacled and subdued in the rear seat. "I've got his confession already, and he'll pay for this. The letter is enough, by itself, to convict him. Oh, by the way, I have a copy of the letter for you. Here! The original is evidence for the courts. My friend Luigi has had the last word in this matter."

Pietro agreed. "The letter spoke of how Dominic tortured Luigi to learn the location of the art cache. It explained his plan to send the altered painting to my mother-in-law in Chicago, but it does not reveal how it wound up in an arts and crafts sale in a Naples schoolyard."

Mario smiled and answered him. "Obviously, the clue's alteration affected the worth of the painting when Dominic went to sell it to his favorite dealer in Naples, so he merely dumped it where he could, for whatever price. A phone call to the dealer revealed similar sales in the past—at least one for every unfaded space on that parlor wall inside. It seems the man has outstanding gambling debts and considerable pressure to pay them more promptly."

Pietro reasoned, "Then Dominic had no intention of mailing that painting to Andrea's mother—not that she would have understood the clues anyway. It says here in the letter that Luigi had secured his nephew's promise to mail it. How do you trust a man who ties you to a bed for days on end while he runs errands?"

"You don't," responded Bartoli," but there were no viable alternatives open to my desperate friend."

"How did the old man lift the rock?" Pietro wondered. "It was almost too much for the two of us."

"We'll never know for sure," said Bartoli. "But there are at least three possibilities. One, he could have tunneled underneath with a knife. Or two, he found something to use as a pry bar. Or three, he had help. My guess is that he carved his way under with a fishing knife."

Pietro had more questions. "Wasn't Dominic careless to allow Luigi the opportunity to plant the letter? Why would the fiend let him go out in the dinghy to fish? Wouldn't he be afraid the old man would try to escape?"

"Two reasons," replied the sergente. "One, by that time the old man was far too feeble to get very far, and two, he wanted his uncle out of the way while he searched for the paintings. Letting him fish wasn't a bad solution."

"Ah, the rummaging through the house, the digging all over the yard," Pietro expounded. "That explains it. But what about his wishes in the letter to leave all the paintings to his daughter? What becomes of that?"

Bartoli put his hand to his chin and spoke. "But you are the solicitor, aren't you? Isn't that akin to a deathbed request? The poor man believed he was going to die. That should be as good as any will. And don't forget the house and land. Lakefront land here is very valuable. After taxes, your family will still become quite comfortable. But the amazing thing I can't get my head around is the fantastic coincidence of the altered painting falling into your hands in Naples.

"Don't forget my wife's sudden desire to visit Pappo Wigi and discovering and making sense of the clue," Pietro added. "Do you suppose there are unknown forces acting here?"

§

Portrait in Peril

I saw neither risk nor danger in this trip, only an opportunity to expand my skills as an artist. To be able to view Japan's rich history from the art of the warring Shogunate to the present-day business tycoons was not to be denied. So here I am in Hakone (Ha-koh-nay), Japan, as a house guest of one of my fellow students at UCLA.

Kimiko ("Kimi") Sharoda captivated me from the day we met with her heart-shaped face and dark, bowl-cut hair. She stands about five-foot-six, with an athletic, easy-going grace, and radiates a generous personality. Although we've been neighborly pals for four years, we've never had an honest-to-goodness date. Sadly, I must confess, we are not lovers—just best friends and study partners. But five weeks in the same house? How was that going to work out?

Kimi's three-story, twelve-room ancestral home stretched across a green hillside offering a spectacular view of the mountains. A fortress-like stone and glass façade encased the perimeter, while opaque sliding panels framed in teakwood defined the separate rooms. For propriety's sake, my two rooms and bath were on the third floor at the opposite end of the house from Tomo and Misao, the live-in couple who saw to the smooth running of the Sharoda household.

One of my rooms consisted of tatami mats, a black-lacquered table, and a wall of wooden cabinets. The second was more to my liking: a double bed with comforter, real chairs, a small writing desk, and all the closet space missing from Western hotels.

I took an hour to settle in and clean up before wandering down to the living room. Kimi joined me, carrying two lacquered trays laden with fresh fruit, bite-sized sashimi, and triangles of peanut butter and jelly on sweet rice cakes. Misao brought tumblers of milk, and when we finished, the polite old woman cleared and conveyed everything back to the kitchen.

That afternoon Kimi and I strolled to the hilly town center. Many shops on both sides of its spotless streets spoke of Hakone's mightiest claim to fame, the elaborately designed inlaid-wood handicrafts called *Zaiku*. We entered one of these shops and climbed a narrow staircase to a second floor *hamamatsu-ya*, a woodcraft studio. Here an artisan sat cross-legged on a low platform, shaving paper-thin ends from a laminate of local and imported fine woods, noted for their distinct grains and vibrant differences in color.

The crafts of parquetry and marquetry called for the wood lengths to be cut into a variety of shapes, tightly fitted and bonded with glue such that the ends of the laminate formed mosaic patterns. The shaved ends were cut, fitted, and bonded to the skins of numerous tourist items. I became particularly enamored of the rectangular secret puzzle boxes called *himitsu-bako*, an art form created over 100 years ago in Hakone. Six-, twelve-, and twenty-four piece *bako* offered different degrees of difficulty for access and reassembly. I chose a twelve-piece *bako* for my souvenir. After visiting a few more shops, we wisely headed back before dark. The *bako* provided several evenings' worth of late-hour entertainment while I followed the instruction sheet symbols for take-apart. But the reassembly? Ha! I had purchased a stubborn treasure. It took me many tries before I discovered the secret.

One misty morning a week later, Kimi and I boarded the Hakone-Tozan railway to Chokoku-no-mari Station, a forty-minute ride. Though our main purpose was to enroll Kimi in a class at the art academy, the trip offered me a chance to visit the mammoth outdoor sculpture gardens nearby. Her class started that very day, so I strolled among the acres of artworks, many fanciful and surrealistic, during the three hours I waited for her. My favorite was a huge disembodied woman's head lying on its side in a pool, with her hair a dense cover of green leaves. I refilled the memory cards in my digital camera and sketched a few sculptures. While sipping tea and nibbling ginger cakes at the café, I even found an adorable little Japanese girl to sketch. She was maybe seven or eight, with dancing eyes and pigtails. I began swiftly drawing.

Caught up in my own joyous activity, I hadn't noticed a curious man, possibly in his mid-seventies, who had taken a table along the wall outside the café. The waiter made a grand fuss over him—lauding, bowing, and scraping. A second, slightly younger, man with a deformed ear and a long red burn scar on his neck sat quietly at the next table. Occasionally, these men spoke, but only a word or two at the most. The little girl picked up a toy from the grass and ran to hug the older man, perhaps her grandfather.

I began to study him carefully, from his shaven head to the deep, hard lines of his long face, his noble posture, and the narrow, nearly evil, way he smiled. I saw a strange dullness in his eyes, as though he perceived nothing around him. I thought he was blind—until those expressionless eyes came alive as soon as the little girl approached him. I flipped to a fresh page in my sketchbook, and my soft charcoal pencil flew across the paper. Ignoring shapes and proportions, I went for impressions and expressions—the inner man, mainly. Amazingly enough, a strong physical likeness emerged anyway.

My frenzied sketching attracted the waiter's attention. He approached and stood behind me, observing and disrupting my concentration. I gave him my credit card to pay for my food and drink in the hope that I would be free of him long enough to finish my drawing. I saw him go from my table to the grandfather's, and while they exchanged words, the older man's temper rose, and they argued for several minutes before the apologetic waiter disappeared inside. I managed to complete the sketch and sip the last of my tea before he returned with my card and charge slip. He bowed slightly and spoke to me.

"Ah, Misssa Edwa Bunneh. Desk tell me phone fo' you, please."

"I'm Edward Burnette. But are you sure? No one knows I'm here."

"Yes, plenty sure fo' you," he replied.

I signed the credit slip and headed to the front desk. When I got there, the phone was off the hook, but when I picked it up, there was nothing but a dial tone. I held the receiver up questioningly to the desk clerk. She merely shrugged. "They must have hung up, sir," she said, with a fixed grin.

Returning to the café, I retook my seat at the table. Something was wrong. The top page of my sketchbook held the unfinished drawing of the little girl. It should have been the picture of the old man. That was how I left my pad when I went to the telephone. I flipped over the page to where the man's picture should have been. It was missing altogether. A residue strip of the torn page remained inside the spiral rings. I glanced over at the tables where the men had been sitting, but both men and the little girl had gone. At that point I saw the waiter, without his apron, emerge from the café and head for the exit.

I stood and confronted him, putting a gentle hand on his shoulder. "Wait! Did you see anyone remove anything from my table? A page from my sketchbook perhaps?" I spoke softly and calmly so as to not frighten him. He bit his upper lip and shook his head.

"What happened to the two men and the little girl sitting over there?"

"No mans, no girl." He wriggled free of me and hurried through the exit to the street.

I would have foolishly followed the frightened waiter out, but Kimi came up the walk toward me from the academy cottage and I thought better of it. As we walked back to the railway station, I wanted to explain what had happened to me, but she burst into excited chatter about her new art class. My brief encounter with misfortune took a back seat.

We boarded the quaint little train back to Hakone. We had traveled some distance when a standing passenger shifted to our side of the railcar to hold onto a different vertical pole. From my aisle seat I could now see the length of the car. Something else, too. I noticed the same two men and the little girl sitting on the sideways bench near the opposite end of our car. They remained oblivious to our presence.

I removed the sketchbook from my backpack and began to re-draw the grandfather's face. Not knowing whether the driving force was the image in my mind, the memory in the muscles of my hand, or the slightly different view as I eyed him from my railcar seat, a reasonable recovery took place on the paper. The image was definitely the grandfather I'd seen sitting in the café. I wasn't completely satisfied with the finished sketch, but it was something I could fix later when I got back to my rooms.

Placing my backpack on my knees, I started to slide the sketchbook in from the top of the pack. In doing so, I dropped my charcoal pencil into the aisle. I glanced down the railcar as I bent to pick it up, and my eyes met the angry stare of the grandfather. I quickly turned away just as the train came to a stop.

Descending several thousand feet in elevation in limited horizontal space, the train was forced to go through several switchbacks. At each switchback the train rolled into a siding, stopped while the seats were turned to face the opposite way, and then moved out in the new direction on a different track. After the first switchback I couldn't see the two men and the little girl, as I now faced away from them. After the second switchback, they were nowhere to be found. I surmised that they had merely changed railcars.

Upon de-boarding the train in Hakone, Kimi noticed the grandfather and his charge getting into a taxi. I searched about for the man with the deformed ear, but couldn't find him anywhere. This bothered me and, throughout the half-hour walk back to the house, I kept looking over my shoulder for some signs of this man. Once or twice we did notice a gray Toyota Corolla appear at the horizon on the road behind us. Not proof we were being followed, but I was concerned. This vehicle should have passed us several times over. We arrived back at the Sharoda home without further incident and put the episode out of our minds.

In my room later that evening, I removed the sketchpad from my backpack, tore off the drawing of the old man that I had done on the train, and started it over again on a fresh page. My new effort captured all the attributes I included in my original café drawing. I closed the sketchpad and stowed it away in the backpack. The drawing I'd done on the train still lay on the desk where I'd been working. I crumbled it into a ball and tossed it in the wastebasket. It hit the rim and landed on the floor. While straightening up from retrieving it, I happened to glance out the window to the road. My heart skipped a beat. Someone was lurking in the shadows. I couldn't see who it was until he lit up a smoke. The scarred neck gave the man away immediately.

I wondered . . . If the two men had gone to such extremes to acquire the original drawing, wouldn't they pursue my latest drawings as well? I rescued the train drawing from the basket, smoothed out the creases, and left it in plain sight on the writing desk.

Years ago, whenever I became troubled, my mother taught me to write my thoughts down on paper. So I tore the newest drawing of the old man off the sketchpad, turned it over, and wrote every detail of the day's events on the back. Now I needed to hide it. I looked around the room. A perfect hiding place jumped out at me. So I folded the drawing and slipped it into its cache.

I pondered what to do next. Because Scarred Neck hadn't invaded the family's domain or threatened them in any way, there was no need to alarm the Sharoda family by calling the police. On the other hand, I now had an insurance policy if he did act illegally. I wrote my name and an explanation on a second piece of paper, put it in a sealed envelope, and slipped it onto Tadashi Sharoda's desk in his first floor office.

The senior Sharodas would be spending the next few days in Tokyo, leaving Kimi and me to be chaperoned by their trusted servants, Tomo and Misao. Meanwhile, Kimi took us to scenic spots in the green foothills overlooking suburban Hakone, where we painted in watercolors. I purposely left the sketchpad behind in my room.

When we returned the second afternoon, we found a distraught Tomo and Misao waiting for us in the living room, anxiously jabbering away. Kimi interpreted. "Someone has broken into the house!" When she asked what was taken, the servants shook their heads and continued to wail and moan.

"I think I know what might be missing," I said, and climbed the stairs to my room to verify the theft. Sure enough, the creased train drawing had disappeared from the desk.

I still had reservations about going to the police. One reason? I wanted to speak with Kimi's parents before I undertook such a drastic move. Two, no one had been hurt, and the house had been left intact. And three, wouldn't Scarred Neck and the old man be placated now that they had what they believed to be the only drawing? So I said nothing, did nothing, and our daily routine continued.

We returned to the same picturesque spot as the day before to finish our paintings. By three in the afternoon, our efforts had produced two pleasing watercolor souvenirs of our time there. Packing up and hanging the still-wet paintings from our backpack straps, we traipsed down the gentle grade to the two-lane dirt road. Following the road, we soon heard a motor off in the distance behind us. That sound slowly got louder and closer until the approaching car forced us to step into the high grass to avoid being run over.

When the car inched to a stop and the doors flew opened, I actually believed some kind soul was offering us a ride back to town. But then I realized it was a gray Toyota Corolla, and I recognized Scarred Neck! We were in for a rough time. He charged at me, while a second thug grabbed Kimi. She screamed, more in rage than in fear. With split-second reflexes, she jabbed a paintbrush handle into her attacker's eye and kicked him in the shin before running off into the six-foot-high bushes beside the road.

My assailant spun me around and painfully twisted my arm up into the small of my back. Holding me helpless this way with his right hand, his left squeezed a smelly rag over my nose and mouth and kept it there until the sickening, sweetish smell made me woozy.

* * * *

Upon regaining consciousness, I discovered I had no idea where I was. A single, low-wattage light bulb hung by wire from the ceiling. I lay on a futon in an empty, windowless room with one door. I heard voices speaking in Japanese in the next room, so I knew nothing of what was said. Not finding myself bound and gagged surprised me. I got to my feet and examined my situation. Other than an aching shoulder, sore arm, and a wooly mouth, I hadn't been harmed. I had no idea how long I'd been out of it. The contents of my backpack were strewn on the wood-planked floor. Trying the doorknob, I discovered it was locked from the other side, and my captives now knew I was up and about. A clattery sound accompanied the key turning in the lock, and the door swung open.

I recognized Scarred Neck. His deformed ear looked even more grotesque as he stepped into the room. With a clenched fist, I tried to take a poke at him, but he put up a defensive arm and stepped out of my reach.

"You may call me Jiro. I went to school in your country," he said in perfect English. "You have nothing to fear from me, young man. I wish you no further harm."

"Jiro, you sure have a strange way of proving that," I said. "You drugged me, kidnapped me, and imprisoned me here, didn't you?"

"Would you have come of your own free will?"

"Hardly," I answered. "What happened to Kimi Sharoda?"

"Ah! Your frisky lady friend. She managed to escape in the deep grass. She did quite a bit of damage to my colleague's eye before she eluded him. But that is of little matter now. My friend Mooki remains a bit uncomfortable, but he'll survive."

"But why did you still pursue us?" I asked, my voice growing shrill. "Why? Evidently you have the drawing from the sculpture garden café and the one from my room at the Sharoda house."

"Of course, but as long as Mr. Yamashita's image remains in your mind's eye, you do pose a rather annoying threat to him."

"Annoying, eh?" I asked. "Yamashita? Is this his house? Is that really his name?"

"Oh, no," Jiro replied. "It's neither his house nor his name. A convenient pseudonym only. He merely wants to make you a conciliatory offer for any inconvenience he might have caused you. You see, Mr. Yamashita has retired from the business world and does not wish to reappear in the public eye."

"In other words, the guy's an out-and-out crook, a gangster, or something worse. And you are one of his hoods?"

"That's a little strong, Mr. Burnette. Let's just say that Mr. Yamashita cultivated both friends and enemies in the harsh world of his profession. He desires only to live out his final years quietly with his children and grandchildren. I believe your idiom is fade into the sunset, *nei?*"

"I'm no threat to him," I told Jiro. "I don't even know his real name or what he's done. In four weeks' time I'll be back in Los Angeles and totally out of his way. What does the guy want from me?"

"The guy, as you call him, wants your assurance that you won't reconstruct his image in any way in the future. For that promise he is willing to pay you $10,000." Jiro held a check out for me.

I wasn't ready to take a bribe, but I was curious to see who had signed the check, so I leaned over to get a look. It was a letdown to find a cashier's check with a machine signature. I shook my head and refused the check. "It wouldn't be right," I told him. "I have no personal beef with the guy. Supposing I just forget all about this business and promise not to reproduce his image anymore?"

"Ah! You are being shrewd and perhaps a little greedy, *nei*? Are you angling for more money? I'm sure Mr. Yamashita would double the figure."

"No, Jiro, that's not it at all," I said, my exasperation rising. "I don't take bribes. I merely wish to be free of you and out of here as soon as possible."

"You must name a figure then. I insist."

I had tried his patience. This whole conversation was beginning to sound so far-fetched that I decided to be just as outrageous. "Okay, then. How about ten million yen? A check made out to a charity of my choice." I guessed that response would get a rise out of him, and it did.

"You can't be serious," he said. My unbroken expression told him I was serious. "This I've got to take back to Mr. Yamashita. Until I return, you'll remain my guest, of course."

He left, locking me in on his way out the door. Several hours passed, and I began to have misgivings about being so bold. My body ached and my stomach cried out for food and water. A bathroom would have been nice, too. I pounded on the wall to reach whoever Jiro had been talking to earlier. I decided it was Mookie, the thug who had grabbed Kimi. I wondered how friendly he would be to my needs. No one answered my pounding.

Later I heard a racket outside—a lot of shouting in Japanese and the splintering of wood. Maybe a door being busted through. More shouting and then I heard a key turning in the lock to my prison. The door swung back, and two uniformed policemen rushed into the room with weapons drawn. The only thing I understood was that they wanted me to follow them back to the police station.

I found Kimi and her father waiting for me there. Kimi and I grasped each other's hands and giggled crazily, so happy were we to see each other. Mr. Yamashita and Jiro were there, too. Jiro was in manacles, pending my pressing kidnapping charges against him. Misguided loyalty and the desire to protect his boss had caused Jiro to act irresponsibly—beyond those measures sanctioned by his boss.

Mr. Yamashita had already renounced his former life of crime, and was cooperating with the authorities to the point where prison became unnecessary. He no longer had the authorities to fear, but he did have to hide from his prior confederates. Being a man of considerable wealth, he had chosen to retire to the Hakone countryside. My drawings posed a threat to that solitude. Kimi explained that we had no intention of exposing him, nor did we wish him any harm; we were willing to drop all charges against Jiro and Mooki.

I turned to Kimi. "Just how did you find me?" I asked.

"Mom and Dad were waiting for us when I got home. They decided not to stay the extra day in Tokyo. When Daddy went to his desk to phone the police, he found your instructions, which led him to ask me about the *himitsu-bako*. I told him that you had purchased one and showed him where it was on your shelf. Daddy's very clever. He knew how to open the *bako* and found your sketch inside and your note on the reverse side. We took the sketch with us to the police station, and the detective lieutenant recognized Mr. Yamashita right away. So we all drove to his place and found the man with the scarred neck and deformed ear there, too."

"That's the creep named Jiro," I told her.

"Mr. Yamashita pressed Jiro. He confessed and told the police where he was holding you. Well, you know the rest."

"But Mooki, the guy you poked in the eye—where has he been all this time?"

"He left you alone and rushed to the doctor," she answered. "He must have been hurting."

"You're a brave girl, Kimi," I said, embracing her in a brotherly hug.

* * * *

I needed to get Mr. Yamashita's image out of my head, out of my system. So I embarked on a pastel painting of the man. It took a week to finish, and I was pleased with the result. I decided to give the painting directly to Mr. Yamashita so that it wouldn't fall into the wrong hands. When Kimi and I knocked on his front door, he answered it himself. The man was so thrilled that he invited us in. His granddaughter presided over a ceremonial tea, during which he presented me with a signed check for ten million yen—approximately $85,000. The space for addressee had been intentionally left blank.

At the end of my stay, and after all we'd been through together, Kimi and I remained best buddies. No more, no less.

Himitsu-bako **Puzzle Box, *Zaiku* Parquetry**
(Purchased by Rosemary and Larry in Hakone, Japan in 2006)

Also by Rosemary and Larry

The Paco and Molly Mystery Series

Locks and Cream Cheese—In scandal-ridden Black Rain Corners, a Chesapeake Bay mansion harbors locked rooms and deadly secrets. A wily detective and a gourmet cook tackle the case.

Hot Grudge Sunday—Bank robbers and conspirators derail the sleuths' blissful honeymoon at the Grand Canyon. Can they nail the suspects after they themselves become targets?

Boston Scream Pie—A teenage girl's nightmare triggers a sinister tale of twins, two warring families, and a blonde bomb-shell who hates being called "Mom."

Available on Amazon.com and as E-Books

Also by Rosemary and Larry

Cry Ohana, Adventure and Suspense in Hawaii—A car accident, blackmail, and murder tear apart a Hawaiian *ohana* (family). Danger erupts at a Filipino wedding, a Maui resort, and the Big Island's volcanic steam vents. Can the family reunite and bring down the killer?

The Dan and Rivka Sherman Mystery Series (#1)

Death Goes Postal—Rare 15th century typesetting artifacts journey through time, leaving a horrifying imprint in their wake. Dan and Rivka risk life and limb to locate the treasures and unmask the murderer. Not quite what they expected when they bought The Olde Victorian Bookstore.

The Dan and Rivka Sherman Mystery Series (#2)

Death Takes A Mistress— After 23 years, Ivy, the daughter of a murdered mistress, seeks revenge on the lover who killed her mother. She follows the cold case clues from London to Maryland, where she discovers her father and killer belong to one of four families. But which one?

At The Olde Victorian Bookstore Ivy finds friendship, advice, love, and caution from Dan and Rivka. Can they solve the mystery before the families destroy Ivy?

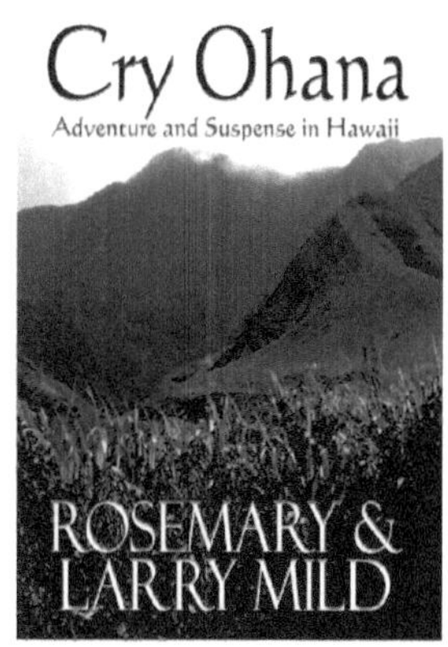

Available on Amazon.com and as E-Books

Also by Rosemary and Larry
A Collection of 8 Short Stories

The Misadventures of Slim O. Witts, Soft-Boiled Detective—If you're looking for a hard-boiled private eye, go see Sam Shade, Flip Marlowe, or Mike Slammer, Should you need an anal cop try Adrian Schmonk. But if you're in the market for a truly soft-boiled gumshoe, you want me, Slim. I'm rarely in charge, frequently behind the 8 ball and seldom paid; but in spite of all that, my case record is remarkably shaky.

Also by Rosemary

Miriam's World—and Mine—Miriam Luby Wolfe, a junior at Syracuse U., spent her fall semester in London exploring her talents: singing, dancing, acting, and writing. But she never made it home. A terrorist bomb destroyed her plane over Lockerbie, Scotland. Learn about Miriam, the Pan Am families, the bombers, and the political fallout.

Love! Laugh! Panic! Life with My Mother—Don't we all have mixed emotions about our mothers? Rosemary Mild's story of her super-achieving, but tough-to-live-with mother. Luby Pollack was a journalist, popular book author, and psychiatrist's wife. Always the Heroine, and sometimes the Villain, from the viewpoint of her loving but ornery daughter.

Available on Amazon.com and as E-Books

214

What do you take away from reading one of our books? We hope that we have not only transported you to another time, place, and adventure, but challenged your mind with worthy puzzles, introduced you to believable characters, and satisfied your sense of fair play and justice. We hope we meet you again on the pages of our books.

Aloha, Rosemary and Larry

Rosemary and Larry Mild coauthor mysteries and thrillers—novels and short stories. Their short stories appear in two anthologies: *Mystery in Paradise: 13 Tales of Suspense* and *Chesapeake Crimes: Homicidal Holidays*. In 2013 the Milds waved goodbye to Severna Park, Maryland, and moved to Honolulu, Hawaii, where they cherish time with their children and grandchildren.

E-mail the Milds at: roselarry@magicile.com

Visit them at: www.magicile.com